LEGACY OF A DREAM

LEGACY OF A DREAM

Stephen P. Matava

Copyright © 1999 by Stephen P. Matava.

Library of Congress Number:		2002090067
ISBN #:	Hardcover	1-4010-3975-8
	Softcover	1-4010-3974-X

All rights reserved. No part of this book may be reproduced or transmitted in any form or by any means, electronic or mechanical, including photocopying, recording, or by any information storage and retrieval system, without permission in writing from the copyright owner.

This is a work of fiction. Names, characters, places and incidents either are the product of the author's imagination or are used fictitiously, and any resemblance to any actual persons, living or dead, events, or locales is entirely coincidental.

This book was printed in the United States of America.

To order additional copies of this book, contact:
Xlibris Corporation
1-888-7-XLIBRIS
www.Xlibris.com
Orders@Xlibris.com

This is dedicated to my three children who listened to my father's stories and learned from them. They have made their father proud.

CHAPTER ONE

It was in the spring of 1901 when young Johan Janek decided to tell his father that he was going to America. He had come from the fields early on this cool, bright sun shining day. He thought, as he rode his horse at a slow pace, that it was a shame to waste such a beautiful day when he should be helping his brothers plant the large field. His brothers, Pavel, Karol and Josef were still out there and he told them that he was finally going to tell their father that he was leaving. His brothers knew how difficult it was going to be so they covered for him because on the Janek farm, the work had to be done. His youngest brother, Stefan and his little sister, Marta were still in school and his mother left for the afternoon so he could get it over with.

He found his father sitting in the backyard, enjoying the sun and a beer. The news was gnawing at him and he had put it off long enough. Now was the time to bring it out into the open and he hoped that his father would not be hurt too badly by the news. They sat silently for a long time, just enjoying the day and watching the clouds float by. The leaves were just starting to peek their little green heads out of the brown branches and the clouds looked like giant fluffy pillows as they came from behind the High Tatra Mountains.

Young Johan finally spoke. "I have thought about leaving our home and our country for some time. I did not make my feelings known until I had actually made the decision to leave. I am going to America where I can make a better life."

A lone tear made a trail down the wrinkled face of the old man and he thought about it before he spoke. He had suspected this for some time and, clearly, did not want his eldest to leave him, but he would not discourage the young man from living out his dream.

"You are a Slovak and your life is here on the farm. You are the oldest and the farm will some day belong to you, but I will not stand in your way. You should go where your heart leads you. Now, tell me how all this came about?"

"In the tavern, I had become friendly with a young man named Anton Krepski and he has an uncle in a little town of Cohoes, New York. The town has some woolen mills that are growing and they produce wool yarn and sweaters that are worn all over the world. There are many Slovaks in this town and they even have their own social club. Anton has been there for six months. I wrote to tell him that I would consider following him and we could rent some living quarters together. This would allow us to share expenses. I am eager to go, but reluctant to leave the farm and our family. With everything that has been happening in this part of the world, I have finally decided to go. I will pave the way for you, mother and the rest of the family to follow, because there is no future for any of us on the farm."

"Does your mother know of this?"

"You know mother better than the rest of us and she knows, but she wanted me to tell you, myself. She said that it was my duty and she wanted you to hear it from me. If you feel strongly about my leaving, I will not go because I would rather not hurt you than go to America. I really do want to go."

He looked at his father who remained silent for a few full minutes.

"It is as if someone put a dagger in my heart, but I can not stand in your way. You have always considered everything very carefully and I am certain that you will succeed in America. You have my permission to leave, but I will miss you, Johan."

They stood up and the father embraced his son. Young Johan thought that he felt a slight shudder go through the body of his father and the emotion started to build, but he fought it because he did not want to harm his father any further.

Johan waited until the harvest was in that fall to buy his ticket and make arrangements to leave. He threw himself into the work on the farm and the time went by very quickly. Before he left, he made one last trip to his favorite spot in the world; he went to the field and sat under the lone oak tree in the wheat field. He was born on that spot while his mother was cutting grain. His father had planted the tree and it had prospered very well. He imagined the roots of the tree going deep into the Slovak soil and how difficult it would be to pull them up. It would be just as difficult for him to pull up his roots and leave the farm. The Magyars (Hungarians) were breathing down his neck and eventually there would be war. The Serbs were the trouble makers, but he felt a kinship with them and the Russians. The Magyars would make him fight for their cause, but he had no interest in their cause and it was time to move on.

It was an emotional day when they stepped on the platform of the train station in Polodencz. His mother cried and he saw tears in his father's eyes. He turned away because he knew that his father did not want his son to see him weep. He gave his father a great embrace and boarded the train before his father could see the tears making their way down Johan's cheeks. Looking out of the window, Johan saw his father's face for the last time. He watched his parents get smaller and smaller as the train moved out of the station. As the train got to full speed, he settled back in the seat and watched the Slovak landscape roll by. This would be the last time he would see the land of his birth and he tried to put many memories into his head; he would never forget this place.

Johan had chosen to leave from Bremerhaven because it was right on the north Atlantic and the schedule told him that it was a few days quicker to Boston. It cost more money, but the ship was larger and he did not want to take the time to travel up the Elbe river from Hamburg; into the open sea. The trip across took exactly one week and following the instructions from Anton, he took a train from Boston to Albany, New York. Anton met him at the train station with a horse and buggy and took him to the home of his father's brother.

Anton said. "In America they call me Tony for short. My uncle's name is Pietr, but we call him Uncle Pete. You will sleep on the living room sofa until we can find an apartment."

As they rode from Albany to Cohoes about fifteen miles, Tony added. "The first custom you should learn is what everyone calls everyone else. Everyone has a nickname for everyone else. If a man is short, they call him "Shorty." If he is thin, they call him "Slim." You will probably be known as "John." It is better to have a name before people at the club pick one for you so I will introduce you as John."

Johan did not know how his parents would react to his name change, but he would write and tell them when he could. They reached Uncle Pete's small house on a side street. It was brown and red and it had a siding that made it look like a brick house. The yard was small with a little fence around it. There were three buildings in back, one was a barn, the second was smaller, a wood shed perhaps and the third was easy to distinguish; that was the privy. The houses, on the street looked alike, but Uncle Pete's house was slightly larger. There were little numbers on each house.

Tony said. "Uncle Pete's address is twelve Oak Street. You should write it down on a piece of paper and keep it with you at all times. If you get lost, you show the paper to a policeman and he will give you the directions home. The policemen are very nice as long as you are within the law. Once a person stepped outside the law, they become very difficult and will lock you up for days before they talk to you."

John had heard that America was an unruly place and the police had to be tough to keep the law. Tony pulled the buggy into the yard just opposite the front door, tied the horse to a fence post in front of the house and said, "We will take care of the horse and buggy later because I want you to meet my Uncle Pete and Aunt Emma."

Johan thought how different things were in America. His father would never allow an animal to be tethered without attention after pulling a wagon for fifteen miles. As he walked up the path and got closer to the house, he noted that the siding, made of tar was fashioned to look like brick. It looked like tar paper that was supposed to resemble brick, but it failed miserably. It was an older house made to accommodate people who worked in the mills.

Tony said. "The owner of the mill had these homes mass produced so people who worked for him, have a place to live. It sold most of them to its workers, allowing them to pay a little each month, with interest until the house was paid for. It takes twenty years to pay for the house and the workers have to pay for all improvements and repairs."

John asked. "If the worker wanted to sell it, could he sell it?"

Tony replied. "He could, but most of the money would go to the owner of the mill because he gets what is owed on the house first."

The inside of the house was as small as it appeared from the outside. Uncle Pete was a short, heavy set man with large muscles in his lower and upper arms. He had a bald head and since he had very little hair, he shaved it all off. His face was round with a short upturned nose and deep blue eyes. The lack of hair made his eyes look more intense and brought the focus of his face to his large ears. John concluded, at once, that Uncle Pete was an intelligent man and this was a man to have as an ally rather than an enemy. He had a thin mustache which he kept trimmed perfectly, but if he allowed it to grow, it would make his ears appear to be smaller. His middle was large and his stomach hung over his belt. He really did not need the belt because he wore wide black suspenders to hold up his pants. His stomach put a strain on his flannel shirt and it looked like the buttons were about to burst. Uncle Pete was a foreman at the mill and this was the only way he could afford this larger home. Most of the houses had one bedroom, but Uncle Pete had two; he could accommodate more people.

Standing behind Uncle Pete, Johan could see his wife, Emma, looking around his ample body. Emma was not a Slovak, but she was accepted by the Slovak community because she was married to one. She came from England many years before and, although, she was younger than Pete, they had a happy marriage. She was small and looked frail, dressed in the ever present apron over a plain house dress. Her hair was tied in a bun in the back to get it out of the way and it was beginning to turn gray. There were streaks of dark gray running from her forehead to the tightly tied bun. Her eyes were bright blue and seemed to twinkle when she became excited; she was excited. When Emma smiled, her small, white teeth gleamed because she took the time to brush them. She wore a flowered house dress and a pale blue apron. She kept wiping her hands on the apron while she waited for her turn to speak.

The first thing Emma said. "We will have to find you some different clothes because we cannot have you walking around like that."

"What is wrong with the clothes that I have on? These are the best clothes that I own."

Emma looked him over, "They may be all right for Slovakia, but they will never do in America. People will know that you just came over on the boat and they will try to take advantage of you. I know many people at the club and I will get you some better clothes."

Emma worked in the knitting mills for ten hours before she came home, made supper, washed clothes and still kept an immaculate house. Her Sundays were spent cleaning one part or another. Pete and Emma wanted children some day, before Emma got too old. They would have to save first because Emma would be out of work for a long time and they needed her money to survive.

Uncle Pete showed Johan around the house. There was wallpaper on the walls and the doors were painted to match each room. The floors were made with narrow boards: fitted together. John did not see any nail holes and he wondered how they got the boards to stay down. The house had the two bedrooms, a kitchen, dining room and a parlor. There was a stove in the parlor that burned wood and heated all the rooms that opened into the parlor. The kitchen was small and had a linoleum floor. The linoleum had a flowered pattern with a six inch border that came to within a few inches of each wall so the wood floor could be seen. There was very little furniture, a table with an oil cloth covering and four wooden chairs. The black, cast iron stove was wood burning and had a shelf where a variety of utensils could be kept. The stove had four rings on the top and a small door. The door was on the bottom where one could put more wood into the stove. John asked what the circles were and Pete took a handle from the shelf, used it to lift off a plate and expose the fire.

Pete told him. "Never leave the handle in the notch on the plate, because it would get too hot and the next person would burn his hand when he went to touch it."

The kitchen sink had a pump that allowed the water to go directly into the sink. There was a drain that sent the waste water outside.

Pete told him. "Most of the houses just pipe the water outside where it forms pools. In the winter, the pools freeze and when spring comes, the ice melts and you can smell the stagnant water. I dug a deep hole by hand, lined the hole with rocks piled one on another until I came to within two feet of the ground level. I put some sheets of tin over the top covered it with tar paper. The end of the drain pipe goes into the covered hole. This way, we do not see the water, it does not freeze, but sinks into the ground the entire year."

John had always thought about getting water into the house on the farm, but he never thought that getting rid of the waste water would be so complicated.

There was a door on each side of the kitchen. One door opened into a cupboard or food storage room. This was a room with shelves on three walls where the canned foods, that Emma put up, were stored.

Pete explained. "There are many orchards and berry farms in the area where we can go and pick our own fruit, for a price. Emma cans these, along with meat we buy from the farmers and salmon we catch in the rivers and channels. We have a vegetable garden in the back of our house and Emma cans the harvest so we will have plenty of vegetables for the winter."

The other door opened into a washroom. It had a table with a bowl and pitcher that was always filled with water. There were cloths hung on racks along one wall. Sitting against the other wall, was a large white tub on legs and it was large enough to accommodate a grown man. He looked into the tub and there was a hole on the bottom.

John looked puzzled and Tony explained, "Water is heated on the stove, poured into the tub and the little hole is plugged with a rubber stopper. The person using the tub gets into it and immerses himself. When he is finished bathing, the stopper is taken away and the water drains into the covered pool in the ground."

John marveled at all the conveniences. He had made the right decision in leaving the "Old Country" for life in this new land and he could not wait until he could send for the rest of his family. John thought that he would have to save his money and get them to America as soon as he could. He placed his belongings in Tony's room which he would share until it was time to go to bed. His bed was made on the sofa and he would have to fold the bed clothes each morning. The board would be a dollar an a half a week for the room with his meals so it was important that he get to work as soon as possible.

John's head was spinning because he had learned so much in a day and he needed time to sort things out. He did not know if one and a half dollars a week was fair, but he had no choice. It turned out that the price for his room and board was very fair. The food was excellent and Aunt Emma washed and ironed his clothes. She had a large cast iron weight which was flat on the bottom and a wooden handle on top. She heated it on the stove and ran it over the clothes to take the wrinkles out. He could not understand where she found time to do all of this work and still work sixty hours a week in the mill besides.

On the day of his arrival, John sat down with his new family and had his first meal in America. Emma served a meat dish of roast beef, potatoes, carrots, turnip and string beans, all cooked in one pot. It was dark and tasty. The juices were thickened with flour and became a gravy. She called the dish "Yankee Pot Roast" and because she was working, Emma made many one pot meals. She made boiled dinners with ham, turnip, cabbage, potatoes and a green vegetable. Emma cooked most of her meals with recipes that she brought from Great Britain and all of the meals were designed to be good, healthy food that a man who did heavy work needed from day to day. Sunday's meal was roast chicken, stuffing, mashed potatoes and a green vegetable. Emma always included a green vegetable in every meal because she wanted her men to stay healthy so they could provide for her.

After supper, as Tony called it, they went to the Slovak Social Club so the family could introduce John to all of his future friends. It was a short walk because Oak Street was within the city limits of Cohoes. One of the main reasons that Pete bought this house was because it was within walking distance to everything he needed. He could walk to work, schools, stores, city offices and most importantly, to the social club.

They walked into a large room with a raised platform at one end and a bar at the other. There were tables and chairs where a few people were talking and drinking beer. A bulletin board that announced coming events in Slovak was on the wall because the mother tongue was still spoken here. They sat at one of the empty tables and Pete bought four glasses of beer, on a tray from the bar. The beer was surprisingly cool and John asked how this was done.

Tony explained, "The keg of beer, once it is tapped, rests in a tub of ice. The ice is brought in everyday and this is paid from the money that the members pay in dues. The bartender, upkeep and other expenses were also paid from the dues. The club has a president, vice president, secretary and treasurer who are elected by the membership, once a year. Each member, whose dues were paid, can vote at the annual meeting which is held on the first Tuesday of January. Pete was elected vice president of the club last year and the vice president is usually elected president the following year. The vice president presides over the monthly meetings when the president could not be here."

As they talked, people came to their table to visit and to meet the new guest. They pulled up a chair and asked John how things were in the old country. They were eager for first hand news since most of the people still considered Slovakia home, no matter how long they lived in America. Most of them had contributed money into "the fund" to free Slovakia. The "cause" was recognized from the east coast, through Chicago and to the west coast. Slovak language newspapers sprang up and printed the accounts of injustices that the Magyars were inflicting on the Slovak people. It was through these social clubs that the word was spread throughout America. John listened to the talk of the people in the hall because they seemed to know more about what was happening in Slovakia than he did.

John asked, "Are there any Slovak newspapers that I might read on the subject?"

Tony answered, "Uncle Pete gets a paper every week called the Jednota which is published in Middletown, Pennsylvania. You could read that paper each week if you want something to read."

John said, "I have not seen any publications in Ruzbachy."

One of the men said, "That was because the Magyars did not allow it. But here, there are plenty of newspapers to read and the government does not interfere."

John learned a great deal about the movement to free Slovakia here, in America. He would keep silent and possibly help the movement at a later date because, after all, he had been in this country for only one day.

On the way home, Uncle Pete said to John, "I have arranged for you to meet with the head of the departments at the mill because there is an opening for a laborer to move the large bales of wool to the machine operators in the carding room. It is heavy work, but you must start some place and the pay is good. You have to report to the mill at seven o'clock and I will introduce you to the head man, Mr. Gallo. He is Italian, but he is a fair person and he rewards men who work hard. When an opening comes, the hardest working men always get the promotion. It will mean more money and the work will not be as hard. Tony has already been promoted to a machine operator following this advice."

The next morning, John woke up and put on his work clothes while Emma made her men breakfast of ham and eggs. They had toast with a fruit spread and coffee before they left the house to walk to work.

Pete said, "It always makes a good impression with Mr. Gallo if you come to work early."

John saw the outside of the factory building from a distance. It was made of brick with huge smoke stacks spewing out streams of dark gray smoke. The fires had to be lit early so that the steam engines would be ready to run before the men came to work. The owner would not tolerate men standing around waiting for the water to turn to steam.

There was a large fence around the factory with a gate that allowed the wagons to come in and out. The gate was locked at night and the factory was patrolled by men and dogs. John wondered why someone would want to go into the plant after working in it all day long. It never occurred to him that the reason for the security was because of the crime, not to keep workmen out. The crime in America was a new concept for him to understand and he would learn more about it as the days went by.

Pete pointed, "That building houses the carding department, the spinning room, the weaving room, dye room and the department that actually makes the finished sweaters. The wool comes in by horse wagons, in bales, and leaves as a finished product. There are Poles, Irishmen, Germans, Italians, Swedes and even Russians working here, but we all keep to ourselves when we are not working. We eat separately and do not mix with each other."

They walked up some steps and stood on a long platform. John could see that this was the area where the horse wagons backed up to unload the bales of wool. There were some small piles of manure that no one had cleaned up and the smell reminded him of his homeland and his family. The bales arrived from the warehouses or the train station where they were loaded on the wagons. There were three wagons loaded with twelve bales of wool, each waiting to be unloaded. John looked around and saw that they were alone and no one else had arrived for work. They went through a door into a huge room, it was clean, but the noise was deafening. John put his hands on his ears to keep out the noise.

Pete shouted over the noise, "You will get used to it."

John did not hear him because there were eight machines lined in a row; all running. The wool was brought to the top of a platform, the restraining ropes were cut so it would fall on a steel lined table. A long pole was used to break apart the wool so it could be fed into the machine. The steam machine was located on the far end of the room, it chugged along and ran a large spindle attached to the ceiling. A rod ran through each spindle that hung from the ceiling. There was a belt about six inches wide which ran from the main shaft to each carding machine. When one wanted to start a machine he took the end of a lever that hung from the ceiling. The lever moved the belt on the main shaft pulley and that would engage the machine. When one wanted to stop the machine, the process was reversed. John noted that even if the pulley was taken off the main shaft, the carding machine would continue to run until it lost its momentum.

There was a small office in the corner of the room with glass on two sides where a small man was sitting at a desk. Tony left them and went to a machine at the end of the room. He took an oil can and poured the brown liquid into the can from a large drum. His job called for him to oil and grease all of the fittings on the machine, every day so the working parts would not wear out. Pete knocked on the glass door and the man motioned for them to come in without looking up. They stood in front of the desk until Mr. Gallo finished reading the papers in front of him. He signed them, stacked them in a neat pile and looked up.

He was looking at John and asked, "Is this the man you told me about?"

Pete said, "This is John Janek and he is new to this country." Mr. Gallo waved Pete out of his office without taking his eyes from John. He looked at John up and down, he did not speak Slovak and John knew very little English, but they seemed to communicate. Mr. Gallo walked over to John's side of the desk and felt his upper arms. John still had muscles from the work on the farm and said the word "strong" as coached by Pete. Mr. Gallo smiled at the obvious coaching by Pete.

He was a short muscular man with an almost bald head and a handlebar mustache. He had on a red plaid shirt with wide red suspenders. The shirt was flannel and it was buttoned all the way up to his chin. It was so tight that he had trouble moving his head, but he would not admit that he was gaining weight on the desk job and even if it was tight, he would keep it buttoned. John thought that this was a stubborn man because he was determined to keep his collar buttoned even if it meant choking to death. His clothes were clean and what John was to find out was all of the workers wore clean clothes on Monday morning and lived in them all week long. By Saturday night, the clothes would stand up by themselves. The wives believed that the clothes would not wear out by wearing them, they would wear out by washing them on the wash board.

John could not imagine that Mr. Gallo ever got his clothes dirty because he did very little physical labor. He had worked in the card room for some time, so he knew how hard the work was. Apparently Pete had brought other Slovaks to work and he felt that John could do the work. Mr. Gallo took out a slip of paper and filled in his name, but when he asked John for his address, John took out the slip of paper with the address on it. Mr. Gallo motioned for Pete to come back in. He needed further information and Pete would have to translate.

Finally, Mr. Gallo went back to his chair, sat down and said, "You are hired, but you have sign this paper. Your pay will be seven dollars a week. You come to work at seven every morning, go home at five at night with a half hour for lunch. You will have to do this six days a week."

John looked at Pete who nodded. John smiled and nodded and Mr. Gallo put out his hand. He took his hand, shook it once and he had a job. The boss smiled back and told him that Pete would show him what to do. John did not understand anything that his employer said, but Pete led him out the door and explained it to him. He asked how much seven dollars was in Slovak crowns and Pete told him; John just smiled.

Pete took him outside and showed him the bales of wool on the wagons. There was a cart that stood upright, with a lip at the bottom of one end and two large wheels on either side. He showed him how to put the lip under the bale of wool, pull it back on the wheels and wheel it to the front of the machines. He stopped in front of a machine. The straps were holding the compressed wool in the bale. Pete had trouble finding the straps and once he did, he cut them with a knife. The wool seemed to expand and as it did, it fell into the semicircular bin in front of the machine. The bin narrowed until the opening of the bin was the size of the machine.

Pete told him, "Your job is to make sure that the feeding of the machines never stopped because if that happened the machine would run empty and that will waste money. The machines have only a limited life and that entire time must be used processing wool."

He took John to where the machine operators worked and showed him how the machine handled the wool. As the wool was fed into the machine, a drum rolled over the wool, the drum had spines on it and separated the wool like thousands of little fingers. The separated wool was twisted until it became yarn and the yarn was rolled on huge spindles that were located above the machine. When the spindles were full, the machine was stopped and the spindles were lifted off the machine with a chain pulley on each end of the spindle. It was pushed to the back of the building and dropped on a waiting cart, which was sent to the dye room. The carting operation was over. John's job, in addition to keeping the wool bins full, was to help the machine operator "doff" the full spindles and replace them with empty ones. The machine operator would start the whole process over again: his job title was a machinist helper.

John's first day was a disaster because he had people calling his name constantly to help with the doffing of the spindles. There were others telling him they were running out of wool. As he emptied a wagon of baled wool, another would be in its place by the time he got back. He was told by the machine operators that he would get the hang of it and the work would become easier as time went on. John did not know how he could continue with this heavy work because, on the farm, others helped with some of the heavy manual labor. He was not accustomed to this type of heavy, continuous work. He could hardly walk home from work and when he got there, he ate his supper and went directly into the parlor. John could barely lie down on the sofa to rest. Pete asked him if he wanted to go to the club, but John just waved his head back and forth. Pete, Emma and Tony, knew enough to let him alone and went to the club without him. They knew he would fall asleep and they did not want to disturb him. When they returned, they found John sound asleep with his clothes still on and Emma covered him with a blanket before she went to bed.

The next morning Pete got up earlier than usual, woke John and had him wash and shave. He said, "A good appearance is favorable for advancement and if you look good and appear to be doing your job with ease, the bosses will consider you ready for promotion."

John had a good meal before he went to work and Emma gave him a pail with some beef between two slices of bread and some fruit. She gave each of them a kiss good-bye and watched her men walk to work. She had already taken a liking to John because he was straight forward and he was clean and honest. She felt that he needed a woman in his life and she would have to talk to the ladies at the club on Saturday night, to see who was available.

Tony had a girl friend named Stella, but that was a stormy relationship. It was an on again, off again affair with much arguing and threats to break off their relationship. Stella was a large girl with a good figure, twenty years old and long blonde hair. When they met at the club, they knew all along, that they were going to a hotel, or anywhere to be alone for obvious reasons. They would disappear from the club and head either to her home, his, or directly to the hotel. When they returned to the club, they both would be flushed and Tony would look over to his friends with a smile on his face. Everyone at the club knew what they were doing. The women thought that it was disgusting, while the men treated Tony as a hero. Emma mentioned this to Pete one day and she wanted to know if he would object to Tony and Stella getting married.

All Pete said, "Why should Tony buy a cow when he is getting his milk for free."

After the first day, the work became easier for John. The machine operators realized that he was trying. He showed the operators that he wanted to do a good job, so they showed him how to cut corners. They knew how long it would take to fill a spindle with yarn, so they showed him how to pace himself. He learned how he could get a bale of wool a bit early, when he had time, and the operator would cut the straps and push the wool into the bin. He made it a point to learn the first names of the operators, which ones were the most demanding and which ones would help him when he was busy. Within a few weeks, the carding room was running smoothly and Mr. Gallo was pleased. He knew which department was running smoothly when he did not have to handle complaints from that part of the plant. He asked the operators how John was doing and they said that he was working out fine. There had been trouble with the previous helper and Mr. Gallo had to let him go, but with John doing so well, he was relieved.

John's body was changing. His waist was slimmer, his shoulders got broader, and he appeared to be healthier than when he first arrived. Emma served good healthy food and it showed on the men in her household. John was becoming more confident especially with the women at the club, but he went there only a few times a week because he did not want to spend the money. He was saving his money and he did not want to discuss why he was saving it. He had promised Pavel, before he left, that he would try to save enough money to bring him over in another two years and he could not let his brother down. John went to the club every Saturday night for the dance, but sometimes he just listened to the music and sometimes, he asked one of the young ladies to dance. He liked the way they smelled when they danced the slow numbers. The hall was kept warm for the dances and when the violin player played a few polkas in a row, the men and women became sweaty so they had to sit down to cool off. John did not prefer one woman over another, but he caught a few looking at him when they thought that he was not looking.

He usually left early because he went to the seven o'clock mass on Sunday and this gave him the rest of the day for himself. On nice days, he would take the horse and wagon and explore the countryside around the small hamlet of Cohoes. He saw the canals that floated the barges of wool down from Lake Erie to the Hudson River. He marveled at the locks that rose from one level to another to allow the barges to complete their journey. John felt that this country was so far ahead of Slovakia, that it would take a generation for his homeland to catch up.

The family that boarded him treated him very well, but he did not see much of Tony because John did not want to interfere with his relationship with Stella. Stella asked him to dance a few times at the club, but he took her over to Tony once the dance was finished. On the slow dances, she pressed her body against his so he could feel the outline of her breasts against his chest. Sometimes, she would run her leg between his and worked it up and down while they danced. This did not go unnoticed by the women at the club, and they noticed that he brought her right to Tony when the dance was finished. He felt no physical attraction towards Stella because he valued his friendship with Tony more.

John noticed that the weather was turning colder and the leaves on the trees were turning red, yellow and orange. The air was crisp and when he walked to work with Pete and Tony, the vapor from his mouth was visible. He liked this time of year when he was on the farm because most of the work had been done and there was now time to go to the tavern to talk with his friends. He had not made many friends in America, yet. He knew many people from the Slovak Social Club, but none that he could really call a friend, except Tony. On Sundays, Tony went to see Stella, while Emma worked around the house humming one of the popular tunes. Pete usually sat in his favorite chair and slept. When John went for a walk, everyone waved as he went by and shouted some greetings, but he was learning to speak English very slowly. Everyone at work spoke Slovak and there was no need to learn English. The area in the town where they lived was in the center of the Slovak community; it was as though someone had taken a Slovak town and transported it over the Atlantic and placed it in Cohoes, New York.

While they were eating supper one night, Emma announced, "I have invited Andy and Mary Baranowski, with their daughter Hana, for Thanksgiving dinner. The owner of the mill has given all of us the day off with pay as a bonus for the good work that we are doing."

John did not understand why everyone was given the day off from work and what the celebration was about.

Pete told him, "This is a holiday to commemorate the day that the first immigrants came from England and started a settlement in Plymouth, Massachusetts. This is a great holiday in America and it comes on the fourth Thursday of November when everyone had a great meal and sits around the house for the rest of the day. We have many holidays in America, many more than we had in Slovakia. We just celebrate because it gives us a day off."

Pete and Emma were good friends with Andy and Mary Baranowski and had been for a long time. Andy's father came to Cohoes many years ago from Presov in Slovakia and Andy and Mary spoke excellent English as well as Slovak. Their daughter,

Hana was nineteen years old and although she was not the prettiest girl in the world, she had a pleasing personality. She worked hard and knew how to handle money. Hana loved children, knew how to cook and would make some man a good wife. The club did not hold any fascination for her because she did not care for the type of men that went there. Hana preferred to stay at home and knit or work on her needlepoint; she made all of her own clothes and sweaters. Her job at the mill was in the sweater knitting room with her mother and Emma. Andy worked with Pete in the spinning department.

The announcement gave John something to look forward to and he did not give Hana another thought; he was looking forward to a day off and a large meal. They never ate all that they wanted on the farm because they had to save some for another day. He asked Emma if he could contribute something towards the meal, but she said that it was all taken care of. She warned him that he would have to rise early because the men would be going out right after breakfast. This was the day that they would go to the farm in the country and buy the turkey because that was the traditional meal for this holiday. Suddenly, the holiday was all that everyone talked about. They talked about what they would do on their day off and how much they were going to eat. John became as excited as the rest of his countrymen and he listened when anyone spoke about the day. People knew that it was to be John's first Thanksgiving in America, so they tried to explain the holiday to him. He listened, but he did not understand all the holidays celebrated in a country that was only a hundred and twenty-four years old. The country of his birth was thousands of years old and it did not have all of the holidays that his new country had; these Americans knew how to celebrate.

CHAPTER TWO

The dawn on the fourth Thursday of November broke clear and cold and Emma let her men sleep until seven o'clock, when the sun started to come up. She had gotten up three hours before to start the process of making bread. She had to knead the dough, let it rise and then knead it again. She prepared the nuts, raisins, cheese and potatoes to go into her breads. When John woke, he smelled the bread baking and it was delicious; just like home. Emma had just taken two loaves out of the oven and was putting butter on the top to make a tasty crust, when John came into the kitchen. Pete and Tony were already there. Emma cut each of her men a piece of nut bread with butter melting into the folds of the steaming bread and gave them each a piece. She wanted to test the inside of the bread before she made more and from the look on the faces, they loved it. She made eggs, kielbasa and fried potatoes for breakfast and since they would not eat dinner until three o'clock, they needed a full breakfast. They each had two cups of coffee and another slice of bread before they left. A loaf was almost gone, but Emma had counted on that. She would finish that loaf herself after they left and she still had seventeen loaves left.

Pete and John hitched the horse to the wagon and the men left Emma in the kitchen to start preparing the meal. They rode to the edge of town and beyond because Pete knew of a Slovak farmer who raised turkeys for this holiday and Christmas. They left the main road about ten miles outside of town, went up a hill and turned on a narrow dirt road. The leaves had fallen from the trees and it seemed that they all settled into the middle of the road. The leaves had fallen some time ago and they could see through the bare branches of the maple trees. Soon, they came to a clearing with a neat little cottage sitting in the middle of a fenced in area. The house was one story and had been recently painted. It was made of wood and the clap boards were painted a light blue. The trim was a darker blue and it looked like one of the homes that John had left in the old country. They stopped while Tony opened the gate and waited for the wagon to pass so he could close it. There were three horses inside the fence watching and the horses followed their every move as they rode to the house. Behind the house was a large barn with a high round building attached to it.

Pete called it a silo and said, "The farms in America have them and they are used to store corn that has been cut into little pieces. The corn feeds the stock during the winter and this allows them to store more food for the animals in less space."

The barn and the silo were painted red, but they had been painted some time ago because the paint was faded and it appeared to be a project for the farmer next summer. John thought that the farmer's wife had a say in what was to be done and she wanted the house painted first. She must be a strong willed Slovak woman to pressure the farmer into painting the house before he did the barns. John remembered stacking the corn in a pile and cutting enough to feed the animals as they needed it. He thought that there was no end to what he would learn about his adopted country; he was thankful for Pete who never tired of explaining everything.

The farmer saw them coming and met them outside because he knew Pete and was expecting him to come on Thanksgiving morning as he had done in the past. Pete introduced them to the farmer whose name was Michel Rusnek. Michel was a small man wearing a wide brimmed straw hat. His face was clean shaved and he had the most intense eyes that John had ever seen. He had bought the farm about ten years before. He and his wife, Eva, had no children and lived mainly off the farm and the produce that they managed to sell. His wife was short, but she had a large stomach and a round red face. John thought that she did not lack for enough to eat. The farm had a large vegetable and herb garden in the back of the house, Eva had canned most of the vegetable and dried the herbs in her kitchen. They raised cows that they sold for meat, poultry and eggs at the road side stand from early spring to late fall. The couple was in their middle forties and had been married in Slovakia before they came to this country.

Michel showed them around the farm and John said, "I grew up on a farm in Ruzbachy, but it was not like this farm."

Michel's barn was equipped with large vats that carried the manure out of the barn to a large pile outside. He had installed an overhead track so he would not have to use a hand pushed cart as they did in Slovakia. Michel took them to the turkey pen where there were about twenty birds feeding. Pete picked one out and Michel went in to fetch it. He tied a twine around the leg of the turkey and gave the other end to Tony. Tony tied his end of the twine around his wrist in case the turkey should get loose.

Michel led them into a storage area where there were baskets of apples, peaches and pears. There were potatoes, turnips and cabbages put up in bags. Pete took a bag of apples, peaches, potatoes and turnips and asked if he had any of Eva's corn relish for sale. Michel gave him a pint jar at no charge.

Pete paid the farmer and as they were preparing to leave, Michel said, "Tony, tie the turkey to the wagon and come in for a cup of coffee."

Eva had the cups on the table when they entered and a loaf of fresh baked cinnamon bread. John had never eaten so much in one day in all of his life and he still had the main meal to look forward to. Tony held the turkey all the way home while John talked about the farm in the old country.

He said, "If my brothers had all of the improvements that Michel has, I would not have wanted to leave the farm and come to America."

When they arrived home, Tony and John unhitched the wagon while Pete took the turkey into the barn to kill it. He hung the bird upside down from a beam, the legs and wings were tied so they would not flap around. He took the head of the turkey in his left hand and with his right, he slid a thin knife into its mouth and pushed it through its brain. He held the neck so the blood drained into a pail which would be washed later. When the turkey was dead, he took it down and started to pull the feathers off because it was easier to pull the feathers while the body was still warm. Once the body had cooled, it would have to be immersed into hot water. Within twenty minutes, he had most of the feathers off while the remaining feathers were burned off with a flaming stick. Pete took the bird into the kitchen to prepare it for baking and one half hour after the turkey was brought to the Krepski's home, it was in the oven.

The Krepski's home was spotless. Emma had spent two days getting everything in order and the stove, even though she had been cooking all morning, was so clean that it was shining. New black polish had been applied a few days before because Pete was proud of his home and told Emma so. He bent over and kissed her, but she shooed him away saying that she was busy. Pete smiled and John, who watched what had happened considered Pete to be a very lucky man.

After John was finished with the horse, he went into the kitchen, washed his hands in the sink and Emma slipped him a piece of warm bread which he ate before he joined the men. The men were sitting in the parlor talking about the mill and John listened to all that was said. He did not understand everything that was going on around him, but he was eager to learn. He had to prepare himself so that he might be able to make it easier for Pavel when he came over. Since it was too early to drink beer, they had just gotten a cup of coffee when a knock came at the door. Tony answered it and one of the machine operators from the carding room who was bored sitting at home, came to visit. The men wandered from house to house while the women spent their time cooking the meal. John recognized him right away and they spoke of the work in the card room. The man's name was Joe Ambrodek and he lived a few houses down from Pete.

Joe said, pointing to John, "You got a good man there. He is learning the job very quickly and he is a hard worker."

Pete was pleased, slapped John on the back and said, "Everyone from Ruzbachy knows what hard work is because they have to work hard to survive. Things are not as easy over there as they are here."

Soon, there were a few more knocks on the door and they took turns answering it. Pete looked at the clock and said, "It is noon, lets have a beer." Tradition dictated that noon was the unofficial time for drinks to be served so Pete went to get the beer. He returned with two large bottles and as many beer mugs as he could carry. While they were drinking their beer, the noise level began to rise. Emma poked her head into the parlor and Pete took this as a sign that the party was getting noisy so he put his finger to his lips and shook a thumb towards the kitchen. They all knew what that meant so one by one they started to leave. It was time to leave, anyway, because most of them were expecting company and they wanted to be there when they arrived.

At one o'clock, the Baranowski family arrived with their daughter, Hana. She was wearing a dark blue overcoat that John helped to take off. The first thing that he noticed about Hana was her smile. She had straight, white teeth and when she smiled, her whole face lit up. John could not hold back his smile, even if he wanted to. She was a thin woman of short stature with straight brown hair. Her eyes were brown, her complexion was milky white and she favored her mother because her father had harsh features. When John took her coat off, he noticed that she smelled of a scented soap. There was no strong smell of perfume that he smelled when he danced with the girls at the club. Her father had a large nose and bushy eyebrows. His hair line was receding in front, the back was kept long and it was apparent that his wife cut his hair. John was very happy that she took after her mother. Pete and Andy spoke to each other after drinks were served, Mary went into the kitchen to help Emma which left John to entertain Hana. When Emma decided to bring a young man and a young woman together, she planned it very well. Hana was shy around young men because her parents kept a short rein on her activities. She had not been alone with a man very often, but she tried to keep the conversation going, knowing that John had been in the country only a short time.

Hana spoke excellent Slovak and said, "My grandfather, Michel made a trip to Ruzbachy many years ago to deliver some money to the priest who was building a new church."

John smiled and said, "That priest, believe it or not, was my grandfather, my father, Johan Janek had been sired by the priest and he was born out of wedlock."

He said it as though it was common knowledge and Hana not hearing the story, raised her eyebrows. John was not ashamed of this fact; he was only stating a true happening. They were looking for common ground and found they had many things in common. John went to the club only to meet people and not to drink, he drank one or two beers, but that was his limit.

John continued, "I cannot understand why some of the young men drink so much that they become drunk. This does not appeal to the young ladies, but has the opposite effect."

Hana said, "I think that the men were trying to exhibit their manhood, but there were other ways of showing that."

She realized what she had said and her face turned red. She did not mean it to come out in the way that it did, but John understood and changed the subject.

He said, "I have heard the story about your grandfather, when two robbers stopped them, your grandfather shot both of them."

She laughed and said, "When my grandfather saw the look in the priest's eyes and my great-uncle Andrej's eyes, he feared them. They must have thought that America was a wild place. What ever happened to my great-uncle Andrej?"

"Your great-uncle became a priest and is still pastor of the church your relatives had helped to build."

They must have talked for more than an hour when, first Mary and then Emma poked their heads out of the kitchen to check on their progress. When the meal was ready, they sat at the table. Pete sat at the head of the table while Emma sat at the other end. John and Hana sat on one side while Andy and Mary sat on the other. Tony had gone to have dinner with Stella's family so no place was set for him. If he did return, a place would have been set quickly since there was more than enough food.

John looked at the table and he had not seen so much food in his entire life. To the others, this seemed like a natural thing, but to John it was too much food for the six of them to eat. He thought of his parents, brothers and sister who barely survived and here he was with enough food to feed his entire family in Slovakia, with enough left over for another week. This was the land of plenty.

As they sat down, Emma asked John to say grace and he quickly tried to think of some of the words that his father had used. He did not want to make a fool of himself, especially in front of Hana.

He took a deep breathe, made the sign of the cross and the rest followed. "Thank you, dear Lord for the good friends that I have made in this wonderful country and help me to be worthy of your blessing. Help us all to be more tolerant of our fellow man's failings. Allow us to help the less fortunate so they may overcome them and we may all go to our reward at your side. Bless this abundance of food that you have provided for us that was prepared with love through your generosity." He made the sign of the cross as all at the table said, "Amen."

Emma beamed as she looked around the table and Andy was impressed. He thought that this country bumpkin could be eloquent when he needed to be. Mary had just made up her mind that Hana must marry this man and she would enlist the help of all the ladies at the club. John did not know it at the time, but his future was sealed as of that moment. Whatever Mary wanted, Mary received so if Hana liked this young man, she would marry him. She was interested to find what other surprises he had in store for her; he was not typical of the other men in the Slovak community. He was different and special and as she sat there and smiled to herself, she would learn more about this man. Mary was sure that he would measure up to her expectations and he would be Hana's husband.

Pete sunk the large, gleaming carving knife into the brown turkey that was placed before him and everyone passed their plates to him. Mary and Hana said enough, but he put on an extra piece anyway. The vegetables were passed around and everyone took a spoonful. There were mashed potatoes with a large spoonful of butter in the center, the turnip was mashed as well, there were small onions, green beans, stuffing, gravy and home made bread. Each person had a glass of wine in front of them, but Hana took only a sip.

Each fall, Pete rode down to the Brotherhood winery in South Washington, New York and bought a case of their rich red wine. This was to last them through the holidays and the men emptied their glasses very quickly. It was excellent wine, made for generations by the friars in the small hamlet. Their vines were brought to America, from France by a friar many years ago and the vineyard flourished. It was not only the excellent wine that impressed them, but the trouble that Pete went through to ride all the way down there to bring it to his guests. This proved that he valued them greatly. The people at the table became silent as they started to eat, but everyone commented on how good the food was. Emma who had been picking and tasting food all morning was not hungry. In a very short time, she was full and just picked at the rest of the meal. Hana who wanted to show the hosts that she did not eat too much, took very little and daintily put small morsels into her mouth. She did not want to create the impression that she would be expensive to support. Andy and Mary did not let the opportunity of a free meal go by without taking full advantage of the situation. They cleaned their plates and Pete got up to carve more meat from the carcass. He thought to himself that next year, the meal would be at the Baranowski home and he would make them pay for this.

Pete did not like leftovers because they had very little room in their icebox and the space was needed for beer. At Emma's insistence, Pete had bought the icebox. It was made of wood with galvanized metal on the inside. The box contained four doors, two on each side with one above the other. The top left side was for the ice which the iceman brought every other day and the compartment beneath was used to catch the melting ice. A pail had to be emptied everyday so it would not leak on the floor. The top compartment on the right was used to store the more perishable foods while the one on the bottom was used for the rest; Pete's beer. The icebox would be full at the end of the day.

Once the second plateful had been eaten, the three men sat back, put their hands on their stomachs. They announced that they were full and could not eat another bite. Emma believed it because she had slaved in the kitchen for two days and they consumed it in thirty minutes. They all complemented the cook and got up from the table. The men went into the parlor where Pete produced some cigars that he had bought for the holiday. The women put on aprons and started to clean the kitchen.

The vegetables were put in glass jars with caps screwed on. The meat was cut off the bone and placed in a large jar. The stuffing and gravy would be stored as well. Emma put the carcass in a large pot with some herbs and water, placed it on the stove and allowed it to boil. When the pot had boiled enough, she would allow it to cool so she could take the meat from the bones with her fingers. She would take out the bones, put in the vegetables and the soup would last for three or four meals. The turkey would also provide a few more meals because Emma knew how to make the food last as long as possible. They would have meals for the rest of this week and a few days into the following week.

It took the women some time to clean the kitchen, but they still did not go into the parlor to sit with the men. They sat at the table with a cup of coffee and talked among themselves. Women did not want to hear any conversation about work, sports or anything else that the men found interesting. They exchanged gossip about the various families in their close knit community. They knew who was dating whom, who was contemplating marriage, who was pregnant and who was beating his wife.

They had ways of combating wife beating and the first step would be to go to the priest who would talk to the husband. If this did not work and the situation became serious, they would go into the home, pack some clothes and take the wife away to one of their homes. The husband would have to confront the man of the house where his battered wife was staying.

Sometimes the matter became serious enough where the women would move the battered wife around to different homes and the husband would have to confront many men. When the husband would come to the club, he would be shunned by the community until he went back to the priest and vowed never to beat his wife again. This usually ended the matter or the man would move away. There was no such thing as a divorce and outside authorities were never called. This was an internal affair within the Slovak community; they would take care of their own. If there were children involved and the father moved away, the women who did not work would care for the children during the day while the mother would work to make ends meet. The women would donate food and clothing to the fatherless family until the children had grown and could work in the mill. No one, outside of the Slovak community, knew about any problems within; matters were handled in the old traditional way.

The afternoon went by and the shadows were becoming long so it was time to go to the social club. This is where they would wish the friends, neighbors and relatives that they have not seen, a happy Thanksgiving. The men were still full and were on their third cigar. The parlor was thick with smoke and Emma opened the windows so it could air out because she did not want John to sleep in the room full of cigar smoke. The more John stayed in America, the more he liked it. The past was dimming in his memory, and all he knew that, before he was finished, he would have his entire family in America.

There was still two more days left in the work week so they

could not stay very long. They did not bother to hitch the wagon, but walked to the club in the cold night air. It got dark early, this time of the year, in the central part of new York state and the moon gave off enough light so a lantern was not needed. The two married couples walked ahead of the others. John and Hana walked more slowly because they wanted to be alone so they could talk to each other without disturbances. They knew that once they got to the club, they would not be alone. It would be nice if they could see each other away from the club and prying eyes, just be together; alone.

John asked, "May I see you at home for a visit?"

She answered, "Yes, but my parents will have to be home since they do not allow me to be alone with any man."

By asking Hana if he would visit her, John had established a relationship where they had an unwritten and unspoken commitment to see each other and no one else. John wanted to get this out in the open before they got into the club or he might lose her attention.

When they arrived at the club, they found people crowded into the hall. The man behind the bar was doing a brisk business selling beer. Someone had spilled a glass of beer at a table in the corner and there were two women on their hands and knees mopping it up. This caused some comments from the other women about men who could not hold their beer. The fiddle player was playing a fast tune and there were couples twirling around on the dance floor in the smoke filled room. John did not like the atmosphere in the hall, with so many people. He found an empty table in the other corner with four chairs and he had the three women sit down while he brought over two more chairs. The table was next to a window so he lifted it up an inch or two to let out some of the smoke. Pete went to the bar and brought back five beers and one sarsaparilla, for Hana because her parents did not allow her to drink beer. They sat and looked at all the activity in the room. The women noted who was dancing with whom and who was sitting with whom. They noticed that Tony was sitting with a group of single young men drinking beer and it was at this table that the beer went all over the floor. They were talking loudly and Pete noted that there were many empty glasses in front of Tony. He must have been there for quite sometime because there was more noise coming from that part of the room than from anywhere else. Emma looked over to the other side of the room and saw Stella sitting with a smaller group of young women. Stella was drinking beer and she had a few empty glasses in front of her. She was talking in a loud voice, trying to be heard over the fiddle player.

Stella was wearing a traditional dress that someone had brought over from the old country. The dress was tight around her waist and the scoop neck was barely keeping her breasts inside. Every time she waved her arms, the breasts were in danger of popping out. The cleavage jiggled because so much of it was exposed. She had rouge on her cheeks, dark red lipstick and some dark makeup to accent her eyes. Her blond hair fell across her exposed shoulders and swayed when she turned her head. She looked over at Tony, said something to her friends and they all laughed. The more they laughed, the angrier Tony became and it was obvious that both of them had been there for a long time and they were engaged in some type of argument. Both were under the influence of the beer that they were drinking.

Finally, Tony got up and walked over to his uncle's table. He pulled up a chair between Pete and Emma so he could talk to them and be understood.

He announced, "Me and Stella have broken up and I will not be seeing her any longer. She told me that either we set a date for the wedding or I could leave because she was not going to wait for me any longer. I walked out of her house and came right here and I did not even have dinner yet. I have been here ever since to wait for my friends to drift in."

Pete told him, "You had a good time while it lasted, but the time has come to shit or get off the pot."

Tony said, "She is great in bed, but I do not want to marry her and spend the rest of my life trying to control her temper. If we got married, I do not know if Stella would be a good mother to any children we might have. She is not the type to stay with one man for the rest of her life and even in our relationship she had gone out with other men. I do not trust her enough to marry her."

Pete and Andy listened to Tony, but did not say a word. Tony was trying to justify his actions and it was a decision that he would have to make by himself; they just let him talk.

Tony went on, "I decided not to marry Stella and I will try to find a girl who is a good Slovak woman. She must be able to take care of a family, work hard to help the family get ahead, go to church and raise the children in the Catholic faith."

Emma who had heard this last comment by Tony, looked at him in disbelief because she thought that it was the beer that was talking and not her nephew. She thought that he was going to begin to cry, but he got up and left the club. No one saw him until the next morning when it was time to go to work. He did not mention Stella again, avoided her when they were at the club and it took Tony months to get over her. He still went to the club, but not as frequently as he had before. He no longer was the carefree young man that he once was, he turned serious, did not drink as much and he went to church with his aunt and uncle. Tony was a changed man and Pete said that he finally grew up.

CHAPTER THREE

John had gone to see Hana at her home on the following Sunday. Hana was in the choir at church and since they were rehearsing for the Christmas concert at six o'clock, he had to leave at five. Mary and Andy never left the house while John visited. They spent their time in the kitchen and let the young people sit in the parlor. They trusted Hana, but they were afraid that some of Tony's influence might have rubbed off on John. John, however, was a perfect gentleman.

He saw Hana at the club more often and she asked to go with her parents in the hopes of seeing John there. The four of them would sit together and sometimes Pete and Emma would join them. The fiddle player would play and John asked Hana to dance. She asked her father who nodded his head and the couple danced under the watchful eyes of Mary and Andy. John decided not to drink beer while he was with Hana and this did not go unnoticed by her parents. Their courtship was progressing along the lines used in the old country and if this couple was to marry one day, the courtship would have to be slow and deliberate. They would have to get to know each other and would not sleep together until they were married.

Christmas fell on a Friday that year and two Sundays before, Pete asked John and Tony to help him pick out a Christmas tree, cut it down, and set it up in the parlor. After breakfast they hitched up the wagon, took a saw and went off into the woods to find a suitable tree. It took them two hours to agree on a tree because it had to be full on all sides even though one side would be against the wall. Emma thought that it was the prettiest tree that they ever had, but she said that every year. They put the tree on a stand that Pete kept in the barn and John watched the three of them decorate the tree with ornaments that had been in the family for generations. Emma had bought new candles, but they would not light them until Christmas Eve; Emma wanted them to last until Christmas. Emma had a rule, she wanted someone in the room while the candles were burning. They kept a large pail of water handy which could be used in the event of a fire.

Emma explained what happened at Christmas, "Our celebration has mixed traditions. Those that we have brought from our old countries and those of our adopted country. There is a midnight Mass which Pete, I and Tony attend and the Mass will be two hours long with the choir singing the High Mass. Before the Mass we will have a Christmas Eve dinner and exchange gifts. Our family does not want you to spend a great deal of money buying gifts, but you should buy a small gift for each of us because we have planned on buying gifts for you. Hana is going to present you with a small gift so you should act accordingly. The gifts would all be placed under the tree before dinner and we will light the candles and open them after the meal. After the opening of presents, we usually visit friends and sing Christmas carols."

She spoke so fast, that he had difficulty keeping up with her, but if he forgot anything, he would to ask Tony. He learned that the traditional Christmas drink was eggnog and it was a drink introduced to them by some Swedish friends. It contained heavy cream and spices to which was added brandy.

Tony, who was standing behind John, clapped him the back and said, "You should not drink too much because the Slovaks add more brandy and make it into a powerful drink. You do not want to miss the Mass because you drank too much eggnog."

John thought this to be an unusual drink. In Slovakia, the cream was prized by all the farmers in Ruzbachy. They either kept it for themselves or sold it for a good price. At his farm they had to sell it to get enough money to buy other things they needed in order to survive. In America everyone had money to buy cream and drank it as if it were an every day food. It was no wonder that the older men had pot bellies and the women gained weight after the children had grown. They could afford to buy these foods. He vowed that he would not allow himself to get a pot belly. It was a good life, but there was no reason to allow the body to grow fat and lazy and in Slovakia, only the very rich men would support a big belly. It was a matter of pride to have a big one, to show everyone how rich you were. Here it just meant that you ate too much.

The matter of a gift for Hana would require some thought. He did not want to give her a gift that was too large because it would show that he was extravagant; he really knew her for only a short time. If he gave her one that was too small, it would give the impression that he was miserly and did not think much of her. He needed help badly so he spoke to Hana's mother, Mary, and asked her what Hana would like.

He thought that he would get a fair answer from her and she thought for a minute and said, "It must be something that you pick out personally or it will not mean much to Hana. I could suggest something that you buy at the company store at a discount, but she will know what you paid for it. She knows that the company allows employees to buy sweaters at the factory at a small discount. She would like a sweater, but to get her a present that she might have worked on, will not mean as much to her. You might get her a scarf or gloves, but that would be too practical. You could get something pretty, something that she would not buy for herself."

John left as confused as he was before he talked to Mary. He did know that he would not buy her anything from the company store and he spoke to Pete who agreed with him. He had bought Emma some presents from the company store, but it will not mean as much as something personal bought elsewhere.

Since the stores in Albany were closed on Sunday, they had to go on a Thursday night when the stores were open until eight o'clock. The three men decided to go on a Christmas shopping trip the following Thursday. Andy asked to go with them because he could use all the help that he could get. There was a large department store in Albany called "Gettermans" which would have a good selection of gifts and they might be able to find something there. Aaron Getterman, the owner, was a Jew so he would have preferred to have his store open on Sunday. His store had to be closed on Saturday, because that was his holy day and he could not find anyone to work on Sunday; he had to bend his religious beliefs and keep the store open on Saturday. He did not go to the store on Saturday, but worked on his accounts on Sunday, when it was quiet. When sundown arrived on Friday night, he dropped whatever he was doing and sat in his chair to read the Old Testament. He did not lift a finger except to turn a page. His meals were brought to him and the gas light was turned on and off by someone else. He did absolutely no manual labor, no matter how trivial, until sundown on Saturday when he would dress and go into his store to see what the receipts were for Friday and Saturday.

On Thursday, the men came home as quickly as they could. They devoured their supper, changed clothes, hitched up the wagon and were on the road in one half hour. Albany was fifteen miles away and by pushing the horse, they were there at six-thirty. That gave them an hour and a half to shop and they were sure that Mr. Getterman would not make cash customers leave at eight o'clock even if they could not make a choice. John found a little music box for Hana. It was twenty-five cents more than he had allotted for the gift, but he was sure that she would like it. It had a ballerina on top and when she wound it up, the ballerina would turn and the music box would play a piece of music that he did not recognize. He thought that Emma would know what it was and he would have to show it to her.

He bought a wool scarf for Emma, a billfold for Pete since he always had money. He found a pair of nice warm gloves for Tony and his Christmas shopping was complete.

Tony was torn as to whether he should buy a gift for Stella. Things had been rather cool between Stella and Tony since the break up at Thanksgiving. She had gone out with several young men, but they never asked her out the second time. Stella did not appear to be her old carefree self. She had buckled down in work and changed her style of dress to call less attention to herself. Her blond hair was worn tied in back. Her clothes were more conservative and she did not flaunt her attributes for every male to see and admire. Stella had changed and Tony had noticed the difference. They met once in a while at the club and even danced a few times and it was evident that neither of them wanted the breakup. Both were stubborn and neither would make the first move towards getting back together again. Tony thought that a little gift might get things to change because he wanted to start over. He just did not want the relationship to get to the point where it was before.

Tony had thought of getting her a small case that held powder and a small mirror, but Stella did not wear much makeup anymore; she looked better without it. She had a healthy, wholesome look and she really was a pretty woman. He did not tell anyone in his group that he was buying a present for Stella, but John knew by what he was examining, that a gift had to be for his old girl friend. Tony finally decided on a silk scarf that she could use even if they did not get together again. He would stop at her home before they opened their gifts and leave it for her. John ended up spending four dollars for gifts and he could not afford to be so extravagant all the time, but these people have been good to him. They have made the transition into this new life much easier. Everyone had finished their shopping and they stopped into a little tavern to celebrate.

The tavern was called Murphy's and most of the customers were of Irish decent, but there were other people. They each ordered a pint and were given a tall glass of dark ale. The first taste was bitter, but by the time they were half way through, it tasted very good. They finished the second glass and left because they still had an hour an a half on the road and it was ten o'clock. The women would be worried and they would have to get up to go to work the next day. John sat next to Tony in the back seat while Andy sat up front with Pete. They were singing old songs and laughing at the words that they made up to replace those that they had forgotten. John felt something wet strike his cheek and at the same time, Andy announced that it was snowing. They still had an hour to ride before they reached home.

Pete said, "I hope that the snow does not accumulate. There is no moon or other light to show us the road."

It started snowing rather heavily and Pete had trouble keeping the wagon on the road. They came to a ditch on the right and the right wheels slid into it. The horse pulled, but the wheels just kept sliding back into the ditch. Pete stopped the horse and the three of them had to lift the wagon out of the ditch. They rode for about one hundred feet when it happened again and Pete just could not see the road. Luckily Pete keep a kerosene lantern in back and he said a little prayer asking that there was fuel in it. They stopped and got out the lantern. It was almost full of fuel so they lit it and one of the men walked with the lantern in the middle of the road while Pete followed. They took turns carrying the lantern until they reached Cohoes. The way had been slow going and they were tired when they saw the lights of home. It was one-thirty in the morning when they finally left Andy off at his home. There was a light in the kitchen so Mary was waiting for her husband. Emma was waiting also and she was so relieved to see them that she did not ask questions, she just hugged all three and took Pete to bed. John volunteered to unhitch the horse and he spent sometime rubbing the horse down. His father had trained him to take care of his horse and always warned him never to leave a wet horse. The horse, left wet, in cold weather could contact a chest cold and die. John knew what to do, although he suspected that this had not been done in the past.

Christmas finally came and John delivered his gift to Hana on the afternoon of Christmas eve. The mill had closed down for the holiday at three in the afternoon, but the machine operators had to clean and oil the machines. John stayed to help. He could have left, but the operators had families and they wanted to get home as soon as they could. The kindness that he showed would be rewarded some time in the future. He walked home, with about three inches of new snow on the ground and he followed the foot prints of Tony and Pete to the house. For some reason, he felt that there would be less snow than they had on the farm. He could not remember getting snow this early, in this amount and the temperature also appeared colder to him. Someday he would find a place where the weather was warm and there would be no snow at all. He would move there and be warm for the rest of his life.

When John arrived home, he found Emma in the kitchen, making the meal for that night. He heated some water, put in into the basin and went into the washroom to take a sponge bath because he did not want to go through the trouble of filling the tub and cleaning it afterward. He had too much to do before Christmas dinner. Hana's gift had to be dropped off and he wanted to go to confession. While at church, he wanted to listen to Hana rehearse with the choir. He loved to watch and distract her so that she would forget her lines and they would laugh about it later. John washed himself, put on his finest clothes, the ones that Emma had gotten for him and left for Hana's house.

Mary greeted him at the door, he kissed her and nervously said, "I have a gift for Hana,"

She smiled as she took it and put it under the tree. He had a cup of coffee and a slice of bread and then left for church. John thought to himself that when you ever visited a Slovak home, you had to have some refreshments before you left. This had not changed from the customs in his home country that went on before time. It was an insult to the hostess if anyone refused her offering and in his time schedule, John had allowed for this.

John loved this church. It was made of cut stone and the steeple was very high. He had never seen such an ornate altar. It was an exact replica of the church with the peak rising to the ceiling. There were stained glassed windows all around the church with a little plate to show who donated each one. He had found the one that was donated by Hana's grandfather which is where Hana always sat. There were painted stations of the cross and beautiful paintings on the wall above them. It was a place where John could sit and just be around the beauty of the house of God. To the right of the altar was a space for the choir and to the left was an ornate pulpit where the priest said the homily.

Confessions ended at five in the afternoon, but when he arrived, he found a long line waiting to go into the confessional. He knew that the priest would stay until he heard every last one. As he waited, a second priest came and set up a confessional at the front end of the church. John went over to that priest since he would be closer to where the choir was rehearsing and he could use his time watching Hana. He succeeded in disrupting her twice and saw her trying to hold back a smile. The choir director saw it, turned around to look at John and glared at him. John had to look away. He did not want to see Hana get into trouble so he did not distract her again. Finally it was time for John to enter the confessional and it did not take long because he had little to confess. He had attended Mass every week and as he contemplated the ten commandments, he could report only a few minor impure thoughts. He received the minimum penance and waved to Hana before he left the church. He arrived home at six o'clock and they were waiting supper for him. Emma was smiling because she knew where he had been.

Tony ate his supper quickly and he was like a little child who could not wait to open his presents. Pete, knowing this, ate very slowly and teased him at every opportunity.

Emma told the men, "Andy dropped by and there was something under the tree for John from Hana. Stella had also dropped by and left something for Tony."

At the mention of her name, Tony's face lit up and he flushed. Emma, looking at Tony remarked, "Stella looked like a different young lady and someone must have had a talk with her. She certainly had changed and I thinks that she still likes you."

Emma did not say that it was she who had talked to Stella on Thanksgiving night in the lady's powder room.

She told Stella, "I am going to give you some motherly advice.

Your relationship with Tony can still flourish, but you both have to give in a little and the type of woman you are portraying, does not appeal to a man who wants to settle down. You cannot go on this way if you want to attract a man; Tony or anyone else. Wear some conservative clothes, do not wear so much make up. It does nothing for you and it costs a great deal of money. You will see that Tony will change toward you."

Emma was pleased that Stella had changed overnight. She told Stella later, "Tony will probably buy you something for Christmas, because I see that Tony still has feelings for you. You do not have to act this way to get Tony's attention because you have had it all along."

After the meal and the kitchen was cleaned, Emma came into the parlor with four cups of eggnog on a tray. Pete lit the candles and said, "Thank you God for allowing us to have another Christmas. Thank you for sending John to us because we consider John and Tony the two sons that we never had."

John looked at Emma and saw tears forming in her eyes so he went over to her and kissed her on the cheek.

He said, "I want to thank God for sending me to you fine people because there are not too many people in this world who have two sets of parents."

There were hand shakes and embracing and Pete said, "Life is good, and I am pleased with my life."

He passed out the presents. Pete waited until every one had his or her presents before he opened his. He was pleased with his billfold and he said, "I feel like a rich man because I have some place to put my money."

Tony said, "I needed new gloves and these are warm ones that will last a long time."

Emma said to John, "I do not deserve the fine scarf that you have given me, I will wear it to church and will be the envy of all the ladies."

Tony gave John two pairs of wool socks and he held them up to admire them, "These will come in handy on the walks back and forth to work."

John put Hana's gift aside and opened Pete and Emma's gift. It was heavy and John ripped the paper off. It was a strong box with a ledger where he could keep track of the money that he was saving to bring his family to America. John did not realize that he had made his goal so obvious, but this was the reason that Pete and Emma would not accept any other money from him except the board that they had agreed upon. John waited until Pete opened his present from Emma. It was a box of cigars that she had ordered through the store from Cuba. She knew how he enjoyed his cigar after a good meal and these, he could keep for himself.

She told him, "These are not to share, You have others that you could share but not these. These are only for you."

Emma opened her present next and Pete waited, impatiently for her to open it. It was a bottle of toilet water that he had found at Getterman's store. He had paid more than he wanted to, but he loved his wife, she had never had a bottle of toilet water before and it was about time that she had the finer things in life.

Now came the time for John to open his present from Hana and he opened the package slowly. It was a box and as he took off the cover, he saw white tissue paper. He was wondering if he would ever come to the present, but he pulled aside the paper and saw a gleaming white dress shirt. It was the first new garment that was made in America and it was something that he would never buy himself.

Emma blurted out, "It is beautiful."

She took it out, opened it up and placed it against John's chest to see if it would fit. She thought that it would fit and took it into the kitchen where she heated her iron on the stove, pressed it and gave it back to him so he could wear it to Mass.

John could not take his eyes off Hana during the Mass, he watched her while she was performing and when she sat down. The choir wore white robes, the men were bareheaded. The women, in accordance with the church rules had to have some coverings on their head. They wore small silver tiaras, and they wore a thick chain with a cross at the end of it. It looked impressive to John because there were no robes in Slovakia and the people did not have as much time to rehearse. When John checked some of the other singers, he was amazed to find Stella singing a few feet away from Hana. He poked Tony with his elbow and motioned with his head towards Stella, but Tony smiled and whispered that he knew. He looked at Tony and noticed that he could not keep his eyes from watching Stella. Hana knew that John was watching her and she smiled for him once in a while. His first Christmas in America would be one that he would remember for a long, long time.

When the Mass was over, the families met outside the church to exchange greetings. A light snow was falling and the gaslights on the church were flickering. People were milling around, shaking hands and embracing each other. Once in a while, John heard laughter and he saw one woman sobbing as she embraced a young man. John wanted to comment on it to Pete when Hana came running over followed by her mother and father.

She put her arms around him, "Thank you for the music box, it is the first gift that you have given me and I will treasure it always."

"Thank you for the shirt. It is the finest shirt that I have ever worn."

They looked into each other's eyes and promised to meet at the club that afternoon"

She kissed him on the cheek and blushed at being so brave. "I have to go with my parents to visit with other people before we go home."

John could see Tony and Stella talking to each other and there was no arguing or motions with their hands. Unconsciously, he rubbed the spot on his cheek where he received the kiss. Tony and Stella were actually talking quietly and calmly. He made a mental note to ask Tony how things were going, but it was beginning to snow a little harder and Emma was getting cold; they decided to go home and go to bed. No one wanted the night to end, the spirit was willing the flesh was weak.

On the way home Emma said, "You should have been in Cohoes

four years before because it had snowed for four days and we got a total of four and one-half feet of snow from that one storm alone. It came in February and everything was shut down for over a week. There was no money coming in and we could not leave the house to buy food."

Pete continued, "Luckily, Emma always had a cache of food and we were able to get by with what we had. We were even able to give some food to our close neighbors, but many people ran out of food and had to trudge through snow to buy food from the company store. The store gave credit when the money ran out and by the end of that week, the store was beginning to run out of food. Some people had to tunnel through the drifts to get out of their homes."

John had never seen that much snow from one storm, but America is a land of many surprises and he felt that there were more in store for him. It felt good to get into his nice warm bed. John could not wait for the next day to come as he lay in his bed trying to sort out his feelings that the kiss on his cheek provoked. He never felt this way about a woman before and he said her name out loud as he drifted off to sleep.

The social club opened at nine a.m. on Christmas morning and by eleven o'clock all the tables were filled. It was bedlam with a great deal of hugging going on between the women, the men were shaking hands and wishing a greeting to each other. As soon as a new family arrived, it started all over again. The bartender was selling eggnog and every adult had a glass of the white creamy liquid. The extra tables usually stored in the backroom were brought out and set up. The chairs began creeping into the dance floor when the room around the tables was used up. Some of the members of the social club made only two visits to the club each year, one was at Christmas and one was at Easter. The five inches of snow that fell during the night, did not stop them from coming. At about noon, Andy, Mary and Hana came in, brushed the snow from their shoes and looked for a place to hang their coats. The pegs on the wall had long since been used and someone started to pile the coats on a table at the entrance. The table was piled high with outer wear and the newcomers just threw their coats on top. Hana looked for John and found him in a crowd of people in the far corner of the room. She motioned to her parents and started her journey around the tables and people to reach him.

When Hana reached the Krepski table, Tony got up and offered her his seat, but she preferred to stand next to John. She said that her mother would be along in a minute and she was sure that she would take it. Tony had been looking for Stella and could not find her and apparently, she had not arrived yet. He had hoped that nothing was wrong and he would talk to her neighbor who had just come in. Tony had wanted to talk to Stella about getting back together. He wanted to start fresh and court her as he would any other young lady. He knew now, that he loved her as a person, and not some one to release his emotions when he felt like it. He waited until four o'clock and when she did not come, he found his coat and set out for her house to talk to her. He rehearsed his speech on the walk over and did not feel the cold wind that came from the northwest across the Great Lakes. It blew into his face as he subconsciously pulled the scarf tighter around his neck.

When he reached the company house there were lights shining in the kitchen so he went to the back of the house and rapped on the door.

Stella's father answered and asked, "What do you want?"

Tony said, "I want to talk to Stella."

Her Father looked angry and said, "She is not here and she has left for good. You will never see Stella again because she packed her things and left town. She left early this morning and went to live with my sister and her husband in New York City. Forget about her and try to find someone else to see. I am going to close the door now because of the cold wind and you had better leave."

Tony walked back to his house with tears frozen on his face. His first thoughts were to find her, but New York was such a large city and if he left work, he would not have a job when he returned.

John, Pete and Emma came home later that evening and found

Tony sitting at the kitchen table in the dark. They had assumed that he had been at Stella's house all this time, and had they known what had happened, they would have come home earlier. Tony told them what Stella's father said, and they looked at each other in amazement. No one had a clue that this was about to happen.

Pete said, "I will get to the bottom of this mystery. Everyone go to bed because we have to work tomorrow."

Tony did not sleep that night, he tossed and turned and thought about what might have been instead of what was really happening. He went to work looking sad, pale and gaunt with dark circles around his eyes. He did not have a productive day. His boss thinking that he might not be feeling well, sent him home early to go to bed and rest. He said that he would cover for him and arrange for him to be paid for the entire day. In the meantime, Pete was asking questions about the mystery, as he called it. He found no answers, and decided that if he could not unravel the course of events, he would speak to Stella's father.

He went to the club that night and found Stella's father, Jan sitting alone at a table drinking a shot and a beer. He bought a beer, sat across the table from him and Jan looked up to see who it was.

Pete, in a very low voice asked, "Jan, do you want to talk?"

Jan took his time answering, he looked up and said, "She was a slut, Pete, she slept with anyone that asked her and we could not control her anymore. She seemed to straighten out, but when we got home after Mass, we found her in bed with a man. I will not tell you who he was, but he left quickly and it was almost as if she wanted to be caught. We packed her things and I took her to the train in Albany. She will live with my sister and her husband, he is very strict and maybe he can straighten her out. She is probably gone for good. I do not want to have this story spread around, you can tell Tony as long as he promises to keep his mouth shut."

Pete did not know what to say so he said nothing and they just sat there in silence. Jan felt better telling his friend about his problem and Pete was glad that he talked to him. He hoped that he had been of some comfort. When he got back home he found Tony talking to Emma and John who were trying to relieve some of the anxiety that Tony was showing for Stella's welfare. He asked to talk to Tony, alone and they went out to the barn and although, it was cold, neither felt it. Tony wanted to know what had happened and Pete wanted to let him down easy so they talked for an hour and finally, Pete began to feel the cold. They went inside and had a glass of brandy to warm their insides.

Pete put his arm around Tony's shoulder and told him, "No matter what you want to do, I will help You."

Tony went to bed and because of the lack of sleep the night before, he fell into a deep sleep.

Nothing was mentioned of Stella, but Tony thought of her often. He did not take anyone to the New Years party at the club and left early. The fun-loving Tony was no more; he was now the serious Tony. John was spending more time with Hana and this left Tony to join his other friends. Since he was no longer any fun, they excluded him more and more from their activities. He spent more time at home and went to the club only on special occasions. Tony decided that it was time to be on his own and started putting money away so he could rent an apartment. There was little room at his aunt and uncle's home and he thought it best that he move out so that John would not have to sleep on the sofa.

In the middle of February, one of the maintenance men came to John and said that Mr. Gallo wanted to see him when things were slow in the afternoon. John made sure all of the machine bins were full and there were no spools coming off before he went to see the boss. He saw Mr. Gallo through the glass and knocked on the door. He motioned for John to enter without looking up and when John came in, he was told to sit. Mr. Gallo finished what he was working on and put the papers in a basket on his desk. John was learning English so he did not need an interpreter any longer and Mr. Gallo spoke slowly so John could understand. John did not need to speak very often, he acknowledged questions by shaking his head.

Mr. Gallo asked John, "How long have you been working for the company?"

John held up four fingers and said, "Four months."

Mr. Gallo smiled and said, "It is a little over four months and I am pleased with your work. It is company policy to reward the good workers and to let the bad workers go. My figures show that the production in the carding room has increased since you started working here and I receive only good reports from the machine operators. They report that you do not have to be asked to help, you do what has to be done, without being told. I have asked and received permission to give you a raise of seventy-five cents a week and you will be making seven dollars and seventy-five cents a week. I will look at your progress at the end of six months and there might be more money if you continue to do a good job."

He got up, walked around the desk, shook his hand and told John to keep up the good work. John took this as a dismissal and said "Pombuk Zaplaz" and to his surprise Mr. Gallo answered "Nema Zazhu."

John could not stop smiling all afternoon, he could not wait to tell Pete, Emma and Tony, but he would have to wait until he saw Hana to tell her.

At supper, John told Pete and Emma,"I got a raise and I want to pay more for room and board."

Pete said, without hesitation. "We do not want any more money. It cost us nothing to have you sleep on the sofa and Emma has to cook, anyway, so it did not cost us much to cook a little more. Besides, you do work in the barn and the horse and wagon never looked better. No, we are happy with you and we want to leave things just as they are. How is your transportation fund coming?"

He reported, "I have fifty-one dollars and sixteen cents in my strong box."

While John was in the barn that night, Tony came out to talk to him. He said, "I am looking for an apartment and want to know if you want to rent one with me and split the cost. I have to know because this means that I would have to look for a two bedroom place instead of a one bedroom one."

John answered, "Look for a two bedroom apartment because if you move out, your aunt and uncle will insist that I move into your room and they could rent the room to someone else for more money. I do not want to put any more of a hardship on Pete and Emma than I already have."

Tony suggested "We should not discuss this with anyone until we have found a place and made our plans."

A few weeks later, Tony announced, "I found a house to rent. It was one big house which was split in two and there was a common wall, but in effect, it was one building with two houses. It has two bedrooms, a kitchen, dining room and a parlor. There was some furniture, but we would have to get quite a bit more. The house is owned by the company that owns the mill and it will rent to employees of the mill for eight dollars a month. We will have to provide our own heat and gas, there are gaslights in the house. The stove and the icebox come with it along with a kitchen table, two chairs, a sink with a pump. There is a septic tank and a bathroom, but the inside needs paint and cleaning."

Tony and John went to look at it and it needed much work because the previous tenant was a widow who did nothing to clean or maintain the house. They found the paint peeling from the walls and the curtains were there for so long that they had rotted and were frayed at the bottom. There had been a leak in the roof, but it had been repaired. Nothing was done to repair the damage that had been done. A new piece of ceiling had to be put in to blend in with the existing ceiling and then painted. The floor was covered with grime and the linoleum was worn through in spots. It would have to be thrown out. There was cold air coming from around the windows and John wondered how the old lady that lived there was able to survive without a man. The one fault that John found in America was that some of the people lived in homes that were so dirty that he would not allow his animals to stay there on the farm.

John looked at the dirty windows and said, "We have a choice here. We can either wash the windows and put up curtains or we can leave the windows dirty because no one can see in anyway."

Tony appeared to be disappointed when he said. "This place is worse than I thought it would be. We can still back out if you want to."

"No, we can get help and we can fix it up and my vote is to rent it. Lets talk to the company to see if they will deduct some rent or, at least, supply some paint. I have never been afraid of hard work and if we can get some materials from them, we can make this into a nice home."

The company said that the mill would supply the materials, but the tenants would have to provide the labor. There would be no choice of colors because the mill had the paint in stock and they would have to use that. John said that he wanted to talk it over with Pete.

Pete and Emma thought that it was a good idea for the boys to be on their own since they were worried that John had tired of sleeping on the sofa. They wanted their house to themselves and it would be a good idea for Tony to start taking care of his own finances and welfare. They even offered to help paint and clean the inside of the house. They also wanted to talk to their friends and see if they could get some furniture donated so they could spend their money on other things. John took Hana, along with her parents to see the house and Hana said. "I could sew some curtains."

Mary and Andy said in unison. "We will help."

The two friends were excited about moving into their new home so they went to the mill and said that they would rent the house jointly. The man at the mill had already talked to their bosses and found them to be good candidates for the rental of the property. They shook hands and the deal was struck.

They signed the papers, gave the first months rent to the mill and moved their belongings. There was some wood in the back which they used for heat. The lease became effective on April 1, 1903 and while there was not enough furniture, they made due with what they had. Emma invited them to supper twice a week for a few weeks and someone donated pots, pans and dishes so they were able to cook at home. There was a shed attached to the back of the house where they were able to store some of their food and they slept on the floor until they could buy some cots from the company store. Within a month, they had the inside of the house painted, cleaned, with curtains on the windows.

John remarked, "Curtains are very important to women, I do not know why, but my mother was always concerned about her curtains."

Emma answered, "You men have no shame. You do not care that people can look into your house, but we women do and that is why curtains are important."

She walked away, shaking her head while Tony and John just looked at each other and said as one, "Oh"

The outside did not need any work until fall because the covering was tar paper that was made to look like brick and it would not need replacing for a little while.

CHAPTER FOUR

John wrote some letters to his mother and he had received some responses. Things were getting worse with the Magyars taking all that they could from the people of Slovakia. He heard some news at the club, although he did not go to the club as often since he had his own home. His rent was half of the amount that it was with Pete and Emma, but he had to buy his own food, pay his monthly gas bill and provide his own heat. The expenses of moving in were higher than he anticipated, and he did not save as much. He had about sixty dollars in his box and he needed to send home, at least, two hundred and fifty dollars. The weather was getting better with the daylight staying longer in the day and they would have to think about cutting enough wood to last them for the following year. They could save money by cutting their own and not buying it, as Pete had been doing.

He sent a letter to Pavel and instructed him, "Do not reveal to anyone that you are coming to America until we have actually made plans for you. You should plan on a time span of a year and a half and that will bring you over after the harvest of 1904 or possibly even later. It will depend on how much money I can save, but if you can put together some money, we can move the date up. I want you to come to America and the two of us can save to bring Karol over. My thoughts are always with my family that I left behind. I need a favor. Would you check on the tree in the middle of the field where I was born? I want to know if the tree is thriving or if the roots had died."

It seemed so important to John, that Pavel wrote back at once, "I went to the field and the tree has grown straight and tall. It is healthy and each year provides enough leaves to fertilize the area around it. I think that I can save close to fifty dollars so I might be coming sooner."

What John did not know was that Olga already knew of Pavel's plans and she was saving money to give to him.

Hana could not visit John in his new home unless Pete and Emma or Mary and Andy were there. They were looking back at what happened to Stella and they were going to steer this relationship on more solid ground. They all wanted John and Hana to marry, but they wanted the couple to build a good foundation of love and trust before they wed. John saw Hana almost every Saturday night and Sunday afternoon because the club had a function almost every Saturday night. With the afternoon sun becoming warmer, the young couple walked through the fields always under the watchful eye of Mary or Andy.

Easter came and went with the meal on Holy Saturday being held at the Baranowski home. Tony had found a new girl that he really liked. She was not beautiful, a little heavy, but she had other qualities that put those characteristics into the background. Her name was Edna Stuchick and she came from a good family. Her family knew, as did everyone else in the community about Tony's relationship with Stella. They also felt that now that he was on his own, he seemed to have grown up and was more responsible.

The dinner table, at the Baranowski house, was set for eight and it was an excellent meal. Edna brought some of her mother's nut bread and some bread that she made herself. She wanted to demonstrate to Tony and his relatives that she could cook. Tony was pleased when his aunt praised the bread and said that it was better than what she had made. Everyone at the table knew better, but no one challenged the statement; Edna smiled and blushed.

The period of Lent was important to the Slovaks. Usually, in the old country, the larders had given out by the time Easter had come about. The church, hundreds of years before had proclaimed that Lent was a time of sacrifice. Christ had died on the cross and the least that people could do was to fast during the time of Lent.

There was little food left and the food, that was left, was on the verge of spoiling so the less that was put into the body, the better. This fit perfectly with the church doctrine until food became more plentiful as it had in America. The people did not remember why they fasted, but were told to sacrifice for the sake of Christ. The "fast," years ago meant that meat of any kind could not be eaten for the six weeks of Lent which started on Ash Wednesday and continued until noon on holy Saturday. Slowly, the church relented and said that meat could only be eaten on Sunday and then, meat could be eaten everyday except Ash Wednesday and Fridays during Lent.

The time of Lent ran from Ash Wednesday, when ashes were placed on the faithful's forehead to symbolize the fact that they were all destined to return to dust. The fast ended at noon on the Saturday before Easter. The fast was broken when a large meal was eaten as a celebration of the end of lent and Christ being elevated to Heaven. It was a time of joy with a huge meal consisting of meat, vegetables, and sweet breads. There was usually a sunrise Mass on Sunday to commemorate the resurrection of Christ from the tomb. In Ruzbachy, the food was saved for the feast which meant that the fast was more severe. The meat was usually "Shunka" (ham) that was left in the smoke house along with kielbasa and any ribs that were not eaten. The meat was smoked to excess, because it had to be preserved. It was dry and dark colored, but it was meat and it had not passed their lips for six weeks.

In America, the ham was cured by professionals and if the ham was not cured properly, then it was not bought. The company store made sure that there was a good stock of hams and smoked sausage for Easter and after the sunrise Mass, people were invited to share the Easter breakfast at different homes. Volunteers cooked breakfast at the social club for people who wanted to share the day with friends who did not want to cook. The breakfasts at the club were generally very good, there were eggs, kielbasa, fried potatoes, all kinds of bread and plenty of coffee. Depending upon the weather, people would linger over coffee for hours, talking to friends and neighbors. The stresses of the week were gone for another day at least, and Lent was over. Lives could now go back to normal with the prospects of spring coming to Cohoes, New York.

Life was different for John Janek in America. In America, he worked harder than he ever did in his life, but he lived so much better. He had more food and a better variety of it. He could buy what ever he wanted, prepare it the way that he wanted and he did not have to worry about spoilage because he had an icebox. The ice man came every other day, except Sundays and he could keep food for a longer time. A man delivered milk in a glass bottle every other day and collected his money at the end of the month. The milkman had a horse and wagon and the milk was delivered before John went to work in the morning.

He read Pete's newspaper "Jednota" which came once a week and Pete gave him the paper a few days after he received it. It was printed in America, but in the Slovak language and gave a great deal of space to conditions in the old country. It also gave an excellent account of attempts of the various groups to get the United States government to intercede in the manner in which the Magyars were governing the Slovaks. The groups were committed to the formation of Slovakia as a free state with self-rule. This would be difficult and would take a great deal of time, but it was a goal worth achieving. Money was coming into these groups and those that became citizens of the United States were trying to elect representatives in Congress who would look kindly on their cause. The Slovaks in America were well off compared to their friends and relatives in the old country and there might have been some feelings of guilt at leaving them behind. The people, in the mother country, were coping with the hardships while those, in America lived very well.

There was no doubt that John was feeling the guilt that was connected with leaving his family across the ocean. He had set a goal of having one of his family join him, at least, every two years. He saved his money and went without some food and new clothes. John worked hard to better himself and that was paying dividends because he heard from Pete, that the next promotion to a machine operator was his. He had made a favorable impression on Mr. Gallo who was a good manager and kept an expert's eye on what was happening.

The people around him knew what John was trying to do and helped him without being obvious. Someone would bring over some food for him to try when they made a new recipe. They said that they wanted his opinion on how it tasted. Someone in the neighborhood outgrew some clothes and it would be a shame to turn them into rags when John could wear them. He was putting money aside to bring Pavel to America and each week, he opened his strong box and counted the money.

John and Hana were together more often and there was not the constant surveillance by Hana's parents. They liked John and felt that he could be trusted, but Andy had told him on various occasions that he would not tolerate any undesirable activity between the couple. Mary had talked to her daughter on the same subject. They were alone more often so they could talk about the future. They knew that someday they would marry, but neither brought the subject up because Hana knew of his commitment to his family; she was patient.

At the end of June, John was told that there would be a picnic on the club grounds for the Fourth of July celebration. He spoke to Pete at the club one Saturday night and asked him, "What is this holiday on July fourth? There are so many holidays and celebrations in America that I can not keep track of them. Every time I turn around, there is going to be another celebration at the club."

Pete smiled and said, "This is "Independence Day. It is to commemorate the day that America became a free nation. The country was finally governing itself instead of being told what to do by a monarch from across the sea. The day of independence came about on July 4, 1776."

John said, "I can not comprehend that so much has been done with this country in such a short time. Slovakia had been trying to gain independence for over a thousand years and people are still being told what to do by someone else. Someday, Slovakia will be free and independent."

Pete frowned, "Not in our lifetime, John. Not in our lifetime."

John and Hana went to the picnic at the club on July 4th. The day was hot and there was no breeze. John was in shirt sleeves and Hana had on the coolest dress that she owned. She wore a long loose skirt of blue cotton and a white sleeveless cotton blouse. The clothes that were worn on hot, humid days were loose so air could circulate around their bodies. It was not considered lady like for a woman to perspire. The women would excuse themselves and go to the powder room and put talcum powder on themselves to keep perspiration down to a minimum. The men would wear long sleeved shirts because it was unbecoming for a woman to touch a man's arm and feel moisture. Shade was at a premium, but they put a blanket under the huge maple tree in back of the club. The club was located at the end of a side street and there was a considerable amount of land. The parking lot had room for only about ten or twelve vehicles because no one at the club owned a car to drive to the festivities; most of the members walked to the club. If someone owned a car, they could drive elsewhere. There were many large maple trees in the back of the building and the members had the grass trimmed short. The few picnic tables that were scattered around could have used a new coat of paint and the people put a blanket on the ground and ate their food sitting there. The tables were used by the older people that had difficulty getting up and down on the ground and could not sit on the ground for any length of time.

Hana had packed a lunch for the two of them. There was cold chicken, potato salad, cold slaw, bread and cold tea that was coming into fashion at the time. All the food was in a basket with cloth napkins and china plates. John looked around and found that everyone else was doing the same thing. Andy and Mary were some distance away with Pete and Emma, so they could be alone and talk. The two older couples were giving the young couple every opportunity so John might ask the all important question. They realized that it was only a matter of time and the two women smiled at each other every time they saw the young couple alone.

John had been thinking of how he should ask Hana to become his wife and the subject of marriage never came up, so he turned to Hana and suddenly said, "I want to get married. Will you marry me?"

Hana blurted out, "Yes!" and added, "I want to wait until you resolved your commitment to your family or at least altered it."

He said, "I want to have my brother Pavel as my best man when we marry and once Pavel is here, I will have paid back the two hundred dollars that my father loaned me for the passage. He will loan it to Pavel so he can come over. The worst part will be to get the initial money. It will be possible to use that money over and over again to bring the rest of them over. Once Pavel was here and had a job, we would be able to get married, buy a home and get on with our lives."

She asked, "How long will it take?"

John answered, "I expect to have Pavel here by October or November of 1904 or about fifteen months from now."

She said, "That will be acceptable, but I want to tell my mother so she can plan on it. They are looking forward to the marriage of their daughter and want to make it a big wedding. Since you can not contribute much, they should start saving as soon as possible."

The conversation was a quiet one. They did not want to appear too excited or they would alert the others that they were discussing something special. They really did not look at each other and they certainly did not want to show any physical signs of what they were up to. They agreed to tell the others at Christmas of that year and they would set a date at that time. Both of them were relieved to bring it out into the open because each had expected the other to approach the subject. Mary had coached Hana on how to bring up the subject of marriage and she followed her instructions. Hana knew that John was brought up in the old world tradition so she did not want to appear too obvious when she brought it up. John did not want to bring it up too early, but he did not want Hana to get impatient and give up on him. They got up, left their picnic site and started to walk around the area. They stopped to visit with Hana's parents and Pete and Emma, appearing very casual. Pete offered them a glass of wine which they drank while looking into each other's eyes. The other couples smiled at each other because they knew that something was going on between them, but they would not ask. They would be told when the time was right.

The young couple put their plans on hold for a while. Hana had always saved her money and made a trip to the bank every week. She made only six dollars a week, but she managed to put away at least half of it. She gave her parents a dollar a week for board and she had a budget for the rest. Hana would buy nothing unless she had the money in hand to pay for it. There was a room in Hana's home where she stored all of the furniture, curtains, pots and pans that she bought or were given to her. Sometimes, Andy would tell her that he did not want a piece of furniture and would tell Hana to put it in "her" room. This meant that it was now hers and she could take it with her. She had a bed and bed clothing stored which were given to her, a chest of drawers, and an armoire that a friend had sold to her. John did not know about these things and she did not want to tell him. She wanted him to marry her for herself, not because of the material things that she would bring with her.

September came and John could not take his mind off the harvest season at the farm. This was his first year away from the farm and he wondered if his younger brothers could handle it. His father was close to sixty years old now and he should not be doing the heavy work. He would write a letter and casually ask how things were going, but it would take over three weeks for a reply and there was nothing he could do in the meantime. He did not expect any changes at work until the first of the year so he continued to work hard, do more than was asked of him and allowed the days blend one into the other.

John received a letter from Pavel about three and a half weeks later, it was dated September 30th and Pavel said, "The crops are in and not to worry. Even Stefan, who is ten years old, is helping and we do not let father do any of the heavy work. Marta is seven now, is helping mother in the kitchen and we do not let mother work in the fields any longer. I am twenty-two years old now and I take charge, but the only problem is, the conditions with the Magyars is getting worse. No country wants to stay in the empire and the Magyars are taking steps to make sure no one leaves. The Serbs are the most vocal and the Russians sided with them. I hope that no one does anything foolish. It will start a war and then there will be no one going to America."

John was reading about this in his issues of "Jednota," but he was getting the views of the Slovaks living in America. He was glad to get the news from the viewpoint of someone who was living the problems and he knew that he must try to save as much as he could.

Since his brothers were not having any problems with the harvest, he would try to get Pavel over sooner. He discussed this with Hana and she was all for it; the sooner the better. John looked in his strong box at the end of October and he had one hundred and twenty-one dollars and sixty-six cents. At this rate, he would have the two hundred dollars saved by next September with a little extra to use for the wedding. The secret was difficult to keep, but by the way the couple was acting, everyone just waited for the formal announcement. John and Hana decided to make the announcement on Christmas Eve at the club because everyone that they knew would be there; that would make it public.

There was still the matter of where to live that troubled them. Tony and John were renting the house and if John moved out, Tony would end up paying all of the bills himself. John and Hana could stay in the house and then Tony would have no place to live. He could always move back with his aunt and uncle, but they had taken in a boarder to rent the extra room. The boarder was now settled in and it would not be fair to have him find another place. Another option would be to rent a house from the company as

Pete and Emma did, but they would need money to put down, furniture and other household items. Hana decided to tell John about her storage room and her money; once they set a date. If they were to rent a house, it would have to be a free standing house, not one that was connected to another such as the one that John and Tony were renting. They would, eventually want to buy a house and a free standing house would cost more, but John thought that if they bought one that needed work, they might be able to buy it cheaper and he could fix it up. He never saw houses in such disrepair. Every one took care of their place in Slovakia whether they owned it or not. In America, one never took care or repaired a home that they did not own and they just allowed it to get worse and worse.

John felt that he should talk to Tony and see what his plans were because much that they wanted to do, depended upon what he was going to do. Before he could bring up the subject, a piece of news hit the community that almost caused Tony to leave.

Pete was having a few beers with Stella's father, Jan and asked, "How is your daughter doing in New York City?"

Jan answered, "Stella had left my sister's home and abandoned her baby."

As soon as he said it, Jan realized that he had made a mistake. No one knew about the baby and it was meant to be a secret, but a few beers and the casual conversation had caused it to come out.

Jan decide to tell Pete the whole story, "Stella was three months pregnant when she left and she was beginning to show. Her clothes were beginning to get tight on her and we were told that she was pregnant. She would not say who the father was, but I suspect that it was Tony. Stella had stopped seeing Tony and started going out with other men, but did not sleep with them. She had hoped to get back together with Tony and possibly get married. She straightened out and was trying to be a model young lady, but this lasted two or three months and she even bought Tony a Christmas present. On Christmas Eve, she had a change of heart because she felt that Tony would always have a question in his mind as to whether he was the father of the child or not. I suggested that she go live with my sister in New York City, put the baby up for adoption and come back later. She needed an excuse to leave so abruptly so she seduced one of her old boyfriends and arranged for us to catch her. It happened just as she had planned and I moved her out. In July, Stella had a baby boy which she named Andre, but she would not put him up for adoption; she decided to keep her son. It became difficult for her to take care of him and even with the money, we sent every once in a while, it was not enough to support her. Both my sister and her husband worked, she is a waitress and he is a bartender. They are home all morning and left for work in the afternoon. One night, they came home to find the baby home alone while Stella was in an apartment down the hall, in bed with a young man who lived in the same building. When she returned home, words were said and Stella took her clothes, and moved in with her male friend because he would take her, but not the baby. She stayed with him for a week and disappeared. My sister had no choice, but to give the baby to the church since they both had to work to survive. The baby was still under the care of the convent when they learned that there was a couple who wanted to adopt him. The mother superior was reluctant to start adoption proceedings until they could locate Stella. No one has heard from her since the middle of July."

Pete did not interrupt the story and when it was over, Jan said, "I think that you should tell Tony."

Jan replied, "I do not want to tell him, but if you want to, then you could."

Pete had not seen Tony for a few days because he and Edna were becoming close, but with this turn of events, he did not know what would happen. He did know that Tony must be told and it had to come out into the open. If Tony and Edna got married and Tony acknowledged the child, it would strain their marriage to the breaking point. The couple would have issues that would never come to a conclusion and questions would always be there. They could not begin a marriage with this hanging over their head; he would have to tell Tony.

Pete did not go over to Tony's house, but waited until he saw him at work. He invited him over for supper, and made it a point not to invite John. He told John that he wanted to talk to Tony, alone on family business. John understood, but could not help but wonder what was so confidential that he could not be included in the group. He would find out from Tony later when they were home alone. John always considered himself as part of the family and hoped that no one was sick or dying. Tony came home late that night and John could not wait up any longer. He went to bed before Tony came home and the next morning, Tony would not discuss it. He did say however that no one was ill or dying. It was a personal matter within the family that he promised not to reveal and the matter was dropped. John never did find out what the secret was until about a year later.

Tony had not discussed marriage with Edna, but his uncle had persuaded him to forget about Stella and to think about marrying Edna. Edna had to be told about Stella and her baby, but he honestly did not know if the baby was his. He knew that he had to clear the air and he would tell Edna before he asked her to marry him. Tony went to Mass with his uncle and aunt the following Sunday. He met with Edna after church and invited her to go for a walk before they went home. It was a bright sunny day, a little cool, but a good day for walking. He wasted no time and told her the story from the beginning to the present time.

He held nothing back and said, "I do not know if the child is mine because Stella slept with many men. I was closest to her, but every time we had an argument, she would pick up a man and lie with him to get even."

He waited for a reaction before he asked his next question. Edna walked in silence for what seemed, like a very long time, when actually it was only a few minutes.

He kept silent, and finally Edna spoke, "What happened in the past could not be changed, my family likes you and you come from a fine Slovak family. Pete and Emma are very well regarded in the community and although you were not raised by them, I am sure that your previous life is behind you. I promise not to repeat the story, but I am glad that you told me before our relationship went further. I would not know what to think if you had told me after a commitment had been made. I will tell my parents and get their advice and I promise not to reveal it to anyone else."

Tony was interested to learn of their reaction to the news. He took her home without asking her to marry him. He would have to ask her after she had discussed his confession with her parents. His life hung in the balance at this point because Edna might come back and call off their relationship or she might say that it made no difference and they could continue as before. If her decision would be the latter, then he would ask her to get married because he was sure that John was waiting for him to make a move before he spoke to Hana. Life in America was becoming complicated. In Slovakia, this dilemma would have been common knowledge in Ruzbachy and Edna would simply walk away. Stella would have the baby, beg forgiveness from her parents, raise the child and that would be the end of it. Edna would have felt betrayed and, more than likely would not have considered marrying Tony. She would have spent the rest of her life as a spinster, long after the incident had been forgotten.

The following Sunday, Tony asked his uncle, "May I borrow the horse and wagon? I want to take Edna for a ride. The leaves are turning all colors, and I would just spend the day with her. Aunt Emma said that she would pack a lunch and we could have a picnic."

Tony had not spoken to Edna, except to ask her to go for a ride with him. She accepted at once, so that was a good sign. He picked her up and took her and her parents to church. He sat with them and went to communion to show her and her family that he was a good Catholic. The night before he had gone to confession which took a long time and he was happy that he had the young priest or he would be doing penance for the rest of his life. The older priest would not have been so understanding, but the younger priest was more his age and understood what urges he possessed.

After church, the young couple was left alone. This was an extremely good sign, because if Edna's parents felt any distrust of Tony, they would not have let her go with him alone. What Tony did not know was that Edna's parents would not have let this incident stop them from giving the couple their blessing in marriage. Their daughter was not the prettiest girl in the world and she had a difficult time controlling her weight. Her mother was after her constantly to keep her weight from soaring. Edna's mother was a large woman. She knew that once Edna was married and she was not there to guide her, she would gain weight quickly, especially after the first baby. This was a chance to have her daughter married to a good family and once married, Edna and her parents could control his activities.

Tony and Edna rode until they were out of sight of the church and the town, when Tony asked, "What did your parents say?"

She told Tony, "What was done, was done! They will only judge you on the relationship that they had with you and that has been good. They like you and the past made no difference so if I wanted to continue the relationship, then they would not interfere."

Tony sighed in relief and he said, "I would like to get married. Would you consider me for a husband?"

She blushed and said, "I would like to get married and I do want to marry you."

She leaned over and gave Tony a kiss on the lips and he felt his urges growing, but he decided to control them for now.

Tony and Edna decided to marry in the spring, Edna picked a date of May 10th and everyone thought it would be a good time to marry. The buds on the trees would be coming out, giving the country side a new life. The yellow forsythia, apple blossoms and dogwood would be in bloom. They could gather the flowers to decorate the church and the social club and Edna's mother wanted to have a traditional folk wedding. The women would make the wedding dress, supply the food for the reception and the couple would have to report to the priest to meet with him before the wedding.

While Edna made wedding plans, Tony and John worked out an arrangement with the house. John would move out and find a place to board until he and Hana decided what to do. Edna's parents suggested that John move in with them for the time being. He could stay there indefinitely, using Edna's room once she moved in with Tony. At that point, Edna's marriage was the first priority and her parents would overcome any obstacle to see her married.

CHAPTER FIVE

Tony and Edna were married in the church of the Sacred Heart. The young priest, Father John performed the ceremony and the entire Slovak community celebrated. John was best man and a cousin of Edna's, Charlotte was maid of honor. The bride had the traditional beaded dress and a special effort had to be made to make the waist as slim as possible, but the large breasts made the waist look slimmer than it actually was. The women had made up her face and she looked beautiful through the thin veil. The groom had on a dark suit that he had borrowed from one of his friends that was close to his size. Tony went out and bought a stiff collared white shirt and he looked uncomfortable for the rest of the day. When he finally took it off at the end of the day, he had a ring of red around his neck. The celebration went on from Friday night until Sunday night and those people that worked on Saturday, rushed home, washed and dressed before going to the celebration. The music played Friday night, all day Saturday and all day Sunday. The bartender opened eight kegs of beer for the celebration and the food kept coming. Emma spent most of her time directing traffic through the buffet lines. Mens' jackets came off and sleeves were rolled up when the dancing got into full swing. There were three members of the band, a violin, a piano, which belonged to the club, and an accordion. The musicians were allowed to stop for a beer once in a while, but not for a very long time.

The young couple left in the late afternoon, on the day of the ceremony and the march of the matriarchs took them from the bride's former home to her new one The guests went back to party some more before they left the club in the small hours of Sunday morning. Not too many guests were in church for the nine o'clock Mass. Those that worked Saturday missed the ceremony, but the most important time of this wedding was the reception. Everyone was exhausted when the weekend ended and there would be little work done in the mill during the following week. John and Hana did not participate a great deal in the celebration because they were observing the festivities. They wanted to know what had to be done when they were married. They still had not set a date, because it depended on how much John could save. He had close to one hundred and eighty dollars at last count and he only had a few more months to save if they wanted to be married by the end of the year. They were both happy that this couple was married and now they could concentrate on their own wedding.

The Saturday of the wedding, all of Edna's belongings were in Tony's home and John moved into Pavel and Josephine Repchuk's home, in the room vacated by Edna. Josephine remodeled the room, from one in which a woman left, to a man's room. Edna took the wall decorations with her, along with the bed clothing and her clothes and personal articles. She took the canopy off the bed and stored it in the attic. John did not see the room when it belonged to Edna so he did not know what had been done and when he entered the room with his belongings, it looked like an ideal room for him. He was charged one dollar and fifty cents a week. They were going to charge him two dollars a week, but they knew that he was trying to save his money to bring his brother over; he was also about to get married. He would probably have a good deal of his meals at Hana's home or with Pete and Emma and as a joke, they said that they were not losing a daughter from the household, but were gaining a son.

The summer went by quickly, with all the holidays and events at the club. In August, Mr. Gallo called John into his office and said, "I am pleased with your work. One of my spinning machine operators has left to go west and there is an opening. I consider you my most stable worker and I know that you would have the intelligence to learn the job quickly. The job pays twelve dollars a week after you showed me that you could do the work. You will start Monday."

John left his office and could hardly control himself so he could tell Hana. She was just as excited when he told her. With more money, he could send for Pavel earlier and they could be married earlier.

She told him, "You will have to learn the job quickly because Mr. Gallo will be watching you and he did not get to where is by being stupid. Mr. Gallo will tell you in two weeks if you can do the work or not."

John found out later that Pete and her father had recommended him to his boss. The machine operators from the carding room did not want to lose him, but they wanted to have him promoted. That was how Slovaks took care of their own.

The following Monday, John started his new job in the spinning room and Mr. Gallo led him into a room where twelve huge machines were running. Each set of three, was run by its own steam engine and there were three other operators; each much older than John. There were two types of spinning machines and John would run three that were called "mules." These machines took yarn from huge spools and wound them on small spools called "bobbins." There were twenty-four bobbins on each machine so he was charged with making sure that seventy-two bobbins were winding yarn. If there was a break, John was to mend the two pieces by twisting them together so they could continue to wind, but he had to watch the seventy-two bobbins all the time. Once the bobbins were full, he would stop the machine and "doff" the bobbins by taking them off the machine and throwing them into a basket which had wheels on it. The basket would be taken into the weaving room and the bobbins would be put on a loom to be woven into a carpet. The mules processed yarn that was heavier and was used for rugs. The frames had lighter yarn that was used for sweaters and clothing.

The four machine operators helped each other when one became very busy. They helped each other doff the machines and to place a new spool on the machine when it was empty. The splicing of the broken yarn took some skill and he had to learn how to start a new set of bobbins when the full ones were taken off. There was not too much to do when all three machines were running, but once one of the machines was full the room became a beehive of activity. John now understood why the job paid so well because it took work and skill to keep the machines going. If they were slow, then the weaving room had no yarn and the looms had to be shut down to wait for more.

The first few days, the activity was high and John was running in all directions at once. The other three operators told him that he would do a good job once he became used to the activity. He realized that the mules were timed so two of them did not doff at the same time and with all the operators helping, they could put the machine back in service very quickly. Two weeks later, Mr. Gallo came into the department and talked to the other three operators. When he finished, he came to John and told him that the job was his and his pay would start on the following week. The other three, who knew what was happening, waved to John when Mr. Gallo left. He had joined the circle of machine operators and was not considered unskilled labor any longer.

John took out his strong box in late September and he counted two hundred and sixteen dollars. He took two hundred dollars, went to the bank and sent the money to his father for Pavel.

It was time to send a letter to Pavel. He wrote, "We are ready for you to come over. You are to book passage on the first ship to come over. The money will be put in the bank in Polodencz and mother and father could draw it out and buy the ticket. Once the ticket was paid for, you can write me a letter telling me when you are docking. You will come into Boston, take a train to Albany so I can meet you there. I have just started a new job and I cannot get time off to meet you in Boston."

With this out of the way, he could sit down and discuss the wedding with Hana. They agreed upon a date in November, two weeks before the Thanksgiving holiday. John made an appointment with Father John so that there would be no conflict with Advent, the start of the new year for the church. Once Advent came about, the priests were busy with preparations for Christmas. He and Hana promised to meet with Father John every other week, until the wedding. The young couple felt that they picked the best time of the year to get married. The leaves would be in full color, the air would be crisp and cool and it would be too early for the snows to come. Hana had her dress made and put it in storage because she knew she would be using it sometime. Her mother and her friends had finished it some time ago. It was a beautiful dress with elaborate embroidery covering the bodice, the lace shawl and veil were also embroidered, matching the dress. The dress was white and came down to floor with a train six feet long. The only matter to be considered was where to live after they were wed. They agreed that they should have a home of their own. Hana did not even consider living with her parents after they were married. The space vacated by Hana in her parents home would be rented to Pavel who would need a place to live. Knowing Pavel, he would not agree to move in with the newly married couple because they needed time to live together and get to know each other.

There were three homes for rent by the company that owned the mill. All three were free standing homes and were almost identical. Each previous renter had made some improvements and the rent was the same for all three. John and Hana visited each one and picked the one that showed the most care by the previous renter. The location was far enough away from Hana's parents where they would not be visiting too frequently and close enough where they would be welcome if they elected to come.

When John discussed the terms of the rental, he asked the agent, "What would it cost to buy the house?"

The agent said, "The price of this home is nine hundred dollars now, but the price of homes near the mill was going up and if you really want to buy the house, I am sure some arrangement could be made."

The agent left the room to discuss it with his superiors and approached John with an option agreement. "You would pay the owner fifty dollars for the option that would run for two years and the rent would be eight dollars a month. If at the end of two years, you decided to buy the house, the rent of $192 plus the $50 would be deducted from the purchase price. The remainder would be financed and the ownership of the house would be transferred to you and your wife. The reason that we are not selling you the house, outright is that you are not married yet, and who knows what could happen. If you get married then you will have lost nothing."

John discussed this with Hana who suggested that they discuss it with her parents and receive any thoughts that they might have. John knew what he was going to do, but out of courtesy to Hana, he agreed to meet with her parents that evening.

As they sat around the kitchen table with a fresh brewed pot of coffee, John explained the agreement, "This was the first time the owners of the mill have offered this type of plan to one of its employees. We would have to pay rent anyway and all that was at risk was fifty dollars which we would get back if we bought the home. If the price of the real estate went up, then we are locked into the lower price. No one feels that the price of real estate in Cohoes would go down."

Hana was watching the intensity on the faces of her mother and father. Andy looked at his wife who gave him a slight nod and he spoke, "I feel that you should rent this house, with an option to buy in two years. We will even loan you the fifty dollars."

They looked at Hana who smiled and said, "I have saved that much and we do not need it."

John looked at Hana with a surprised look on his face because he knew nothing about the money. He said to Andy and Mary, "Since you are paying for the wedding, we do not want to impose an additional burden on you by taking the loan of fifty dollars."

Mary stood up and embraced her future son-in-law. John's face flushed as he hugged her back. Everyone was talking at once and the lights burned a bit later as they discussed their plans. Hana's parents were delighted with the turn of events. Their daughter was marrying a man she loved, who had proven himself to be kind, gentle, intelligent and the most important point of all, he loved their daughter.

On the last day of October, John went to Albany to pick up Pavel at the train station. He was excited in anticipation of meeting the brother that he had not seen in two years; they had many things to discuss. John wanted to know how his parents were doing, their health, the living conditions and to explore the possibility of bringing the rest of the family to America. Since Pavel's train came in at seven in the evening, he was able to pick him up. He saw Pavel as he stepped off the train and he thought that this must be how he looked to Tony when he stepped from the train. He never realized how much he had grown since he came to America and he could teach Pavel all the ins and outs on how to survive in this country. They greeted each other with an embrace and then John stepped back to look at his brother. He was thin, his cheeks were hollow and he looked as if he had not had a decent meal since he left home. The handle bar mustache made him looked even more gaunt. John looked at Pavel's homemade suit, his old world hat, his boots, the calloused hands and he thought that he must have worked hard just before he left home. His coat just hung on him and someone must have given it to him to make his journey to America. His boots looked worn and they have seen better days; John would have thrown them out long ago. He smelled of stale sweat and it was obvious that he had not washed himself since he left home. There was no mistaking the steel gaze of his brown eyes and the broad Janek smile. They rode to Cohoes slowly as John wanted to spend as much time as possible with Pavel before he met the people that were to be his friends for the rest of his life. Pavel was tired, but he answered all the questions that John asked while the luggage that Pavel brought with him bounced about in the back of the wagon. There was only one suitcase and that was filled with dirty clothes. Pavel carried everything valuable on his person because he was warned that there were many thieves who looked to liberate an unsuspecting person's valuables from him. They finally arrived at the Repchuk home and Hana came running from the house. She had been waiting for them, walking from window to window and when she first caught sight of them, she threw her coat on and ran out. It was getting dark so neither Hana or Pavel could see each other very well until they entered the house. John ushered Pavel in and introduced him to Mrs. and Mr. Repchuk and Hana. Hana already had her arm around his waist and had accepted John's only relative in America. Pavel was overwhelmed. He was hungry, but did not think of food as he smelled from the long trip and needed to wash and put on clean clothes. John had some clothes ready for him, but they would be big for Pavel. John said. "You will grow into them." Josephine took the suitcase into John's room and sat Pavel down at the table. The first thing one received in a Slovak home was food and John and Pavel ate while the rest watched. John thought that life was getting better and better all the time.

Hana had insisted on two things for her wedding. She wanted to have the men dressed in tuxedos, a very formal suit that one rented for the occasion. The other condition was that they hire a photographer who would take pictures of the wedding and preserve the moment for all time. She also wanted to send pictures to Olga and Johan in Slovakia so they could see her two sons dressed for the wedding. John agreed because he wanted his parents to see Hana and how beautiful she would be in her traditional dress. He wanted his people to know that the traditions from their heritage were not forgotten, but lived on through their children in America. John did not wait long before he took Pavel to the tailor in Albany to measure him for his formal suit.

On the ride to Albany, John said, "We waited to be married because I wanted you to stand up for me at my wedding. It was a long time and Hana agreed so we are very happy that you are here. There is no one that I would rather have here than you. You will be very happy in America. I felt so alone and now that I have you here, there is nothing that we cannot do. Now, we have to solve the problem of finding you some work."

John was looking straight ahead and he did not see the tear that was finding its way down Pavel's cheek. Pavel turned his head away so his brother would not see him wipe it away. Once the matter of the suit was taken care of, Pavel took one day to rest and the following morning, John brought him to work with him. He had spoken to Mr. Gallo about his brother and took him right in to see if he could be put to work. John had paid Josephine the first week of the board for Pavel so he could wait a short time until he found work.

Mr. Gallo looked at Pavel and said, "There will be a job opening in a few weeks, and if you can wait that long, you may have the job. Your job would be transporting the bobbins from the spinning room to the weaving room. You will also be required to help doff the mule and the frame machines. In your spare time, you will oil the machines and keep the spinning room floor clean. The job pays six dollars a week."

He looked at Pavel who was looking at John. John was nodding his head up and down and Pavel gratefully accepted. The thing that impressed Mr. Gallo was the calloused hands he felt when he shook hands with Pavel. Mr. Gallo referred to Pavel as "Paul" because it was much easier for him to say.

When they left, John told him, "Everyone in America has a nickname so everyone will call you Paul. Everyone calls me John instead of Johan and I feel that as long as I live in America, I will answer to that name."

Paul spent the next three weeks exploring the area. He was introduced to the Slovak Social Club and had no shortage of friends when he went there. Some of the older men who could not handle the work at the mill any longer, spent their days at the club playing cards and catching up on the latest gossip. They asked Paul questions about their homeland, and shook their heads back and forth when they heard the news. They did not remember the hard times that they endured across the ocean because the better life in

America had caused those memories to fade into the recesses of their minds. They would finish their days in America and did not want to return to the "Old Country." Paul borrowed the horse and wagon from Pete and spent sometime riding around the countryside. The splash of colors caused by the changing of the leaves caused him to arrive back to Pete's barn later than he wanted, but he still rubbed down the horse. He fed him, talked to him and made sure that the horse was well cared for.

Pete had remarked at the club more than once. "Those Janek boys know how to take care of horses."

The weekend of the wedding finally arrived and along with it the news that Paul would start work on the following Monday. John had gotten off work early on Friday, but he had to take the day off on Saturday without pay. People gathered at the club on Friday night with the food. Soon the tables were filled and people were sitting along the walls to see the festivities. John and Hana walked around and met the guests while they were still single. There were a great many stories told of previous weddings and the young couple were teased about the upcoming wedding and the wedding night. John introduced his brother to people that he had not met and the celebration started in earnest. The band began to play, the beer began to flow and people started to dance. They started with the oberek, a three quarter time dance and as the people consumed more beer, the music got into the polka and then the tsardise. The latter is a dance imported from Russia, where the men sat on their heels and kicked their feet out in time to the music. Paul knew the dance very well and since he was the leanest, he did it very well. He was the hit of the party and all the girls wanted to dance with him.

The party started to break up about two in the morning because Hana and her parents left early so Hana could get some sleep. Mary said, "Unless Hana got six hours of sleep, her face would be puffy and that would be preserved for all time on the photographs."

Paul and John stayed until the end and when they did get home, they both fell on their beds; exhausted. They fell asleep at once and the next thing they heard was a rapping at their door. It was seven o'clock and Josephine told them to get up because they had only three hours until the ceremony. She gave them a good breakfast since they would not get a full meal for the rest of the day. They could pick and eat food all day long, but they would be too busy to eat a complete meal. They spent the next hour washing and getting dressed in their tuxedos. Paul left his mustache on, although John would have preferred to have him shave it off.

Paul said, "Since photographs will be taken, I will always look back and show people how I looked with a handle bar mustache. I will feel naked without it. It would be like wearing no shirt. You would not want our mother to see the pictures of the wedding where I was not wearing a shirt."

John laughed, "You have not lost your sense of humor. Do not ever lose it. Keep it forever."

A knock came at the door and Pete walked in, he had decorated the horse and wagon and it was parked outside.

Hana was up early and found that her father was still asleep, but her mother had been up for hours. She had been cooking and baking for days and she had to have everything ready. Some friends would carry the food to the club. The photographer had arrived with his big box on a tripod so she finished putting out the food and woke Andy. He got up and had a large breakfast, because he would be busy all day meeting and greeting people. He and Mary dressed in their traditional embroidered costumes and sat in the parlor while neighbors gathered around them. At nine o'clock, Hana came in dressed in her embroidered dress to bid her mother and father a moving farewell, before going to church. The father, by tradition, had a to show reluctance in allowing his little girl to leave his home and protection. After about fifteen minutes, he agreed and Hana was led by the maid of honor to the waiting carriage driven by the best man. The carriage was driven very slowly towards the church so everyone could see how beautiful the bride was and those that did not have to work, went to the church to attend the ceremony.

Paul had already dropped John off at the church where he had an hour to wait before the marriage ceremony would begin. Everyone went into the church where Andy would lead Hana down the aisle to meet her intended. The even flow of the ceremony was halted while the photographer took a picture with his box and flame. The veil would cover Hana's face until they were man and wife because it was considered a bad omen if the groom saw his bride's face before they were wed. The ceremony consisted of a High Mass which was interrupted for the marriage ceremony and then everyone went to communion to honor the newly weds. After the wedding, the bride and groom were put into the carriage and driven to a spot behind the club that was selected because of the color for the pictures. Even though the pictures would be in black and white, it would remind the couple of the colors for the rest of their lives.

The guests went into the club and did not wait for the guests of honor to arrive before the festivities began, the bartender was already pouring beer and the music had started. When the newly weds arrived, the guests let out a mighty cheer and the couple made their way to the head table. Two married women brought them some food, but they were never given a chance to eat it. The people going to the food line stopped at the head table to kiss the bride and shake hands with the groom. When the last of the people went by, it was time to go visit all the guests at their tables. The music became louder and those who had finished eating, wanted to dance with the bride and groom. After each drink, the noise level got higher and higher and the smoke from the cigars that were on the bar, settled in a blue haze about a foot from the ceiling. The doors were opened in an attempt to air out the room, but that did little good.

Although the foyer of the hall had a table filled with gifts, some hand made and some store purchased, each man that danced with the bride slipped her a dollar or two. By the middle of the afternoon, she had at least fifty dollars in her hand. The music continued and as food was eaten, more would suddenly materialized on the table. People ate until they could eat no more, some of the men went outside for some air and to find the large tree growing behind the hall. With all the beer being consumed, no one could wait for the little privy to be empty so they just went out of sight and used the large maple tree. Over the years it was no wonder that this tree grew larger than the rest.

The celebration continued into the evening when it was customary for the best man to drive the married couple to their new home where they were to spend their first night. As they bid their farewell, all the guests gathered around the carriage, teasing them about their first night together. Paul started the wagon and the married women at the wedding lined up behind it; the march of the matriarchs had begun. They carried all of the wedding gifts and other necessities such as pots and pans, bed clothes, dishes, and table wear. Once they arrived at the bride's new home, they proceeded to set up the bedroom and kitchen for the couple. When they were finished, the married women returned to the club to join in the celebration. With the newlyweds finally gone, the guests would continue the celebration, until they or the beer gave out, whichever came first. While they were being driven to their home, John asked Paul to go back to the club and bring them some food because John had not eaten since early that morning and Hana did not eat at all. John confessed that he had forgotten to put food into the house so Paul dropped them off and went back to the club. He asked Mary to put up some food for the couple, but she said that it was all taken care of. When John and Hana arrived home, they found the table set for two, with food on the stove and the wine chilled. The theory behind making the new home perfect for the first night, was that everything must be made comfortable for the couple. When they went to bed that evening, they could perform their respective function. This was the reason to marry, to start a family and procreate, the love making was incidental.

The next morning after Mass, the club again filled up with people since some were not there the day before. The couple was not expected to be at the club because they were expected to start their new life together. The people at the club did not need the bride and groom to continue the celebration; they could do very well without them until the small hours of Monday morning. The people running the mill realized that the day after a wedding of this size was not going to be their most productive day so they bit the bullet and allowed the day to go on without much interference.

CHAPTER SIX

Paul went to work with John the following day and was left with Mr. Gallo. His boss took Paul to his immediate superior who showed him what his duties were while John went to tend his machines. Paul's supervisor was a Slovak named Carl (Karol) Paskudnek and Mr. Gallo wanted Paul to work with some one who understood his language. The duties were simple and very soon, Paul would be left on this own. Paul felt that as long as he was busy, the time would go by faster. He took directions quickly so his instructor had to tell him only once and he knew what to do. In his enthusiasm to please, he became gullible and became the object of some practical jokes. One man sent him to the carding room to get a left handed monkey wrench and Paul dutifully went. He asked one of the machine operators who sent him to another while they all laughed at the naive immigrant. They told him that he would have to wait until one became free, so he went back and relayed the message. Another operator told him to get a pail of steam so a frozen nut could be taken off. Again, Paul went back and tried to find a pail of steam. He was told they were out of steam so he would have to come back. In the meantime, a mule operator heard what they were doing and told John, who immediately went to find Paul. He explained that the men were playing tricks on him and he should think before he ran these errands.

Instead of getting angry, Paul decided to turn the tables on his tricksters. The next day, he brought a bottle of sarsparilla to work to refresh himself during the day. The fluid was dark and the bottle had a lever type top on it. He drank about a third of the liquid and filled the rest with oil that was used on the machines. He left the bottle in sight and asked the man who was sending him all over the mill to watch it because he had to go into the weaving room. He knew what would happen and it did. As soon as he left the room, the trickster took the bottle of pop and drank it down at once. He thought that it tasted peculiar, but he attributed this to a difference in taste by the foreigner. When asked who drank his pop, everyone pointed to one another and laughed, but Paul just waited and watched the man who was supposed to be guarding his refreshment. Within a half an hour, the man ran to the outside toilet, stayed there for an hour and came back very pale. No sooner had he returned when he ran outside again and came back looking even more pale. The other men watched what was happening, but no one said a word and covered for the man that had suddenly became ill.

One of the machine operators smelled the empty bottle of soda. He knew at once that there was oil in it and he looked at Paul who just smiled.

The machine operator came to Paul, clapped him on his back and said, "I hope that there are no hard feelings."

Paul had sent the message that he was not the "greenhorn" that they took him to be and he was, from that day on, "one of the "boys." He was invited to meet at the club and made friends with everyone except the man who drank the pop who spent two days in pure agony. Paul realized this and kept his eye on him from then on. John told him a few nights later that the story had spread through the mill. While some felt that it was a harsh trick, most said that it was about time that someone had stood up to this man and gave him a dose of his own medicine. The Janek boys were building a reputation as being, hard working, fair and were not to be mocked. If someone made them the target of any mischief, then he would have to watch his back for the retaliation. Paul's job became easier now that he learned his duties, the men accepted him as one of their own, helped him and he helped the machine operators when they were busy. Word went around that Paul was a good man to have around when the going got tough.

The weather was turning colder so he could not spend as much time out of doors and the club was the only activity in Cohoes in the winter time. He was invited to dinner with John and Hana and took the opportunity to talk to them about life in America. They explained the various holidays and what they were going to celebrate. Paul was amazed at all the food there was to eat and said, "Americans wasted more food than we ate in Slovakia."

John brought up the subject of the two hundred dollars that he had loaned to Paul. John wanted Paul to save the same sum so he could send it back home for Karol to use for his fare. Since Josef was fifteen and Stefan was only twelve years old, there was time to bring them over. They planned to send the money over in two years and worry about the final three later. They also considered bringing their mother and father over with Stefan, but they would have to plan on doing something with the farm.

John said, "We will have to make plans so tell me, from time to time, how much you have saved until we have enough to bring Karol over. Hana and I have an opportunity to buy this house, but we had to pay fifty dollars for an option and we still have to pay rent for two years. We do not want to lose that money by not buying the house."

They agreed upon a plan and John and Paul turned to the task of fixing John's home. They worked on the inside during the winter and when spring arrived they started on the outside because the house needed landscaping and some repair of the windows and siding. Some of the siding had to be replaced, a few of the windows were rotted and needed to be replaced and they needed to make the house air tight to save heat. They could not do anything to the structure, but they repaired the cracks around the windows and doors. The Janek men went over the entire roof and replaced some of the tar paper that had blown away. They heated tar and filled in the holes that were not too big and did not need to be replaced. Pete came to help often and showed them how to buy materials that were unfamiliar to them. Pete loaned them the wagon and they went into the woods at the edge of town and dug some plants and trees that they planted around the house.

"John said, "It is a good thing that our father learned about these plants from Brother Jan at the Abbey because we could not afford to buy them."

Paul nodded as he wiped the sweat from his brow with his red handkerchief, "It would be better if we brought Brother Jan over here to do this for us."

The Janek boys were no strangers to work and it made them feel good, to be able to work together. They would make the home into show place by the end of summer.

In March of that year, Hana announced to John, "I am pregnant."

"Great news." Said John "When are you due?"

"Sometime in the middle of October. I have not figured it out yet, but you can be sure my mother will have a date. The baby is due at the right time of the year. I can wear the same clothes until I have the baby and I do not have to buy winter maternity clothes which are so expensive."

It became common practice for pregnant women to borrow maternity clothes from each other rather than spend the money to buy them. The baby, however would need clothes, a crib and other furniture. The other bedroom that they were using as the spare room, would have to be turned into a nursery. This would mean that John and Hana could not save a great deal of money, especially when Hana had to stop working. Paul understood that he would have the greater burden of saving to bring Karol to America.

Paul was promoted from the spinning room to the carding room where the work was heavier, but the pay was more. He made a dollar a week more which meant that he could put more money into their savings fund.

John and Hana took Paul to the fourth of July picnic where he met a young lady whose name was Maria Solotsky. Maria worked with Hana in the weaving room and the meeting, unknown to Paul, was set up by Hana with the express purpose of having Maria meet Paul. Maria brought her meal over to the Janek's spot on the grass and shared her food with Paul. She did not own very many clothes and it appeared that she wore the same ones all the time. She was still wearing the clothes left by her mother. The dresses were faded, but they were always clean and ironed. She wore a babushka on her head most of the time and did not adapt to the young ladies' style of going bare headed. Paul did not know it at the time, but this meeting would have a great impact on his life. She was two years older than Paul and she was approaching the age where men looked at her and wondered why she was not married. They assumed that there was something wrong with her and with the added burden of her disabled father, they stayed away.

Maria was actually a hard working, diligent woman but she was rather shy and did not mingle in the social circles very well. Her father did not work after he had an accident in the mill. His right hand was caught in the carding machine and it had to be amputated just below the elbow. He could not do the heavy work any longer nor could he work on the machines because he could not splice the yarn. Her mother had died when she was sixteen and she left school to go to work. The mill gave her father a small pension which helped support him. He owned his home and did not owe any money on it; they survived very well. Maria was a small woman with a trim frame, her hair was light brown and tied in a bun in back and this made her seem older than she was. This was one of the reasons that the young men left her alone. Her eyes were brown and even without makeup, they appeared very large and fluid. The eyes seemed to sparkle and laugh all the time and they were her most attractive feature.

Maria and her father went to church every Sunday and Paul had remembered her with the one-armed man when he went to Mass.

She told Paul, "You should speak in English, since you will have to learn the language anyway. I am going to help you learn the language and do not get angry when I correct you."

John said, "It is no small task to educate a Janek in anything and I admire your courage in attempting to do it."

Hana knew Maria for a very long time and she liked her so the two couples were at ease with each other and they had a pleasant time at the picnic. They promised to see each other again and Maria would go to the club more often so she could get to see more of Paul. Hana was pleased with herself.

Later that night, at home with John, she said, "I should be a marriage broker since I am so good at it."

John liked the idea that Paul met someone and could get on with his own life. He smiled, but said nothing about Hana's remark.

John Janek, Jr. was born at home on October 5, 1906. He weighed eight pounds and twelve ounces. The chubby little boy was eighteen and a half inches long and looked like he was six months old when he was born. The women could not resist the temptation to squeeze his chubby little cheeks when they looked at him. Paul was the godfather and Maria was the godmother. Maria had a yearning look in her eye every time she looked at the baby and this did not go unnoticed by Paul. It was about time that he was thinking about getting married and Maria was a fine, strong woman who came from a good Slovak family. He decided to steer a course towards marriage and follow in John's footsteps.

Paul saved his money by following the examples of John and his parents. He bought only what he needed at the time and did absolutely, no impulsive buying. John could not save much because Hana had to stay home and take care of the baby while he was nursing. Young Johnny was always hungry and demanded a great deal of attention. It took Paul twenty months to save enough money to send for Karol and he postponed his marriage until his brother could be with him. In the meantime, Hana announced that she was going to have another baby in February of 1909. She had gone back to work six months after Johnny was born while her mother cared for the child. Hana would rise early, feed and dress him and then take him over to her mother's house. Since Mary and Andy had paid off the mortgage on their home, Mary decided that she did not want to work any longer. The real reason was that Mary wanted to help her daughter, by taking care of Johnny. On the way home from work, Hana would pick up Johnny, take him home and then make supper. Weekends were spent in cleaning, washing clothes and cooking. John would finish supper, play with Johnny and then spend the rest of the evening at the club because this was the only time that he saw his brother, Paul.

The difficult schedule was taking its toll on Hana. She lost weight and dark rings had formed under her eyes. Her mother had noticed the changes, but she did not interfere. She and Andy had discussed it and Andy suggested that she bring Johnny home a few hours early and handle a few of the chores that she could do. This would give Hana more time to rest after the supper dishes were cleaned up. John had noticed that Mary was spending more time at their home and he realized what was happening. He would see that Hana was having problems and he would stay home to help her clean up after supper or spend more time with Johnny so Hana could get a few things done. The other alternative, would be to allow Hana to stay home from work and care for the household. The house had been purchased about a year before and the money that they needed to live on stabilized, so Hana really did not have to work.

They talked about it one night and John said, "Your mother is spending more time here than she used to. She is a good help and things are getting better, but she is getting older. How are you feeling? You look tired all the time."

She said, "My mother is coming over a few hours before I get home so she can help me because I am having a difficult time with managing the house, the work, Johnny and my pregnancy."

Since Hana handled the finances, he and his wife went over what had been coming in, what was going out and John said, "Paul is saving money and when Karol comes over, the both of them will worry about getting Josef to come over. We can afford to let you stay home and when the children become older and go to school, you can return to work if you want to."

Hana said, "I could economize by staying home because I could make better meals, keep a better house and bring Johnny up the way he should be brought up."

John had not realized that he was spending so much time at the club and resolved to spend more time with Johnny. He had many stories to tell him about life in the old country, and he wanted to pass on the history of his family. Hana would leave work and become a housewife.

CHAPTER SEVEN

Paul missed seeing John at the club, but John's place was taken by Maria. Paul had sent the money for Karol's fare, to the bank in Polodencz and he was due to come over in February of 1909. The time passed very quickly for Paul because he was seeing Maria at least four times a week and he was invited for dinner twice a week. She had to show Paul that she could cook and keep a house. She even offered to take Johnny on picnics so she could show Paul how well she could take care of children. She also felt that she could give John and Hana a day off, once in a while to spend the time alone. Maria knew that Paul was a good provider, and understood that he would take care of a family by the way he saved. Bringing his brother over was his first priority. They were getting to know each other and this was the game that was usually played to prepare them for marriage. One had to make friends with the future in-laws and that was easy for Maria. It was more difficult for Paul, because he had to deal with Maria's father, Joe. Her father was demanding equal time for Maria's attention because he was dependent upon her. Maria had always taken care of her father and although, he was not as handicapped as he made out, he did not want his dependence on her to slip away.

Paul and Maria had decided to be married in May of 1909. Since Maria and her father were surviving, the young couple would have to put on the wedding and could not rely upon him for help. The women at the club would help, but the couple had to put aside money for liquor and pictures. They would not have a wedding that would compare to that of John, but it would bind them together. Paul would move in with Maria and her father and some day, the house would be hers. If Maria and her father were able to survive before Paul came to live with them, with his money, they could live very well. When Paul asked Joe for Maria's hand in marriage, as was the custom in the old country, Joe merely shrugged his shoulders and said that he would consent to the wedding and they had his blessing. Paul took Joe to the club that night and they announced it to the members that were there. That was equivalent to announcing it to the entire Slovak population of Cohoes. The next morning, everyone in the Slovak community knew that the young couple was to be married.

Paul and John borrowed Pete's carriage and met Karol at the train station in Albany on February 2, 1909. Karol had gotten older and looked thin, his clothes were too large for his frame. He had not eaten in two days so they stopped in a tavern and bought him two bowls of potato soup with plenty of bread. Karol was the smallest of the Janek family and the thinnest. He did not have a mustache, but he had the intense eyes and the Janek smile. His hands were calloused so badly that he had a problem making a fist. John took the battered hat that he wore and threw it into the refuse barrel right at the train station.

John said, "You will not need that any longer, we will get you a new one when we arrive home."

As the horse plotted to Cohoes, Karol told his brothers, "We should consider getting the rest of the family to America before the war broke out. All that will be required is a spark and the whole continent will be shooting at one another."

They all agreed that Marta and Josef would be next to come over and they would have to take their chances with Stefan and their parents.

Karol told them things that Olga would not put into a letter, "Food is scarce with the Magyars demanding more and more from the small towns. Ruzbachy now has a Magyar notary who keeps track of what everyone owns and produces so he will know how much to take away. Josef works hard, but father can not do the things that he used to. Stefan is fifteen, he helps way beyond his years and Marta helps her mother in the house. Sometimes, when needed, Marta will have go out into the fields and work like a man."

John and Paul had read about the happenings in Slovakia, in the "Jednota" but they had not realized that the problems were extending into the countryside. The Magyars had left the smaller towns on the outskirts of the empire alone, but the conditions had worsened in the empire. In order to finance their lust for more territory, they had to go to the towns such as Ruzbachy.

John told his brothers, "Hana no longer works and not having two pay checks coming into the household, means that I have to economize in order to survive. With Hana due to deliver our second child any day now, it means that I cannot not contribute much."

Paul said, "I will keep on saving and once we put Karol to work, we might be able to save enough to bring Marta and Josef to America in at least two years. If the war will hold off for two years after that, we might manage to bring the final three to this country. Our goal is to bring the whole family to join us. We cannot begin to better themselves until our entire family is together."

They made a pact that day, to work hard until the entire family was safely in America.

Karol made friends quickly at the club because he was the clown of the family. He could make anyone laugh with his antics and he kept everyone entertained with his impersonation of the notary in Ruzbachy. Everyone offered to buy him a beer just to hear his stories.

John spoke to Mr. Gallo who asked, "How many other brothers do you have waiting in the wings?"

John answered, "We have two brothers and one sister left in Slovakia who will be looking for jobs sometime in the future."

The only job open was the job of driving the wagons with the bales of wool from the train station in Albany to the mill in Cohoes. It took a team of four horses to pull the wagon and some skill to get the animals to work together, but Karol knew horses and he could do the work. The only draw back was that it was an outside job, it was winter and although the wagons were equipped with a cab that was used to protect the driver, there was no heat and the wind whistled through the open spaces. The mill had many applicants for the job in the spring, summer and fall, but they would all leave in the winter. Karol took the job because it paid ten dollars a week and, for ten dollars a week, Karol would drive the wagon for nine months until the cold weather became again. It would give him some time to find something better.

Ten days after Karol arrived, Hana delivered a baby girl that they named Catherine. Cathy was a small baby by Janek standards as she weighed seven pounds and four ounces and she was a pretty baby with pink cheeks on both ends. They asked Karol, who had his name shortened to Karl by his friends, to be godfather and Hana's cousin, who was her maid of honor to be the godmother. This was Karl's first duty for the family in his new country. Pictures were taken of the entire family and sent to Olga and Johan because the family was growing and in the following years it would exceed everyone's expectations. Paul had made arrangements for Karl to stay at a boarding house. He slept in a dormitory style room until Paul was married. Paul would move out of his room so Karl could take his place. They had gotten Karl some warm clothing so that he could survive the cold wagon trips and he made three trips a day from Cohoes to Albany. He left on his first trip at seven in the morning, waited for his wagon to be loaded with eight bales of wool and start back. The wagon would be backed into the stall at the factory, left to be unloaded while he hitched his team to another wagon. The last trip would bring him into Cohoes at five in the afternoon. He would unhitch the horses, feed and groom them and take them to the stables.

On May 23, 1909, Maria and Paul were married in the church of the Sacred Heart in Cohoes. There were no rented suits and the expenses of the wedding were kept at a minimum. The custom of carrying the brides belongings to her new home could not be done because Paul would move in with his new wife. Joe beamed through the whole ceremony since he felt that his daughter's marriage ended his years of hardship. Joe knew that Maria had to work overtime to keep them in food and shelter and now, she could spend more time taking care of him. The reception was held at the club with the women of the community providing the food, the fiddle player donated the music for the dancing and Paul bought one keg of beer. When that ran out, everyone had to buy their own. Pete loaned his carriage to take the bride to the church and the married couple to the reception.

Maria and Paul started their life together with items that were borrowed, a suit from his brother John and Maria borrowed her dress from Hana. She had to tuck it in here and there in order to make it fit. After the reception, John drove them home, while Joe stayed with a friend so the newly weds could spend their first night of their marriage alone. When they arrived at their home, they found the table set, food on the stove, a bottle of wine on the table with two candles. It was a poor wedding, but the world had not seen a happier couple. Joe stayed away at his friend's insistence for three days and when he arrived home, he found Maria humming a tune in the kitchen as she cooked. Paul was fixing a broken window pane that had been covered over with a board.

Karl loved his job and he had gotten to know the horses who became familiar with his driving. They knew the route very well and did not need to be led so Karl could have slept on his trips back and forth to Albany. When October came, Mr. Gallo called him into his office and asked if he was going to stay the winter. Before Karl could answer yes, he offered him a dollar more a week to continue driving the team. Karl accepted and left thinking that he should not have been so quick in expressing himself because he still did not understand these Americans. No one said what he thought, they all said what they thought you wanted to hear. The way to handle these people would be to let them talk themselves out, then try to understand what they really meant. In Slovakia, unless you were bartering, you said what was on your mind so everyone had the same understanding.

John and Paul had the pleasant duty of taking Karl through the various holidays and celebrations. Karl said the same thing as the other two when they arrived into the country. These Americans celebrate all the time. There is never a shortage of holidays and the only month in which there was no holiday was in the month of August; it was too hot to dance. Karl did not consider his job hard work and enjoyed the trips with the changing of the seasons. He looked around him and found pleasure in everything he saw, he saw deer early in the morning, along with foxes and raccoons. Once in a while he caught a glimpse of a large cat with pointed ears and no tail. One of the men at the club said. "That cat is a bob cat and stay away from it. It is a mean feline and the only reason that it comes so close to people is because it is hungry."

That winter, one of Karl's horses slipped on a icy portion of the road, broke its leg and the animal had to be destroyed. Karl spent the next two months in a depressed state while he trained the replacement, or rather the other three horses trained him. All Karl had to do was to go on as usual and the new horse would follow the lead of the other three. John and Paul could not understand why he felt so bad about losing a horse, but Karl looked upon the team as his friends and they had learned to trust him. At this point, it would be difficult for someone new to come in and take over the team because no two people held the reins the same way, or put the same amount of pressure on them. All these years of listening to his father were now paying dividends. Karl would make it difficult for anyone else to do his job, so as soon as Mr. Gallo realized this, he would get more money.

Karl and Paul were saving their money regularly, but it would take over two years to get enough to bring Marta and Josef to America. In September of 1909, Maria said that she was pregnant and Paul glowed with joy when she told him. He could not wait to tell his brothers and met them at the club that evening. As Paul told his brother, John did not appear to be too excited.

John said, "I am very happy for you, Paul, but Hana and I are not going to have anymore children. Having more children means that I will have more responsibility and I do not want to be responsible for more children. I want to give our two children all that I can give them, such as food, clothing, shelter, a good education. I want to send them out into the world well equipped."

Paul and Karl looked at each other and Paul said, "We will have all the children that God would allow us to have."

At the club, at the Christmas day celebration, Karl met a young lady by the name of Anna Valigursky. She was two years older that Karl, but she was as fun loving as he was and they found that they viewed life the same way. Life was meant to be laughed at and except for the death of his friend, the horse, Karl never took anything seriously; Anna was the same way. Because of this, her friends called her Honcha and she loved the name. They looked forward to seeing each other at the club because they made each other laugh, but there was only one thing that bothered Honcha about Karl. In the winter, he always smelled like a horse. She took Maria aside one day and told her of the problem, Maria passed it on to Paul who spoke to Karl. Karl had never even suspected that he had that problem, but he took some clean clothes into the stable and hung them in the tack room. Each day after he came in, he would wash and change clothes before he went home and this solved the problem. Honcha never brought it up again.

Karl and Honcha saw a great deal of each other over the winter months and at Easter, Honcha decided to take Karl to meet her parents. Her father, John liked Karl immediately, but her mother, Agnes was disturbed by his sense of humor. She said "Karl will never be serious about anything and therefore will not be able to raise children properly."

John tried to reassure, "Karl was serious when it became time to be serious and he did not take such matters lightly."

Agnes was thinking back to the days when she and John were first married and she could not get him to discipline the children. He did not meet his problems squarely and felt that everything would take care of itself. It took her twenty-five years to get him to handle his children properly. They had three sons and one daughter and their household was always full of laughter. Their only daughter took after her father and that troubled her even more.

She told her husband, "I do not like the nickname, Honcha. My daughter's name is Anna. I do not know where her nickname came from, but everyone should call her Anna."

In March of that year, Maria gave birth to a baby girl. They named her Susan and she was a thin and pale baby. It took eight months of nursing to bring her up to weight and color that she should have had at that age. She was an intelligent girl and did all the usual things before any other children. She walked at an early age, talked and displayed a mind of her own before other children had progressed to that point. Maria and Paul were patient with her and their patience paid for itself. The fact that she was sickly at that early age, allowed her parents to give her more attention which made her progress earlier.

The three brothers met at John's home before the Christmas of 1911 to formulate plans to get Josef and Marta to America. They counted all the money they had and found themselves to be fifty dollars short. Paul had put away the most with Karl next and even John had been able to put away thirty-three dollars. They wanted to bring them both over before the war broke out, but with the money that they had, they could bring only one over. Marta was only fourteen, so she should not come over alone. If they brought Josef, it would leave Marta there and if war broke out, they would never get her over. They were not worried about Stefan, since he was the youngest and he had to stay until they got enough money to bring their parents over. Stefan would have to wait out the war while he helped his parents.

They argued all options and were looking at the alternatives when John's father-in-law, Andy came into the kitchen.

He noted the serious conversation and asked, "Is there something that I can help you with?"

John asked him to sit down and poured him a beer. Paul said, "We are trying to find a way to bring our brother and sister over to this country, but we do not have enough money. Marta is too young to come over by herself and if we brought Josef, she would be stranded there if war should break out. We are about fifty dollars short."

Andy, who was on the finance committee of the club told them, "The club has a contingency fund for members and it was used for just such matters. There is two hundred and forty dollars in the fund and if you agree, I will try to get fifty dollars from the fund. It has to be approved by the officers of the club along with the directors, but I do not see it as much of a problem. You will not have to pay it back if you are not able to do so, but most people do and there would be nothing said if you cannot not pay it back."

The brothers were delighted and told Andy to go ahead with the understanding that the money will be paid back.

Andy said, "The board meets on the first Wednesday of the month and I will bring it up."

Karl looked at his brothers and said, "This will be the best Christmas ever." He told Andy, "You cannot imagine the living conditions over there and to bring our brother and sister here would be the greatest gift in the world."

The second week of January, Andy brought over fifty dollars in cash and nothing was signed or recorded. It was put in the minutes of the board and that was the only record made of the transaction. After work the following night, John went to the bank and sent four hundred and fifty dollars to the bank in Polodencz.

He sent a telegram to Josef. "The money is in the bank. Gather up Marta and take the next available ship to America. Let us know the name of the ship, and when it would dock."

They knew from Karl's instructions that they were to take the train to Albany and would be picked up there. Now all they had to worry about was whether they would arrive safely. There were news reports that ships were being sunk by the Germans with a boat that went under water and they would just wait and pray.

CHAPTER EIGHT

The wait for the three brothers was agonizing. Each day they checked the mails and waited for a message from their brother. For eight weeks, they read the newspapers, asked their friends who read the English newspapers to let them know if there were any problems on the seas. At the end of February, a telegram came to John's home and Hana put it on the table for John to read when he returned home. It was in English, but he knew what it said. It said, "The S.S. Albatross docked in Boston. Marta and I to spend the night. Arrive in Albany at twelve minutes after twelve tomorrow." It was signed, "Josef." He ran over to Pete's house and had him read it to confirm what he had read and he ran to tell his brothers.

Karl said, "I will be at the train station at eleven and I will wait for them so no one has to miss work. I will have to work an extra hour and I will be home later tomorrow." He looked at John, "When you go to work tomorrow, explain it Mr. Gallo. There is enough wool at the factory to keep them going for the day and I will be there at nine-thirty with the first load."

They would see their brother and sister the next day.

Karl waited at the train station with a loaded wagon for two hours. The train was an hour late, but he finally met his brother and sister. Josef was wearing a beard and a mustache, but he could not mistake the piercing brown eyes of a Janek. Josef recognized his brother immediately as he held Marta's hand with one hand and carried most of the luggage with the other. They each had two small cardboard suitcases and he carried two in one hand and one under his arm; Marta carried the fourth one. Marta was a thin, frail little girl. She was shorter than most of the girls at her age, but she had a determined look about her. She reminded Karl of their mother, Olga because nothing seemed to frighten her. If she had half of the obstinacy that her mother had, she would do very well in America. He embraced them both, took them to the wagon where he seated Marta in between two bales of wool so she would be away from the wind and cold. He rushed the horses to make up some of the time he lost. Karl spoke to Josef on the way back and the problems about home had gotten worse since Karl left. The notary was getting braver while the residents of Ruzbachy were getting weaker.

Josef explained, "I expect war to break out soon because the Austrians and the Serbs are two armed camps waiting to pounce on each other. Germany and Russia are waiting in the wings although Russia has weakened considerably under the tsar. I do not know how mother and father will survive. If it was not for Stefan, Kada and Andrej, we would have starved a long time ago. The farm was in good shape when we left, but the Magyars are taking what they want. Some of the farmers are taking their cattle to the High Tatra plains and turning them loose instead of leaving them to be taken by the Magyars."

Karl listened and felt a deep sorrow because they could not bring their parents and Stefan for a while. He prayed that the war would hold off until they could bring them over.

Karl left Josef and Marta at John's house; Paul and John were waiting for them. The brothers were worried that something had happened to them and they were lying on the side of the road freezing to death, but Karl explained that the train was late. With the cold weather, more heat was needed to keep the temperature in the boilers of the train up. Since the fuel could not be put into the furnace quickly enough, the train slowed down. Karl went to unload the wagon and left as quickly as possible and the other two had to go back to work. They had someone covering for them in the event that they were late getting back from lunch. It was now a quarter to three and they would have to repay the favors later.

Marta was to stay with John and Hana and she could help take care of the children. John had put a temporary bed in the children's room and Josef had to go to the boarding house until other sleeping arrangements could be made. John had spoken to Mr. Gallo and had gotten Josef a job at the mill. He would work in the weaving room with the ladies who ran the looms. He would be responsible for bringing wool to the looms in various colors to be sure that the right color went into the right place. If an error occurred, the cloth would have to be torn out and the process started over again. The pay was nine dollars a week and Josef could start as soon as possible.

John had arranged for Marta to start school the following fall. There was only three months left to this school year and Marta did not understand English so she would have to get a grasp of the language before she started school. John had a friend who would come over to the house twice a week to tutor her in English until she started school. John committed himself for the sum of six dollars to be paid after Marta started school. It was a great deal of money, but the young lady would have to learn the language if she was going to be educated in the American schools. They had no idea what grade she would assigned because they had no way to test her.

The family decided to shorten Marta's name to Mary and they called Josef, Joe for short. They told Mary and Joe that everyone in America used nicknames so they would blend in and they were going to be called Mary and Joe.

Joe did not care for the boarding house. He had to sleep in a large room with eleven men and there was only one toilet outside. He was constantly waiting before he could use it. Most of the men just went behind the little building and if there was a lapse in snow storms, the area behind the toilet was covered with yellow urine. Joe refused to go back there so he either had to wait his turn or go when he got to work. They looked for a room in a private home for Joe and finally found one with a family named Sikorski. Vech and Lotta Sikorski were Polish; they were a childless couple who were pleasant and they both worked at the mill.

When Joe spoke to Vech, he was told. "We are trying to have children and you can have the room only until Lotta becomes pregnant and then you will have to leave."

Vech was a machine operator on the frames and Lotta sewed sweaters. They were trying to save some money for the time Lotta got pregnant and she would have to stop work. They were also sending some money to Poland to help Lotta's family and they needed the extra income.

Karl and Honcha were becoming very popular in their circle of friends because they livened up any gathering with their funny stories. They went to all the functions and attended every family activity; even Honcha's mother started to warm up to Karl. He always had a rugged look about him since he spent most of his time outdoors and he had a compact body from pulling and pushing the bales of wool.

He was so dependable, that Mr. Gallo remarked, "People could set their clocks when Karl went by."

The four brothers were doing well in their adopted country and saving enough money to bring their brother and parents to America was becoming harder and harder. Karl was not cooperating because he found it difficult to save any money when he and Honcha lived only to have a good time. He did manage to save a little, but it did not meet with the approval of his brothers. It had become an irritation that would separate them in the future.

Karl finally announced that he and Honcha were getting married and they set a date of May 30, 1913. Karl had asked Honcha's father while they were having a few beers at the club and he gave his blessing.

Honcha's father said, "You do not have ask her mother because she will agree with anything I say."

They spent the rest of the night drinking beer. The next morning both of them had trouble getting up to go to work and Karl thought that the day would never end. He did not go to the club that night, but decided to go to sleep early. He tossed and turned most of the night from his lack of sleep the previous night. He was also worried about Honcha's mother and knew that even if she consented to the marriage, she could still be a problem. He waited for a few days before he went to the club because he did not want to confront Honcha's mother, Agnes. He was allowing enough time to go by so her husband would tell her. He knew that he was not one of Agnes' favorite people and he wanted to be sure that there would be no problems when he saw her.

Agnes was not pleased with the coming wedding of her daughter to Karl. She considered Karl a buffoon who would never amount to anything and she saw a life for Honcha, filled with false hopes and disappointments. If John had consulted her about her blessing before he gave it freely, she would not have consented to the marriage, but it was too late now. By voicing her opinion now, she would only serve to embarrass her husband and cause problems for the couple. Things had progressed so far that she could not stop the wedding so she decided to suffer in silence and not bring the matter up again. Agnes would do all the things that the mother of the bride should do. She would treat her future son-in-law with respect, especially around other people, and hope that Karl would change over the years as her husband had done. What she did not realize was that her husband had not changed, but it was she who had become more tolerant. When his failings became so common, she became used to them and stopped seeing them as flaws in his nature.

Karl had much to do before the wedding. He had to find a place for them to live, he had to find some furniture and he had to make arrangements for the wedding itself. He and Honcha met with the priest and that went smoothly. He enlisted the aid of John and Paul and they found a small house for him and Honcha to rent. John and Paul picked up a few pieces of furniture that some people were going to throw away and a friend of John's made a kitchen table for them. The priest announced at Mass that the couple needed furniture and strangers met him after Mass to donate some pieces. He had used some of his savings to buy a bed, mattress and other bedroom furniture. His brothers were not pleased with that, but no one brought it up to Karl. Honcha had been given some bed clothing and kitchen utensils by her mother. This was the custom, since Honcha was the only daughter, Agnes did not hold back anything. The young couple would start their life together as well if not better than most of the married couples in the Slovak community of Cohoes.

The day of the wedding came and the couple became man and wife in the church of the Sacred Heart. The women of the community marched to the couples home with all of the brides possessions and any other articles that they wanted to donate. They set up the marriage bed, cooked the couple's first meal and decorated the house with dogwood, apple blossoms and lilacs. The guests at the wedding reception were kept laughing by the antics of the newlyweds to the point where it embarrassed the mother and father of the bride. They went along with the fun shaking their heads at the couple and waited for a reasonable time to leave the reception and go home. It was the custom for the bride's parents to invite some friends and relatives to their home after the reception, but no one was invited. Honcha's brothers stayed until the end of the reception as did Karl's brothers. Mary Janek left early because the fun poked at the couple was not suitable for her tender years. Joe, the best man did not understand the language or some of the banter and he spent most of the evening just smiling at everyone. That night the marriage of Karl and Honcha started in earnest, and neither of them got much sleep.

CHAPTER NINE

The Janek men were still worried about the events that were happening in Slovakia. Joe kept telling them of the problems that the Magyars were causing with the food supply. The Austria Hungary Empire was preparing for war, and the spark to set it off could come at any time. They knew how serious it was, but they did not have enough money to bring the rest of their family over and they still had to pay back the amount that the Slovak Community Club had advanced them. Karl was not adding to the sum and there was no way that they could make him do it.

Each time they brought it up, he would say, "I am doing the best that I can, after just getting married. You know that newlyweds start off with so little and we needed so much."

John wrote to his mother and found out that Karl had not paid back the money that was loaned to him for the passage to the new country. One of the other operators told him that Karl had been offered a promotion into the mill. He turned it down because he liked the freedom of the open road. Karl reasoned that the extra money would only have to be turned over to John and he would have to work harder to earn it; he was better off staying where he was.

They read the newspaper, "Jednota" on a regular basis and by the time the brothers had all read it, the paper was folded and refolded so it could not be read any longer. The word, Jednota, meant union and it was edited by Joseph Husek who devoted his life to freeing the Slovaks in Europe. The Janek family heard of the "Slovak league of America", which was founded to aid the plight of all Slovaks, but most of the people supporting the cause were priests who had very little money. All that they could do was preach from the pulpit for a free and autonomous Slovakia. The league lobbied United States congressmen and senators for help, but there was little that the United States government could do in the internal affairs of the Austria-Hungary Empire. There were Slovak communities in Bridgeport, Connecticut, one in Pittsburgh, Pennsylvania, Albany, New York; and New York City. These were separated by distance and no united front was organized.

The brothers knew that if they did not unite the family in America before war broke out, there was no hope of bringing them to America until it was over. Many things could happen, their parents who were now getting on in years could die during the war and they would never see them again. Stefan was of the age where he would certainly be inducted into the army of the empire. They knew that Franz Josef used Slovaks as cannon fodder and they would not see their brother again. They sat for hours in John's home, trying to find a solution before war erupted. Sometimes Karl would put in an appearance and sometimes he would not, but when he did come, he always found an excuse to leave early. To complicate matters, Karl announced in November that Honcha was pregnant. She would deliver in April, so he had other obligations to consider.

John asked his brothers. "Why is there always someone in the family who is independent and does not conform to the wishes of the rest of the family?"

They all shook their heads and could not answer his question. They agreed that they would have to give up on him because they could not count on him. John was supporting his sister who was in school, paying a mortgage on his home and bringing up two children. Hana did not work and he still managed to save some money; Karl and Honcha could not. He simply could not understand his younger brother. They finally stopped inviting him to their meetings and other that his supply of free beer, Karl could care less. He was happy to be free of the commitment and stopped seeing his brothers except at the club and at work.

Joe was promoted to a loom operator, but could not master the skills to weave the cloth so when an opening appeared in the spinning room, he was transferred there. He worked on the frame machines and after a considerable time and patient help from the other operators, he was doing an adequate job. It did mean more money for him so he could put away more. Joe took Mary to the July 4th picnic where Hana, up to her old tricks, introduced him to a young lady by the name of Sophie Vetek. She had seen Joe at the club and spoke to Hana about meeting him. That relationship flowered and they started seeing each other on a regular basis. Sophie went to church every Sunday. Joe started to go with her and after church, they went to Sophie's house. She lived with her uncle Henri and aunt Anna Bechinsky. There had no children of their own. Henri and Anna tried, but try as they might, Anna could not conceive. When Sophie's parents died of the cholera in Pennsylvania, Henri went to pick up his sister's five year old daughter. He took her in as his own daughter and they became family. She grew up in Cohoes and always considered Henri and Anna her parents. She was told that her parents had died when she was young to explain the different last names. The Bechinsky's did not formally adopt Sophie, but she was a member of the family and they loved her dearly. Sophie knew that the Bechinsky's loved her. She loved them in return and she was a better daughter than many other girls her age because she realized how fortunate she was.

Henri and Anna thought very well of Josef and would have been delighted to have him marry Sophie. They encouraged the girl to continue seeing Josef because the men of the Janek family treated their women very well. They did not abuse them as sometimes was the custom in Cohoes, and allowed their women to participate in the decision making processes in family matters. They thought that Karl was a little too foot loose, but he was an exception to the rule and Josef had a different make-up. He worked hard and was much more ambitious than Karl; Josef would make a good husband.

* * *

In September of 1913, Mary went to the school about a mile away from John's home. There was no other way to get there except on foot, but there were three other children in the neighborhood that went to the same school. John felt that there were safety in numbers and two of the children were big boys who would protect the smaller ones. Hana asked her mother to stay with the children because she insisted that she take Mary to school for the first few days and she wanted to meet the young lady when she came out. Hana had gotten some clothes from the neighbors so Mary would not have to wear the clothes that she brought with her. She thought that the other children would laugh at her if she wore the clothes from the old country. She did not want Mary to stand out from the other children, but to blend in because she was going to have enough problems trying to adjust to the different language. The weather was still warm and walking to school was not problem now, but Hana did not know how she would get to school when the weather turned cold and the snow began to fall. They would have to wait and handle that problem later.

The school building had three rooms with a teacher in each one. One room was for the very little children that ranged from age six to ten. The second room had children from age eleven to fourteen and the last room was devoted to children that ranged from fifteen to eighteen. The class with the older children was the smallest and was mainly used for the children who wanted to further their education. They could go to a college either in that area or elsewhere in the country. There were excellent schools this area and other areas in the northeast such as Boston, New Haven, Providence, Philadelphia and New York City. The boys that finished the third level, had a choice of going to college or to a technical school in Albany. The school in Albany had no facilities to house the students so they had to travel every day and return home each night. Most had horses to ride or a horse and carriage that could take other students for a small charge. The school charged a small tuition, but it was well worth the price for a young man to receive a technical education. With new inventions such as the motor car coming into use, there would be a need for men with technical knowledge.

On the first day of school, Emma brought the carriage to Hana's house when she came to care for the children and Hana gave all the children a ride to school. Mary had learned a little English, her tutor had taught her only the classic English, but she knew enough to get by. She would learn the slang words from the other children. Because of her limited knowledge of the language, she was placed in the middle class and, if she showed progress, she would be promoted into the next class during the year. Mary did not attend school for very long in Slovakia, because her mother felt that it was more important for her to learn to sew, cook, clean and keep house. The men had to learn to deal with numbers, reading and writing. Mary was bright and competitive and it was not long before she was put in the next class. She had to be told only once, and when her reading skills improved, she could look things up herself. Her homework was accurate and handed in on time so her teacher, recognizing her ability, gave her extra attention until she progressed into the next level.

Mary liked school very much and she applied the skills that she learned from her mother to help Hana with the children. She translated news from English to Slovak for her brothers and by the time she was finished with the third level, she was ready for a job in the office of the mill. She did not have to work in the weaving room or the sewing room like her sisters-in-law. She would go to work dressed up and not have to perform manual labor because she was the first one in the family to finish school. When she was graduated, the whole family even the little ones, came to the ceremony and no one was prouder than her brothers. The next day, she went to the mill for a job, but the office staff was filled and the women had been a stable work force for many years; she was not hired.

While speaking to the man who did the hiring, she learned that the mill had some space that they were not using. The mill planned to hold out the carpets and sweaters that had slight defects to sell to the employees and people in town at a discount. They now had to pack and ship the goods and they could pass this on as savings to the people of Cohoes.

Mary said to the man, "I would like to work in this new endeavor because I know how to make change, keep books and I like to deal with people."

He liked the way she spoke and her determination and hired her, on the spot, to work with the manager to set up the enterprise. The manager's name was Amos Tuttle. He ran a small boot store in town that he sold and they persuaded him to open the new store. The store would be known as "The Mill Outlet" store and would be one the first of its kind in the area. There were some of these stores in the south, but none that were in the same building where the goods were made and the only one that sold only products made at the mill.

Mary came to work on a Monday morning to an empty store. Mr Tuttle was there with a carpenter employed by the mill by the name of Michael Dobrek. Mike was about five foot six and small in build, he was twenty years old, single and he lived with his mother and father in Troy, New York, a neighboring town. He was a good carpenter, but he did very little work in Cohoes. Michael's hair was blond, it was very thick and a tuft of hair always seemed to be over his eyes. He was constantly brushing it away with his arm. When he bent over a board or something else, it would fall back over his forehead. His skin was fair, not like Mary's olive colored skin and he had freckles. When he smiled, his big broad smile, he looked comical, but there was nothing comical about his attitude; he was a determined young man.

Amos Tuttle had hired Mike to work for him in the past and he had done excellent work so he persuaded the mill owners to hire him for this job. He was not a part of the Cohoes Slovak community nor did he belong to the Slovak Club. He looked Mary up and down as he entered the room and when she spoke, he knew that he would have to get to know her better. He had assumed that she was born in America because she spoke so well and she handled herself as if she had lived in the country all of her life. Mary suggested where to place the shelves and tables that were accepted by Amos. She had a table built to be placed by the door where people could pay for their purchases and could not leave the store without being seen. The lights had to be placed so that the products could be made more attractive and there had to be a place for a stove, because no one would come into a cold store to look at carpets and sweaters; they had to make the store look attractive and comfortable

The three of them worked on the store for three weeks and Mary would bring in coffee for them while Mike would pick up some pastry at a bakery once in a while. Mary liked working in the shop and when Mike finished a row of shelves or a table, Amos would bring in a cart of sweaters or carpets so Mary could set them up and mark them with prices. She went to various stores and checked prices to be sure to sell the sweaters cheaper and Amos did the same with the carpets. They had to be sure that they would be selling their products at the lowest prices in the entire area. The target date for the grand opening was August 1st, but there was still much work to be done. The three of them had to work well into the night to be ready to open by the appointed date. Mary came home from work after dark and Mike went with her to make sure that she arrived home safely.

Paul did not want to see his only sister working such long hours, but Mary said. "Once the store was opened, I will not have to work so hard and so long. It will only be for a few days more."

Paul did not mention it again.

The store opened on time, the whole town was there and since the employees had to work, Mr Gallo gave everyone a half hour off to tour the store. He allowed them to arrange their schedules so there would not be too many people leaving their jobs at one time. The sidewalk outside the store was packed with people who had waited for the store to open and when Amos opened the door, the people rushed in. The store was in shambles in just a few minutes and stayed that way until closing. Mary spent the day at the counter where the people, mostly women, paid for their merchandise. They closed the store at six o'clock and spent another hour straightening the tables and the shelves. They had to bring out more merchandise to restock the store.

Amos said, "Some of the articles have been in the warehouse for years and by lowering the price, we have sold them very quickly. People feel that they are getting a bargain so they actually fight over who has seen something first and who has a right to buy it." Amos made a large sign that said " All sale were final and nothing may be returned."

Mary got home after dark again and she was so tired that she ate a light supper that Hana kept warm and went right to bed. She did not have to be in work until eight the next morning, but she arrived a half hour early to prepare for the customers. When she arrived at the store, there were people there all lined up, waiting to enter.

She told them. "The doors would open at eight o"clock and you will have to wait until then."

She noticed that Amos had put a note on the door that listed the hours that the store would be open. It would be open for business from eight in the morning to six at night, Monday through Saturday. The receipts for the first day went beyond expectations and the mill owners had decided to include those articles that had no defects. They were getting a better price than they were getting from their sales to the retailers and there was no shipping charges; the store was there to stay.

Working in the store was a new experience for Mary because she liked talking to people, giving them advice, pointing out the different features of their products and taking the money from the people. She noticed that the sales slowed down as the novelty wore off, but she also noticed that people came in from other towns and as far away as Albany. The store was getting a reputation for selling quality goods at a cheaper price. A few weeks went by and Amos hired another woman to restock the shelves and tables while Mary handled the people who were paying for their purchases. The best part of the enterprise was that most of the money spent at the store stayed in the community which allowed the mill owners to expand their production by hiring people. The store was packed in the morning and at the end of the day, there were noticeable spaces where the sweaters and carpets had been. Amos made up a name for the carpets that he called "Native American Carpets", after the Indian tribes that ran through the woods many years before. It gave a native American quality to the carpets and, although, they were not made by the native Americans, it gave the impression that they were of the same quality.

Mary and Mike were seeing a great deal of each other in the months following the opening of the store. On Sundays, they went on picnics or for long walks through the countryside. They explored the locks that allowed the water traffic to navigate the canals from the higher ground to the Mohawk river. Mike had not been very religious nor did he go to church on a regular basis. When he started to see Mary he wanted to spend more time with her so he started to attend Mass. He met with the priest at Sacred Heart to establish a relationship with him in the event he and Mary decided to marry. The priest did a good job in bringing Mike back into the church, because he not only attended Mass, but he went on retreats and other church functions. The priest obtained tickets to the installation of the new bishop at the cathedral in Albany and gave them to Mary and Mike. They attended the high Mass and Mike was impressed. Mass was no longer a place to be with Mary, it was a place to hear the choir, listen to the homily and be at peace with himself. It gave him a time to meditate and to use the quiet serenity to plan his future.

It was at Mass, specifically during the time where the bread is symbolically changed to the body of Christ, that he decided to take Mary as his wife. He took this as a sign from God that he was to marry this woman and from that day forward, there was no greater believer in Christ than Michael Dobrek. They were married a year later with the understanding that she still had to help with the family's goal of bringing her relatives to be with her. He accepted this and after the marriage, helped her raise some of the money. He was a skilled carpenter and was demanding more money for his work and with Mary working, they could put all of her money away. They agreed that they would only have children when the rest of the family arrived into the country. She wanted her mother to take care or her children while she worked and they would be married for nine years before they would have children.

* * *

The almost certain war in Europe was in everyone's thoughts. It was discussed at work and at the club. The "Jednota" gave an account of the events, but the newspapers written in English went into much more detail. It seemed that Paul was more concerned than anyone else. John had been in the country longer than anyone else, but the memory of the way of life in the old country was fading from his memory. Karl was more concerned about himself and his wife and Josef was just happy to be in the country. Mary was doing very well in work and she could now translate the newspaper for her brothers.

The Germans had the better equipped army and they were aligned with Franz-Josef of Austria. The French had a large army while her ally, Britain had a small volunteer army, but it was well trained. The focus of Britain's attention was the Royal Navy, the largest sea force in the world, but they were also concerned about the build up of the German Navy. If allowed to surpass that of Britain, it could prevent British merchant ships from delivering food and other supplies. As one grew, the other matched it with larger ships and larger guns. The German ships were smaller in number, but they were more modern and the Germans used the lighter than air dirigibles known as Zeppelins, named after their inventor, Ferdinand Graf von Zeppelin. They were used on the high seas for patrolling and scouting and were a distinct advantage to the Germans because they could fly at such heights that no weapons could reach them.

* * *

On June 28, 1914, Archduke Ferdinand and his wife were assassinated by a Serb terrorist in Sarajevo. Austria accused the Serbs of ordering the deed and, eager to expand their territory in the Balkans, declared war on Serbia and bombarded Belgrade, the Capital. Russia went to the aid of Serbia, and Germany declared war on Russia. Germany declared war on France and marched toward them through Belgium. Great Britain had an alliance with Belgium to protect its neutrality and declared war against Germany. Italy temporarily remained neutral, satisfied to sit back and watch the activities from a distance. Stefan was sure to be dragged into the war that he did not understand.

John received a letter, one of the very few that he had gotten during the war, from his mother, "The war has finally arrived and claimed your brother. Stefan is gone. He had to report to Franz-Josef's army in Bratislava and the hired help, Kada and Andrej stayed to work on the farm. Somehow Andrej has been able to avoid the conscription into the army and he is just one of the many young men who live in Ruzbachy that has avoided the attention of the notary."

The brothers assumed that Stefan would be fighting in the Balkans against the Serbs or even the Russians and at least, he was not assigned to a German Army where a Slovak life meant very little. The Janek family waited for news of the war every day and they were eager for news from anyone. They heard of the massive loss of lives on both sides and they prayed that Stefan was a survivor. They were confident that he would come out of the war alive, but if something happened to Stefan, one of the family would have to go to Slovakia after the war and bring their parents over.

There was another problem that reared its ugly head. If America joined the war, the Janek men might find themselves in the American army fighting against their countrymen. Although America was not in the war and President Wilson was working hard to keep the country out of it, the German U-boats sank an American tanker "Gulflight" causing loss of life. Later the "Lusitania," a British luxury liner, was sunk without warning off the Irish coast with the loss of 124 American lives. Feelings were running high for America to join the war. A few months later, the British liner "Arabic" was sunk with the loss of more American lives. The men of the Janek family did not want to be drafted into the Army and be sent to Europe to fight because it would be brother against brother and they wanted to avoid this at all costs. As it happened, none of the Janek men, living in America, were forced into the army and sent to the conflict.

About two years later, a letter came through from their mother. She wrote, "Stefan has been wounded and a comrade carried him on his back from the front to a hospital in the rear. The doctors had cut part of his stomach away so he would live and he will be all right. He might come home to get well. The Magyars have come and taken all of our food and animals to feed its armies, but Kada was resourceful and has gotten food from some gypsy friends or we would not have survived. Andrej turned some animals loose in the high ranges of the Tatras, hoping to get them back when it has become safe."

Joe listened to the letter with tears in his eyes and said, "I never should have left. Our parents are alone and I could have helped."

John pointed out, "It is a good thing that you did, you would have been sent to the front and could have been killed. We have you here with us, alive."

Mary said, "If Stefan was wounded, they might not send him back to the front."

Paul answered, "Our little brother is still in danger. The central powers of Germany and Austria are fighting on so many fronts, it is highly unlikely that Stefan would remain away from the front."

This was the last letter the Janek family would receive from their family in Slovakia until the end of the war.

* * *

The 1916 Presidential election was one of the closest in American history. Wilson defeated his rival, Justice Charles Evans Hughes, with the Democratic slogan "He kept us out of the War." He broke off all diplomatic relations with Germany when the Germans announced that they were resuming their unrestricted submarine warfare. A British intelligence agent intercepted a message written by the German Foreign Minister to the German Ambassador in Mexico. The message decoded by the British said that if Mexico joined the war against the United States, the Germans offered them the States of Texas, New Mexico and Arizona for their help. War was declared by the United States against Germany on April 16, 1917, while war was not declared against Austria-Hungry until December 7th.

The Americans had an army of only 200,000 men with General John Pershing in command. His plan was to send a force of one million men to Europe by May of 1918 and an additional three million men at a later date. The United States Selective Service act was passed on May 18, 1917 and John felt that he and his brothers should prepare to be inducted into the Army of the United States. They watched the mail everyday, but nothing came and they watched the news from the eastern front, which was closest to their homeland. News came in the "Jednota" that the workers of Petrograd, the capital of Russia had rebelled. They paid little attention to this bit of news since no one would expect Tsar Nicholas to stand for such nonsense, but then the Tsar abdicated, the government of the Russian Republic took over. The new government pledged itself to continue the war against Germany and her allies until the Central Powers were defeated. The Russian Army began falling apart and realizing that they could not continue the fighting, signed a truce and abandoned the war effort. With a sweep of a pen, Russia was out of World War I.

Everything that the family heard was tied to their entering the war against their brother and the situation was grim. The allies were being beaten back on the western front, Russia had collapsed, but their ally to the south, Italy was on the verge of entering the war against the Germans. The Germans were using submarine warfare that threatened the flow of supplies from America to Europe and Britain and France was on the defensive when American troops entered the war. American troops reinforced the tired troops of the allies and the German lines began to crumble. An exchange of messages between the German chancellor, Prince Max, of Baden, and President Wilson, resulted in an armistice that was signed on November 11, 1918. Apparently, there were other Slovaks relieved that the war was over because the celebration went well into the next day and the mill lost one day of work.

One of the brighter spots of the war with Germany, was that the mill had a steady customer for its sweaters because they changed the color to that required by the military and mass produced their product. The people worked overtime, wages went up and the Janek family had the sum of seven hundred and fifty dollars waiting to be sent to Slovakia. Karl had bought a home and was making an extra trip to Albany each day, receiving extra pay. Joe and Sophie were married and bought a home before the prices went up. They anticipated that values would appreciate when the troops came home from the war and needed homes.

The children were coming fast and furious, but John had only two children and no more. Paul had two children, while Karl had one and one on the way. With the extra work and pay, the families had money to improve their homes and to put more money away. With the war's end, most of the tensions were relieved. They were worried because they still had not heard from their parents or Stefan and they did not know if their brother was dead or alive. They wrote to their parents, but did not receive a reply because there was no news to tell. They were worried about their parents and Mary suggested that if they did not hear from them after the first of the year, someone had to go after them. They could not allow them to suffer without Stefan and they did not know what was going to happen to their country. They were afraid that either it would remain with the Magyars or be united with the Czechs to form a new republic. No matter what happened, there would be hardships.

They waited until the first of the year when John sent a letter to his father saying, "We want to send one of us to Slovakia to arrange for you to come to America."

There were many meetings and discussions as to who should go, what was to be brought back and what was to be done with the farm.

About a week later, a letter came addressed to Johan Janek which brought good news, it read;

"Dear Johan, Stefan is safe at home. He came on Christmas Eve and it was the most wonderful Christmas present that we could wish for. He rode home on a huge thoroughbred stallion, in a blinding snow storm, he came out of the snow like a ghost and we had to feel him to be sure that it was, indeed, our Stefan. He had been stationed in the Alps fighting the Italians when he was captured by the Americans who had some men stationed there. He had saved some horses from death in a fire and the Americans gave him the horse as a reward. It is still too early to tell what was going to happen to the country, but Stefan said that he wanted to come to America as soon as possible."

It was signed, " Your grateful mother"

John called the family together and read the letter and Mary could not stop crying because she was the closest to Stefan. They all went to the club to celebrate, the children wrapped up against the cold went with them because this was family celebration.

Mary said, "I will write to Stefan and arrange for them to come to join us. I do not care how much it costs, I want our mother and father and our brother here with us." Her family agreed.

Mary received another letter, from her mother, saying, "Stefan is going to marry Kada and your father is not pleased with the union, but Stefan is going to marry her anyway. The marriage will take place in late May and we will make plans to leave after that. The fate of the farm is still undecided and it depends on what happens when the powers decided what is to be done with Slovakia. No matter what happens, we will come to America, only now there would be four."

* * *

The events occurring in Europe were still closely followed by the Janek family in America. In 1918, all universities, as well as other schools, fell under control of the Slovak government which made attendance compulsory from age six to fourteen. There were state conflicts with the church over the traditional role of the church in the education of citizens. The main populace wanted to retain the church's role, while those attempting to rule the country, wanted control to be with them. The communists attempted a coup to take over the country, but failed and pushed the country to join with the Czech Republic. President Wilson wanted both countries to unite into one republic to solve the problem. Rumors were flying both in Slovakia and in the Slovak community in America. The Janek family did not know what would happen to the country. They were wrestling with the problem when bad news came for their mother.

"My dear children, your father has been afflicted with a lung disease, called tuberculosis. He is confined to his bed. He has to be fed, taken care of and only come into contract with people who wore masks as the disease is highly infectious. No one is allowed to come in contact with him except me and the doctor. Dr. Josef is taking care of him, but he does not have much hope of a cure and it is a matter of weeks or even days before he lapses into a coma and dies. It is a shame that we have survived the greatest conflict on earth and God has now seen fit to take this proud and strong-willed man away from us. Pray for us, my children."

There would be more news coming and the letters would be more frequent. The Janek family went to the Sacred Heart church and arranged for a special Mass to be said for their father. All though no one outside of the family knew their father, the church was crowded to the point where there was standing room only. John was allowed to come to the pulpit and express the family's appreciation for the concern shown to their father because it was the low point in the lives of the Janek family in America.

A telegram arrived the day after the Mass. "Johan Janek has died and will be buried next to his father in the abbey cemetery." The telegram was signed "Pray for him" Stefan. A memorial Mass was scheduled for the following Sunday and Mass cards were delivered to John's home. He had a large basket full of cards which was placed in front of the altar in the church of the Sacred Heart.

John gave the eulogy, "Johan Janek was found on the steps of the abbey a few weeks after he was born and was brought up by Father Damian, the priest in charge of the abbey. He was educated at the abbey and spent eight years of his life studying to be a friar when he fell in love with my mother. My mother was born when my grandmother came over the mountains and died giving birth. The result of that union produced five men and one woman who were raised in the tradition of the Holy Roman Catholic Church."

He told his story in such a moving manner that sobbing could be heard over the entire church. John never felt closer to his entire family then he did while he was on the pulpit that day. Tears flowed down his cheeks and when he finished he bowed his head and went to his seat.

* * *

The coming of Olga, Stefan and Kada was postponed due to the uncertainty of the status of the farm. Stefan and Kada were married after a time of mourning for his father had passed. It was a subdued wedding following the old traditions of their heritage. The only ones from Kada's side of the family to attend was Kada's brother, Andrej and Kada's mother. With the wedding over, the Janek family could concentrate on disposing of the farm. There were no buyers for any of the farms because of the uncertainty of what the central government was going to do. No one had any money to buy anything, anyway even though the prices had depressed to an all time low; they could only wait to see what would happen.

In the early months of 1920, a constitution was signed declaring Czechoslovakia a sovereign state. Stefan wrote, "I am disappointed that we have just thrown off the yoke of the Magyars only to have the Czechs place another one across our backs. There is no self rule for the Slovaks, and Slovaks are not included in the cabinet. There are hard times ahead for the Slovaks."

John wrote back, "Just leave the farm. All you have to do is pack what you can take with you."

Stefan was worried about Andrej who had no ownership of the farm and he could be expelled from it without a place to go. Stefan promised to explore that further and would advise the rest of the family of the progress.

Stefan wrote back, "A land reform act was passed with transfer of farms to the state. All farms in excess of six hundred and eighteen acres will be taken over. Our farm consists of more than that amount and the state will name a manager. We will lose the farm, but there is a good chance that Andrej will be the manager. I have talked to the notary when he and his crew came to take inventory and the way is now clear for all of us come to America."

Mary sent the money to the bank in Polodencz and told Stefan to book passage as soon as possible. The earliest they could leave was in the middle of March in 1921, but Stefan did not tell his family that Kada was pregnant, or they might change their mind about financing their trip. Stefan and Andrej worked to leave Andrej with enough food for him and his bride to be. The Janek family would miss the wedding, but they did not want the notary to know that they were leaving in the dead of night. In a little over a week after they left, Olga, Stefan, Kada and little Joe arrived in Boston.

CHAPTER TEN

Joe and Mary went to Boston to meet the rest of the family. They arrived on the day that the liner docked, went to the immigration department in the large building and asked to see their mother, their brother and his wife; they did not know about their nephew. They were told that they were unavailable. Mary, the firebrand, did all the talking and demanded to see the person in charge, but was told that the processing of new immigrants took priority. They came back the next day and were kept waiting all day without word. Mary stopped anyone that went by, but could not get an answer. They were told to come back the next day and there should be some news. They stayed for a second night and came back early the next morning, but again, they could get no answers. The people in Cohoes expected them the day before and they had no news to give them. They left the building at six-forty-five and missed Kada, who wandered out the building and was being escorted back, by fifteen minutes.

The next morning, they went to the great room and found it almost empty except for two desks with an official behind each one and an occasional person walking from one end of the room to the other. Mary saw that one of the interviewers was alone and she went over to him before anyone else came. She had fire in her eye and she demanded to speak to Stefan Janek, at once. He pointed to a door that had just opened and there was Stefan, Olga and Kada who was carrying a bundle. They ran towards each other with open arms. The meeting was a happy one and Mary embraced her brother while Joe lifted his mother off the floor. Kada stood aside, tears running down her cheeks. When Mary saw her, she ran over to embrace her until she saw what Kada had in her arms. She looked at the baby and screamed, "It is beautiful!"

Kada told her, "Your nephew was born on the ship, on St. Josef's day. His name is Stephen Josef, but everyone on the ship called him Joe."

The five of them all tried to talk at once when a man came over and led the new immigrants to a desk with three chairs.

He said to Joe and Mary, "You two will have to wait in another area because there would be another ship docking in a few hours and the room would soon be filled with people. You can all leave together as soon as possible."

Mary asked, "Can I hold the baby while you talk?"

The man smiled and said, "That would be all right, but I want you to hurry or they will be here for another three days. Within a few hours, this room will chaos. There is another ship load coming in. We really have to hurry."

Within twenty minutes, they walked out of a dark room and into the bright American sunlight. They were free at last, and they wanted the family to be united as soon as possible. They walked away from the pier to the north station and boarded a train for Albany, New York. Mary stopped to send a telegram to John telling him that they were on their way and would arrive in Albany at three that afternoon.

John took the afternoon off, took his father-in-law's new touring sedan and met them when they stepped off the train. John wanted his mother to see how well he has done since coming to America. Stefan was surprised to see the touring car and John was quick to tell him that it was not his. Olga was afraid to ride in it because she had never seen a motor car. Stefan had seen automobiles in the army, but never one this large and he was anxious to ride in it. They finally talked Olga into getting into the automobile and they were on their way to their home in Cohoes.

John explained, "The touring car belongs to my father-in-law, Pete and I borrowed it so I could bring all the people and luggage in one trip. Hana's father taught me how to drive it and at top speed, it would travel twenty five miles an hour."

Olga said, "Ten miles an hour is fast enough for me."

John continued, "The automobile was made in Hartford, Connecticut and has been hand tooled. A man, Henry Ford, is making some on an assembly line somewhere in the Midwest. It is black and he calls it a model T. If the price of the car came down, I might consider buying one, but I will have to convince my wife, Hana."

They rode to John's home where Hana and the grandchildren were waiting to meet the rest of the family. She had arranged a family reunion at the club and the whole Slovak community was invited.

As the family got together at John's home, Olga was introduced to her new daughters-in-law and her grandchildren. They were sitting around and talking, with the children running from one adult to another. The new arrivals would stay with Paul because he had the most room and the party at the club would be Saturday night. Olga was overwhelmed as she sat looking at the scene in front of her and she suddenly started to cry. Her daughters-in-law rushed to her aid, fussed over her, brought her water and when she did not respond, John asked his mother what was wrong.

She looked around her and in between sobs, she said, "If only your father was alive to see all this beauty around me."

Stefan said, "He is seeing the beauty around us from above. Look around and see what he has given us and he is looking at us and smiling."

Olga calmed down and said, "All of you remind me of your father. Yes, Stefan, you are right. He is in all of you and all I have to do is look at any one of you and I will see him. Just promise me one thing, you will always be proud of your heritage, pass it on to your children and keep it alive"

It was obvious that Olga missed her homeland and it would take an effort on everyone's part to make grandma happy in this new country. The family was never closer than they were at this moment.

The family had found Stefan and his family a place to live, had found Stefan a job at the mill and it was not long before they were involved in the life of the community. The party was held at the club to introduce the remaining members of the family and the entire Slovak community came to celebrate.

Olga never met so many people and she remarked, "There is no one left in the homeland because everyone is here in America."

Hana told her. "My grandfather was the man who came to Ruzbachy with the money to build the church and he was the one who shot the two robbers that tried to steal his money."

Olga said, "The church would never have been built if it was not for that money and the town is still grateful."

Many people came to see her and talked in perfect Slovak and Olga was pleased that the customs, language and traditions were being passed on to future generations. She was convinced that her sons had chosen the right path to follow and she began to look forward to her new life in America.

Kada was given a job in the sewing room of the mill because they had to pay back the family for their loan used to bring them to America. The family did not want Olga's passage, only that of Stefan and Kada. The rest of the family took Kada into the fold and Mary took it upon herself to educate Kada. She taught her how to exchange money, how to shop and how best to economize in running the household. It was the custom for the Janek family to turn over all the money to the woman of the house. The husband put his trust in his wife so she would spend it wisely. Kada understood this and she and Stefan had very few disagreements about money. They both made decisions about major purchases, but the day to day expenses were Kada's responsibilities and she handled them well.

John asked Stefan, who was now called Steve, "Tell me about the tree in the field, the one that father planted on the spot where I was born."

Steve told him, "Since there are no more of our family in Slovakia, and no more roots, I told Andrej to cut it down and use it for firewood, at least it would do him some good. We must now set a new set of roots here in America."

It took John's mind back to the old country, he was silent for a long while and he finally said. "It was probably the wisest thing to do since we will never go back."

Steve said, "I will never go back because the Magyars have conscripted me for six years of duty in the army and if hostilities broke out again, I will have to report for duty. I still have a year to run on my six years and I am concerned that they would consider me a deserter and put me in prison."

John pointed out. "The empire is no more and you are now a citizen of Czechoslovakia."

Steve said, "I do not want to take any chances no matter who is in charge."

* * *

Life was good to the Janek family in Cohoes. It took Steve and Kada two years to pay back the five hundred dollars and they were beginning to save a little money for themselves. Olga took care of all the children during the day while their mothers worked. She took care of them at Steve's house and still managed to help Kada with the housework, cooking and laundry. Olga enjoyed her time with her grandchildren and would have taken care of them for nothing, but her daughters-in-law paid her a small sum. She saved half and gave half to Kada for room and board, Olga would not hear of any other arrangement, she wanted to pay her own way.

Two years after she arrived, Kada had a little girl which they named Medka and one or more of the Janek women was pregnant at any given time. John still had two children, a boy and a girl. Paul now had two girls, Karl had two girls and Joe had a little girl. Mary and Mike were trying, but they still did not have any children. There were only two grandchildren that Olga took care of while the others went to school and she doled on them. They were both small and thin, but they were intelligent and could solve problems by using their thought processes. John vowed that his son would never work in the mill, and put money away for his education.

John said, "My son will have all the education that he wants, but my daughter is destined to be a housewife so the only education she needs is to keep house, rear children and handle finances."

Mary took exception to this and pointed to herself as an example. John and Mary had many arguments about that subject. She felt that his daughter should have the same education as his son but John disagreed, his son would go to advance training in one of the highly respected colleges around Albany and his daughter would not be educated any further than high school.

Olga played with her grandchildren as much as she could, told them stories about life in Slovakia and they listened eagerly. When she sat down to tell a story, they stopped what they were doing and gathered around her, sitting on the floor in a semi circle.

She told them, "Your grandfather was left on the steps of the abbey when he was a few weeks old. He had been brought up in the shadow of God and he lived that way for the rest of his life. I never knew my mother because she died when I born. The trip across the High Tatras had taken all the life out of her, but she was stubborn and held on until I was born. Once she saw that I was born and healthy, she died. My father thought that God had punished him for forcing my mother through the hardships of the journey and shut the church from his life. It was your great-grandfather that brought him back to the church of God. Your great-grandfather was a priest and a saint."

There was much to be learned from Olga's stories. It was in this way that Olga preserved the traditions and history of the Janek family. The children had a right to know their roots.

One Sunday in the summer, Pete invited John to take a trip with him in his touring car. They went on a day's outing to Saratoga where the horses raced. Each of them took ten dollars to wager on the horses. Since Pete had been there before and usually lost all of his money, he still enjoyed the thrill of the race. He would win on one race and lose it on three others and he told John that he should never bet more money than he could afford to lose. Pete saved his money for the trip and once he lost it, he would bet no more. John had never bet on anything in his life and the thought of winning money so easily thrilled him. When they arrived, Pete showed him how to place his bet at the window. There was a half dollar minimum and after Pete explained the odds, John made his first bet of fifty cents on a horse that paid ten to one. He lost his money on the race and bet on the next one. After losing that, he bet a dollar on the next four races and he had lost five dollars and nothing to show for it except worthless tickets. Pete thought that he would stop betting, but John bet his last five dollars on a horse that paid twenty to one and they found a place at the rail to watch the race.

The horses took off and John watched his horse go from fifth place to first on the back stretch. The horse held his position and won the race, John turned in his ticket and the man gave him five twenty dollar bills. John did not bet anymore that day, but the win had an effect on him for the rest of his life. He had been bitten by the gambling bug.

John could not wait to show Hana his winnings and she was pleased to see the money, but was not pleased with the enthusiasm that he was showing. She had hoped that the thrill would wear off, but she knew her husband only too well and she dreaded the time when he would return to the races.

She tried to convey her fears to Pete, and said, "I worry about him because he is enthusiastic and he will not give it up."

Pete told her, "John was just lucky that day and once he lost a few times, the novelty would wear off and he would forget about it. Do not worry about it, it will pass."

She told her father, "You do not know the Janek men. They are all the same, and either they did not get involved with an undertaking or they went after it completely. There is no middle ground with them. That is why they did so well at the mill and any other endeavor. Please do not take him to the track again."

Pete laughed and said, "You are overreacting. It really is not a problem."

Hana had looked into the future and she did not like what she saw. John put the winnings into his son's college fund and looked forward to his next trip to Saratoga. Hana's prediction to her friend was coming true because John had gone with Pete several times. When Pete did not want to go, he either went with one of his friends at the club or he went alone. He had lost much more than the hundred dollars that he had won previously and Hana began to feel the lack of money from the budget. She decided to talk to him about it. If that did not work then she would have to bring it up to Olga because she needed help and she did not care where she got it.

One day, she got up enough nerve to talk to John, "You are gambling away too much of our household money."

"I am not," he said, "I cannot believe that there is a problem."

She took out her ledger book to show him how much she was spending to run the household and there was not enough money left at the end of the month to pay all the bills.

She told John. "You are spending thirty to forty dollars a month on your gambling and we are not putting anything away for John Jr's college fund. You are robbing your son of a good education."

He looked at the figures and agreed to stop going to the races. Hana felt that she would have to watch the situation closely, but she could not watch John all the time.

* * *

Business was good at the mill and the employees were working longer hours, but they were not being paid extra for their overtime hours, only straight time. Some of the other mills in Troy and Albany were paying their people time and a half after forty-eight hours. Some were not working Saturdays, but had three shifts which employed more people. The Cohoes mills became a target as the next mill to be unionized by the textile union. There were rough looking men handing out leaflets when the employees went home at the end of the day. The union wanted the employees of the mill to vote to see if they wanted a union to represent them. The union representatives went to the various social clubs to explain what the union could do for them. Most of the Slovaks working at the mill felt that they were being treated fairly and they did not want to use the weapons that the union said they could use. The union said that it could get the workers better wages, working conditions and benefits. Mr. Gallo had been good to them and allowed them time off when they had a good reason. He promoted people from within the mill and left those that did not deserve a promotion in their old jobs. The Janek men were promoted regularly. John was a foreman, Paul and Joe were machine operators and Karl drove the new truck back and forth between Albany and Cohoes. Steve worked hard and it was just a matter of time before he was promoted. They were making a good living compared to the old country and wanted to leave things as they were.

Those men that did not work very hard or did only as much as they needed to get by, were the ones that were not satisfied. They wanted to get the benefits without doing more work and those were the men that the union targeted to cause unrest. The union was organizing these men to hold an election, but the employees were about evenly divided in the vote to allow the textile union to represent the employees. A ballot was passed out to all of the employees with instructions on how to use it. This was the first time that the Janek men had been exposed to the democratic process and they did not know how to react. The Magyars told them what to do and how to do it, now someone was asking them what they wanted to do and this was foreign to them. They did not know what the unions were capable of doing and if they sided with them, they did not know how their relationship with the owners of the mill would change. John was a foreman and part of management, so he would have no problem, but the rest of the men had to decide what they wanted to do.

Steve called a meeting at his home and this did not include John who understood why he was not invited. The brothers each gave his account as he understood it, on how joining the union would help them.

Steve said "If I joined the union, then my promotion might be in jeopardy, so I want to take a back seat in the election and not vote at all."

Paul told Steve "If you do not vote, that would be one vote for the union that will not be challenged. If many workers do not vote, then the union will be voted in because you can be sure that the union enlists all the pro union workers to vote."

Paul understood the democratic process better than his brothers, but Steve was bewildered by the notion of being given a choice on how his life would be controlled. He wanted to leave things as they were and Paul told him that he must vote against the union in order to see this happen.

Paul said, "I heard that if the union is voted in and management does not approve changes that the union wanted, the workers will strike. That means that everyone connected with the union will walk out and we will not be paid by the mill owner." The discussions went deep into the night, but the vote was not due for a few weeks. They agreed to meet again just before the election and decide what to do at that time. Each man was supposed to ask questions and learn as much as he could before the meeting.

No one discussed the meeting with John, but he knew his brothers and did not try to influence them in any way. He had read in the "Jednota" that the unions were the wave of the future and they were here to stay, but it did not mean much to him, one way or another. His job was secure and he was not in the decision making circle of the company. The union was the object of discussion at the club and the Janek men listened. They did not contribute any ideas because they were still in the learning process, but they listened and then discussed what they heard with each other.

About a week before the election, the company made some moves to ensure that the union would not win. The managers, who apparently had been planning a strategy to combat the union for some time, announced a series of promotions. They took the most popular and influential people and promoted them into management. They gave everyone a small raise saying that the previous year had been profitable and the company decided to share the profit with the workers, who had made the profit for them. They were planning to shut the mill down for two weeks in the summer. The shut down would give them time to install new lighting, paint the entire inside of the mill and install wash rooms with running water in every department. The union made a special effort to win the election, by passing out leaflets in English, Slovak, Italian and German. They held a rally with officers of the union as speakers and a dinner dance at the club. The voter turn out was sparse and the union lost its bid to represent the workers by an overwhelming margin. Within a week, the union was forgotten and work went on as usual while the union decided to direct there energies elsewhere. They wanted to allow sometime to pass before they tried again

CHAPTER ELEVEN

Steve worked at the mill for seven years. He and Kada had three children and Kada was pregnant with the fourth. They had paid back the money that was loaned to them and they managed to put some money away to buy a house. With the mill paying more money and everyone working overtime, the cost of homes kept going up. Every time Kada had another child, she had to stay out of work for a while and they just got by on what Steve made. Olga still lived with Steve and Kada since John's children were older and they were helping Olga with the care of the rest of the children. Mary had two boys who were taken to Steve's home and stayed with Olga while Mary worked.

In March of 1928, Kada gave birth to a little girl which they named Josephine. Joe was seven, Medka was five and Magda was two years old. Along with Mary's two sons, John and Joe, the five children kept Olga busy. She enjoyed her times with her grandchildren and at night, she had gotten into the habit of talking to her husband while lying in bed.

She told him, "Our grandchildren are clever, bright and intelligent. They are having a much better life than they would have had if they had stayed in Slovakia. I will never be tired of playing with our grandchildren. I only wish that you could play with them also. They are sad that they never met you or played with you, and I told them that it was God's will. I think that they understand. Kada's new baby looks just like you. I will be reminded of you every time that I look at her. I am so happy here and the only thing missing is you, my dear husband. We will be together again when I come up to see you. I had better go to sleep because I will have a busy day tomorrow. Good night, my love. I will talk to you tomorrow."

She was so proud of her children's children and thankful for the time that she could stay with them. When she felt that Johan was smiling down on her from somewhere above, she closed her eyes and fell into a deep sleep. Olga did not realize how much the children tired her during the day, but now that Kada was home for a while, she helped. She would go back to work soon and Olga would be alone again with her little friends.

Steve could not understand why they were not saving more money with the pay they were both bringing home. With the mill running at full capacity, the banks in Cohoes were solid, but he had heard of banks failing and people were losing their money elsewhere. The Slovaks had little to do with banks in the old country. They felt more secure if they could take the money from the strong box and actually feel it; they very rarely counted it as they added to it. They had it hidden under the floorboard of the bedroom and only two people knew where it was. Steve did not realize that inflation was creeping into the country. The money, not earning interest in the floor boards of the bedroom was losing its value as the years went by. They were putting some away, but that was because of the overtime. The cost of living kept going up so they were spending more to live especially with the addition of each child. He was earning more, but he was also spending more.

The year of 1928 brought about changes to Steve and Kada's house hold. Olga became ill with pneumonia and could not handle the children even with help from John's children. Cathy came when she could, but she was seeing a young man and was spending less and less time with the family. John, had been accepted into a good engineering school called Rensallaer Technical Institute and he was beginning classes in the fall, so he would be gone. This meant that Kada would have to leave work in the summer and take care of the children until Joe became old enough to help. The mill had started to slow down in the summer of 1928 and people were told to go home because there was no work. The women were the first to go while the men took over their jobs. Everyone had to tighten their belts in order to survive; the down cycle had begun.

It took Olga six months to recover from her illness and Steve tried not to think of what life would be like without his mother. Kada stopped work and stayed home to take care of the children and Mary brought her sons over to her house while she worked. She paid Kada a small amount, but announced that it would stop. Mary was pregnant and she would have to stay home from work after her baby was born. The times were becoming bleak, but the Janek family did not realize how low the situation would become. The mill was letting more people go and only the hard workers were kept. There was no method to determine who was to stay and who was to go because the foremen made the decisions and usually the relatives were allowed to stay. John had made many friends among the foremen and used his influence to keep his brothers working. Management remembered who spoke for the union and who did not, so the Janek brothers kept on working.

In October of 1929, the stock market crashed with huge losses and it started a traumatic period for the family. Kada was pregnant again and announced it about the time that the news of the crash came to Cohoes. No one really knew what the stock market was or how it influenced their lives, but everyone attached so much importance to it, that Steve realized they were in trouble. In the winter of 1930, he was told not to come to work anymore, but he could stay in the house he rented from the company until he could make other arrangements. He tried to make some money by working by the day for farmers in the area, but there was no work in the winter. A few months after he lost his job, he received the news that the mill had closed and everyone was out of a job. The reason, as he understood it, was there was no one to buy the sweaters or carpets and the warehouses were full. With no one paying for the products, there was no money to pay the employees to make more.

The club provided a meal for families that needed food and the church provided as much as it could. Those families that had food shared with those that had none. Somehow, the Janek brothers and their families received just enough food to survive, but one of the worst problems for Steve, was to find enough to do to fill the days. He became bored even after reading the "Jednota" two or three times. He was learning a great deal from reading the newspaper. He would take it from John when he was finished and pour over it until he understood what the newspaper was telling him. The stocks on the exchange had lost eighty percent of their value and forty-four percent of the banks had failed. Steve tried to stay out of his savings which no one knew about, but it became impossible and slowly, the money in the strong box began to dwindle. He was happy that they did not put their money in the bank because if they had and the bank failed, they would have nothing. He read that the industries most effected were the construction companies, textiles, coal mining, and railroads. It was time to make a move because he saw no future in Cohoes and he started to formulate plans to leave.

Kada was due to deliver another baby in the middle of April and she had grown huge. She was so big that she could not sit down, lie down or get up without help. This was much worse than she was when she was pregnant with Joe and Steve had to be sure that he was around in the event that she needed help. One night in bed, she woke him up and said that she was having pains and it was not the same as those with the other children. Steve woke Joe and sent him to the mid-wife's home since the doctor lived many miles away and there was no time. He tried to make her as comfortable as possible while he waited for the mid-wife. He looked at his wife and saw her huge bulk, she looked so much larger lying in bed, he tried to understand why she had gotten so large this time. He thought about the type of food that she had been eating and realized what had happened. They had been eating very little meat, and quite a bit of soup and bread. The soup was made mostly from potatoes and other starches and the diet was not right for his wife while she was pregnant; this was no way to treat his family.

The mid-wife came to the house and tried to help, but the baby was too large to be delivered the conventional way. Kada was in pain and screaming in agony. The mid-wife's husband had brought her over in their carriage and as soon as he dropped her off, he rode to fetch the doctor. An hour later he arrived with the sleepy eyed doctor who suddenly became alert when he saw Kada. He knew what had to be done and sent everyone out except the mid-wife. He had boiling water brought in and went to the carriage for some equipment. He knew Kada and knew that she delivered large babies so he knew what to bring. He brought in his instruments, alcohol and ether. He put Kada to sleep and prepared to deliver the baby by caesarian section. When he was able to reach the baby, he found that it was a little girl, the cord had twisted around her neck and strangled her. He took the lifeless infant, untangled the cord and placed the baby on the scale that he brought with him. The infant weighed eighteen pounds and four ounces so it was no wonder that Kada was not able to deliver the child. The midwife took care of the baby while the doctor closed the incision and went out to explain to Steve what had happened.

As the doctor came from the bedroom, he saw Steve sitting on the floor with his mother and four children. The doctor took him aside, spoke to him for a few minutes and left. There were tears in Steve's eyes when he told his mother and the children.

He said, "We are going to leave this place as soon as possible. We have to go to a place where there is work and we can buy food. We cannot live like this any longer. Mother, will you come with us?"

Olga answered while she dabbed her eyes, "Yes, my son, Kada needs all the help that we can give her. I will go where ever you take me."

The girl was named Kada after her mother. She was cleaned and placed in the basket that the family used for the new born. The basket was placed on a stand in the parlor and Olga and the children went to bed. The mid-wife stayed with Kada until she woke up, while Steve sat in a chair and looked at his dead daughter all night. He looked at her features, her hair, her nose and the shape of her face. She would have been a beautiful woman, he thought as he memorized everything about the girl. He had to tell Kada about her because she would be buried in a few days and Kada might not get an opportunity to study her as he had.

The next morning, the mid-wife came out and told Steve that his wife was awake, but in pain. The doctor had left some pills for her to take when the pain came back, but she was not to be moved for two weeks. Olga had woke early and made the mid-wife breakfast before she left. Steve sat on the bed to tell his wife that their new born daughter was dead. Kada was still a little groggy, but she understood and they sat in silence for a long time. Neither one knew what to say until Kada said that she wanted to have her children around her. She spent the day with her children and did not see her daughter until the next day when Steve brought her in. She looked at her for a few minutes and waved him out. He took the baby out and she was buried in the cemetery of the Sacred Heart Church with only Steve and the children being present. Olga would have much to tell her husband that night.

Friends and relatives of the family came every day, once little Kada was buried. They helped with the cleaning, laundry and cooking. Meals came from all directions so the family had plenty to eat. Someone was always present to take care of Kada and sometimes when there was nothing to do, one of the women would sit on the edge of the bed and talk to her. She was healing quickly, but it still would take some time. Kada asked Hana to go into the woods and look for certain herbs which she knew would help her heal faster. Hana did not understand, but she spent the day gathering herbs for her sister-in-law.

One of Kada's former co-workers stopped in to talk to Kada about a mutual friend, Anna Sophcak, who came to America. She married and settled in a little town in Connecticut. Her maiden name was Kolepek and Kada had worked with her at the resort in the High Tatras. She remembered her well and they spoke of her for a long time. Anna had been corresponding with her friend and knew of Kada's tragedy. She was coming to visit and wanted to stop by and see Kada. This cheered her up and Kada was excited when she told Steve. Steve knew the family, but did not remember Anna because she left Ruzbachy before the war and he would not have known her. Stefan was happy for any news that would cheer Kada up.

A few weeks later, when Anna entered Kada's room, she recognized her at once. She had grown taller and had put on a few pounds, but they hugged, and cried at their reunion. Anna's husbands name was Albert and they came by car, it did not appear that the hard times had bothered them. Steve talked with Albert, over a few beers, and they spoke of the old times in their former country. Albert came to America before the war and Steve told him all about his four years in the army. He spoke of being captured by Americans in Italy which probably saved his life. He spoke of the lack of work in Cohoes and that he would have to move as soon as Kada was able.

Albert said "I have few relatives or friends in Connecticut and Anna would like to have Kada and your family move to be with her. They had not seen each other for twenty years and it was about time that they renewed their friendship."

Steve saw this as an answer to his problems and said. "I want to talk it over with Kada and we will let you know. Do you know of any work in Connecticut?"

Albert smiled, "I am a foreman in a paper mill and it might take some time, but I am sure that I can get you into the mill. It is hard work, but it is honest work and the starting pay is not too good, but it will get better. You and your family can stay with us until you find a place of your own, I have two cows so there would be plenty of milk. We have two children who were fourteen and twelve and they could help Kada while Anna worked."

Albert had it all figured out, and unknown to both of them, the two women were discussing the same thing upstairs. Kada was ready to go as soon as she was able and once the four of them were together, they made arrangements to move to Avon, Connecticut at the end of April of 1930. Albert and his son, John, would ride up in the wagon and it would take them fourteen hours to make the trip. They would arrive on a Friday night load up the wagon by Saturday afternoon and leave very early on Sunday morning. It would be a long and hard weekend, but that was all the time that Albert could get off. Steve and Kada could use the time to make arrangements to leave and the Sophcaks would need the time to make their home ready for seven more people. Steve and Kada insisted on making financial arrangements then and there, before they moved and before Albert and Anna left. An agreement was reached and Steve and his family would move to Connecticut.

There were not many arrangements to make before they left. The house had to be packed and only the essential furniture and other belongings could be taken. The rest would be stored for them by Paul who had the most room in his barn. Weekends were a busy time in the house as friends and relatives came to help pack and cook. The one thing that could be said about Slovaks was their commitment to each other. By the end of April, they were ready to move and the only unknown, was the size of the wagon that Albert would bring. The night before Albert arrived, a reception was held at the club to say goodbye to Steve, Kada and their family. They had journeyed into the unknown before, but now they had four little ones and Kada was still weak from her ordeal. They still looked forward to a new adventure and to a new life. At last, there was a promise of a job so that Steve could support his family.

Albert came right on time with his son. John was large for his age and very strong, quiet, but eager to help. Kada thought that he was just shy, but as she got to know him better, she found out that he was deeply religious. He knelt down each night and said the rosary and he was worried that he would not be able to go to church on Sunday. When he came into the room, Kada smiled, but had to hold back a giggle. He was about five foot ten inches tall, with a stocky build and he appeared to be a grown man, but he was dressed like a little boy. It was apparent that Albert had cut his hair because he must have put a bowl on his head and cut all the hair that was below the rim of the bowl. His arms dangled out of his shirt and jacket and his trousers came somewhere between his knees and ankles. He had high topped shoes that had seen better days, but his grin was genuine. The children took to him at once and Joe followed him around trying to help him.

The wagon was larger than Steve though it would be and they loaded it, leaving only a small load which Paul took to his barn. They all went over to John's house for supper and Kada, Olga and the three girls could stay there. The four males slept on the floor at Steve's house and the next morning they loaded all the children and women in the back. Steve assigned Joe the task of taking care of the women and children. His chest grew two sizes that day. Hana and Sophie made food so they would not have to stop as often except for the children to go into the woods. There were two large horses, but the load was heavy and Albert thought that they should stop and rest the horses while they ate the noon meal. This would make them later, but at least, they would arrive. Olga played with the girls to keep them occupied and Joe asked to sit in front with the men. Steve smiled and changed places with him while it was someone else's turn to drive the team.

They left New York state and entered Massachusetts following the road south. The road passed by North Adams and Pittsfield, into Lennox, Stockbridge and Great Barrington. Albert said that they would leave the main road and take a short cut through the woods near New Marlboro, where they would enter Connecticut close to the little town of Winsted. They would turn left and head southeast along another main road until they came to Avon. Steve thought that it was about the same distance from Ruzbachy to Bratislava that his grandfather had traveled so often. When they came to Winsted, Steve saw a sign showing the road to Torrington.

Steve commented, "That is a funny name for a town."

Albert said, "The town was growing and industry was moving there. Connecticut has less unemployment then Cohoes because the jobs are not limited to one industry. Things are not so bad in this area."

They finally arrived on Orchard St., in the little town of Avon.

The girls had slept for the last five hours while Joe was wide awake and observed everything around him. They pulled the wagon around to the back door and the Janek family got the first look at the inside of their new home for the next few weeks. They would have to unload that night because some of the furniture would be used and the wagon had to be back at the paper mill early the next morning. Steve looked surprised when some men from the neighborhood came to help unload the wagon and stated carrying the furniture into the house. Apparently, Albert and his family were well liked and they had helped some of them in the past so now, it was their turn. Anna had food ready and the children were fed first while the men worked. The additional beds were set up and the girls and Joe went to bed. Joe fought sleep as long as he could, but he finally dosed off, and the adults sat at the long table and ate their meal. Steve and Kada met all the neighbors who helped and Steve made on observation and that there were less Slovaks here so he really would have to learn English.

When Steve woke up the next morning, Kada and the children were still asleep. Anna was sitting at the table drinking a cup of coffee with John and her daughter, Helen. They were waiting for their new visitors to awake. Albert had gone to work with the wagon and he would come home that evening, but Steve was too excited to eat and wanted to walk around the area. The center of Avon was located on the main road about five miles away, but they did all of their shopping and activities in the small town of Unionville which was only about a half mile away. The house was located on a road that was not used much because there were few houses on it and it did not serve as a short cut to any where. Anna and Albert owned a large tract of land behind their house which contained a barn that was painted a bright red. Next to the barn was a chicken coop, a pig sty and the toilet. The house and grounds looked like a picture on a postcard. It was very well kept and the grounds were manicured.

Steve noticed two sheep in the front yard and he asked Anna when he returned, "Are the sheep yours? I did not know that you owned sheep."

Anna smiled and replied, "Albert calls them his lawn mower and they do a very good job. We sell the wool and in the spring, we have lamb."

The Avon town line was only a stone's throw away. The paper mill was in Unionville along with the schools, and the church. The church did not abide by the town boundaries and the family belonged to St. Mary, Star of the Sea, parish. John left to go to school and Helen went with him, because it was only a short walk, just a half mile down the hill.

Steve was fascinated with John and asked Anna, "Is John going to work in the mill?"

She answered quickly, "No, he was going to graduate from high school and go to the seminary to become a priest. John wants to become a missionary for the church."

Steve understood more about John from that time on and treated his decision with respect. The Janek family stayed with the Sophcak's for four weeks.

Steve worked around the house for the first week and Albert had recommended him for an opening at the mill; Steve finally went to work. He was paid twelve dollars a week, but he had Saturdays off so it gave him two days a week to look for a house. Albert told him that houses were cheap now and the banks were loaning money. All they had to do was find a house and go to a lawyer who would handle the whole transaction. The lawyer would arrange with the First National Bank to give him a loan because the bank was happy to give loans to Slovaks, Poles and Italians; those people had a good repayment record. About two weeks later, they found two houses that peaked their interest and began to negociate. One house was located a mile outside of town and it had ten acres of land that went with it. It was a smaller house than the one in the center of town. The home in the center of town was larger, but was situated on a small lot. It had a large barn and a small garage and the children could walk to school. The center of the little town provided better police and fire protection.

Steve and Kada discussed the options to some length and Kada wanted land, which she never had in the old country, while Steve felt that the education of the children was most important. When the children became educated and found good jobs, they could buy their own land. Finally, Kada gave in and they went to see the lawyer, John Ryan to hire him for the purchase of the house on Railroad Avenue. A man named James Coody owned the house and he was asking thirteen hundred dollars. The lawyer went to the bank; he was a director of the bank so he had no trouble arranging a loan of twelve hundred dollars. Steve, Kada and the lawyer talked to Mr. Coody and the deal was struck for twelve hundred dollars. The closing was a week later and Kada and Steve owned the house. At the closing, John Ryan gave Steve a bill for ten dollars for his services, he usually changed more, but he noticed that the family had four children and he decided that he wanted only ten dollars. He asked Steve if he wanted to come to his house for a few weeks and do some gardening and he would forget the ten dollars, but Steve took out a ten dollar bill, gave it to the lawyer who marked the bill paid. They shook hands and Steve had an attorney that he relied upon for the rest of his life.

The family of Stefan Janek moved into its new home the following weekend. The furniture was brought in and placed where it belonged and the boxes were unpacked. There were three bedrooms upstairs and two small bedrooms downstairs. Mr. Coody had left the wood stove, a Columbia in the kitchen. This provided heat for the downstairs except for the living room and two small bedrooms. Kada and Steve took the bedroom closest to the street and Olga got the other bedroom on the first floor. Josie and Magda shared a room, Medka got her own room as did Joe. The living room had a coal burning stove on a metal base and this heated the living room, the two bedrooms. Since the chimney heated up when the stove was being used, there was heat for the three bedrooms upstairs. The whole front of the house had a porch with a railing facing north, so the porch was in the shade from noon on in the summer. The kitchen contained a walk-in pantry, while the entire back of the house was a woodshed. The toilet was in back next to the barn and this left plenty of space for a garden.

The house was six feet away from the sidewalk that ran along side of the road and there were rows of homes across the street. The back yards of those homes bordered the Farmington River. If one stood in one of these yards and looked south, he would see a small covered wooden bridge and just across the bridge was the mill where Steve worked. The back of the new property had a four foot picket fence and just twelve feet west of the tracks of the Hartford/New Haven Railroad. The train carried freight twice a day from Hartford to Collinsville and points in between.

There were no closets in this home, so the first thing that Steve did was to build wardrobes with shelves for each room. It was too late to start a garden, although the two apple trees and the peach tree had small fruit on them already. He cleaned out the shed and made that ready for wood and built a coal bin in the cellar, under the window where the coal would be deposited into the cellar away from the cold and snow. He made arrangements to have Joe, Medka and Magda start school in the fall and he assigned Joe the task of bringing the girls to and from school. They had to walk across the wooden bridge and this was dangerous, but he was sure that Joe would handle it. The mill was located on the river on the south side of the main road so Steve did not have to buy a car or a wagon to get back and forth to work because, if it snowed some of the walk went under the covered bridge. An opening came about in the factory for the second shift, the hours were from three in the afternoon until midnight. It paid more money and Steve jumped at the chance to have his mornings off to work around the house.

The family was content and the children were making friends. The neighbor across the street was Anna Sophcak's friend from Slovakia, Agnes Mortek and Kada never met her in the old country. She was younger than Anna, but she came over with her and they turned out to be best friends for the rest of their lives. Agnes husband's name was John. He drove a car with a back seat and when the weather was good, they went for a ride on a Sunday afternoon.

John smoked a curved pipe and he was never without it. He called his pipe, "Fika" and no one remembered where he got the name. Everyone referred to the pipe as fika and treated it like a human and John's best friend. There was always a thin wisp of smoke curling over John's head and he learned how to talk and be understood without taking fika out of his mouth. He always smelled of stale smoke and even when he was met out of doors, everyone made sure that they were down wind of him. Agnes and her daughters became used to it and thought nothing of it, but the smell was always there. Agnes did not allow John to smoke in the dining room, living room or in the bed room and the ceiling of the kitchen was turning brown from the smoke. John tried to spend more time out of doors so he could take fika with him.

During the summer, John put Steve in touch with a farmer from Avon named Andy Ruskin. Andy sold wood and he delivered two truck loads of wood which was cut, but needed to be split. Joe helped with the splitting and soon it was all piled neatly in the wood shed. The next thing he did was order two tons of coal which was sent to the cellar in a metal chute and the Janek household was now ready for a cold winter.

In September, Kada told Steve that she was pregnant again.

Steve said, "This time, I hope that it will be a boy. We need a little boy around here. After three girls, I want to raise a boy."

He sent her to see Doctor Drake who had an office just across the bridge because he remembered what happened the last time. This time he was worried and he did not want it to happen again. She was scheduled to see Dr. Drake once a month until she gave birth. He did not live very far away from their home and he had a car so he could be there very quickly. The doctor gave Kada a diet to follow so she would not gain too much weight and when he examined her, he found the scar on her abdomen and questioned her about it. The doctor knew that he would have to watch this pregnancy very carefully. Steve was also determined to allow this pregnancy to go full term without any problems.

The children were all in school except Josie who was still too young and she stayed home with her mother. Steve got everything ready for winter, but it was going be a lean Christmas because of the expenses in buying a new home. The house needed insulation, new doors, new paint inside and out and a new roof, but this would have to wait until next spring.

They went to church as a family each Sunday, rain or shine. One sunny day, after Mass, the priest stopped Steve and introduced himself as Father Sullivan. He was a in his early sixties and had been at St. Mary's for seventeen years. He knew everyone in the parish, and had seen the family at Mass several times.

He asked, "Has Joe made his first holy communion?"

Steve answered, "Yes, Father, he had made it at the Scared Heart parish in Cohoes New York, but he had not gone to confession for sometime."

The priest asked, "I would like to visit you at home and take all the information I need for the parish census."

Steve was happy that he met the priest because this was one more step in becoming part of the community.

When Father Sullivan visited their home on the following Thursday, Kada, remarked in Slovak, "I am surprised at your knowledge of the Slovaks. You speak Slovak very well."

Kada saw his smile and the twinkle in his eyes, "With so many Slovak families in the parish, I have to learn the language and I also have to learn Italian. All the Slovaks sit on the left side in Church, all the Italians sit on the right and the Irish along with everyone else sat in the middle."

Kada had already noticed this and when they went to church, they sat on the left under the statue of the Blessed Virgin Mary. Father Sullivan enrolled the two older girls into catechism class every Sunday at nine while the others were at Mass. They would be making their First Holy Communion in May of the following year. In another year, Joe would be confirmed, so he would have to take class on Tuesday afternoons. Everyone was so friendly in this little town that Kada vowed to stay, raise her children here and live out the rest of her live in this quiet, sleepy little town.

The winter was a cold one and Steve knew that he must take steps to seal the house from the cold winds of winter. They burned more fuel than they had anticipated and called Andy to drop off another load of wood which they just left outside and split as it was needed. They did not count on this in the budget and although Andy said he would wait until spring for the money, Steve wanted to pay him at once. This meant that they would have to cut back on food.

Agnes had two older daughters and she gave Kada some clothes that they had outgrown. The girls had warm coats and boots for the walk back and forth to school. Joe also was given a coat by a friend of Steve's at work, so the children would not be cold.

On the corner of the street opposite Railroad Avenue, was a small meat market owned and operated by a man named Abel Stein. Abel was a Jew and there was only one other Jewish family in Unionville. Two brothers, Aaron and Nathan Nieman ran a restaurant on Farmington Avenue called the "Green Garden." The restaurant was well known and people from all the neighboring towns came to enjoy the food. Abel took a liking to Kada and because of her struggle to provide meals for her husband and children, he would slip extra food into her shopping bag once in a while. He also saved the bones and poorer cuts of meat that he had trouble selling. He gave them to her and Kada would make soup or goulash that would feed her family for days. Abel also let her charge some small items when money was short, knowing that Kada would not let the bill become too large before she paid it. Steve had no knowledge that Kada had these arrangements and she did not tell him. Kada wanted him to believe that he was providing for his family with no problems. This was very important to Stefan Janek

The neighborhood became very close and the women exchanged

clothes which they did not need for those clothes that other children could wear. No one felt that they were being treated unfairly and since Kada's children were younger, she was given more of the out grown clothes than she gave. She was thankful that God had put her into this community. All but two families on Railroad Avenue were Slovak. One family was Italian and one family was Polish, but everyone spoke Slovak. Either they learned the language, or they did not communicate and everyone suspected that Mr. Coody sold his home because he really did not fit into the neighborhood.

In April of 1932, Kada gave birth to a not so little boy. Peter was fourteen pounds and fifteen ounces as Dr. Drake managed to keep Kada's weight down, but not the baby's size. The doctor delivered the boy without trouble, although he had to cut Kada to get at the baby. The baby, according to Agnes, looked to be a year old on the day he was born. The women in the neighborhood came over to see the boy and could not resist pinching the cheeks at both ends. Peter slept in the room with his parents for a year and then was transferred upstairs into Joe's room so Joe could help take care of him. He was a happy baby as long as he was well fed. A gate was put on the top of the stairs so he could not fall down the open stair well. He was brought down every morning and returned to his crib every night. Once Peter was able to negociate the stairs, the gate was taken down. Toilet training was a pot with a cover that was put under the bed so if the boys had to go at night, they could use that instead of going outside; Peter watched what Joe did.

CHAPTER TWELVE

Peter was two and one half years old and he was playing in the kitchen while Kada was making supper. He was a big boy and started walking late because with five women in the house, when he reached for something, it was handed to him and he did not have to walk. He did not have to talk either because all he had to do was point and grunt and it was handed to him. He walked around the kitchen using chairs, a table or any other object for support. This day, he walked to the stove and pulled on the handle of a pot full of boiling water. Suddenly there was a scream, the water came down and splashed on his head; Kada panicked. She lifted him up and put his head under the cold water tap, but the damage had been done. She put him into her bed, sent Josie to fetch Agnes. She arrived in just a few minutes and determined quickly what had happened. Peter was lying in the big bed and he looked so small. His head was red and it looked like it would blister at any moment. Agnes ran to the store and called the doctor's office. Although he had a waiting room full of patients, he took his black bag, ran out his office and burst into the Janek home. He applied a salve on Peter's head right away. Agnes ran to the paper mill and told Steve who got some one to cover for him and ran home. He arrived just as the doctor was finishing with the bandage around Peter's head.

Dr. Drake asked Kada, "What did you do when you saw what had happened?"

She explained, "I put his head under the cold water, I did not know what else to do."

The doctor said, "That was the worst thing that you could

have done. The next time this happens, put some butter on his burn as soon as you can. We will have to watch the boy carefully. I will come back tomorrow."

Now that Peter was taken care of, Steve went back to work and Agnes took Josie and Frank to her house so Kada could devote all of her time to Peter. The boy seemed hot so she gave him a spoonful of the medicine that Dr. Drake had left. She just sat there and swayed back and forth blaming herself for what had happened because she felt that she should have been watching the child more closely. The rest of the children came home from school and Kada assigned each a task to keep them busy. Joe fixed supper and the older girls helped, but Kada did not eat that night. Joe fixed his father's supper and took it to him. Kada would not sleep that night, she sat with Peter who whimpered all night.

The next morning, the doctor came and took the bandages off. He noted that Peter's little head was blistered and told Kada, "You have to be careful not to break even one blister or the pain would be unbearable. Peter is not to be moved until the blisters dried up."

The doctor came the next day and stopped in for the next seven days. He went to church at ten o'clock and stopped in after Mass, it took about two weeks for the blisters to dry up, but Peter developed another problem, his lungs were filling up with fluid.

Doctor Drake said, "The onset of pneumonia is common with patients that have to lie still for so long a time, but I have never seen it happen to a person so young."

Peter developed a fever and a cough and the doctor left some medicine to be taken every two hours, twenty-four hours a day and promised to return the next day. Kada reached way back in her memory for the remedy that the gypsies used. She got a large box of epsom salt, some sauerkraut juice, boiled thyme and made a paste. She and Olga covered Peter's entire body except for the eyes, nose, mouth and ears with the paste. Within a few hours the paste had dried into a cast and the next morning the cast was wet from the sweat of the little boy, but he felt cooler and he did not cough as much.

The doctor walked in, took one look at Peter, and started to take the cast from Peter's body. He became very angry and told Kada, "Do not ever do this again!"

He examined Peter, gave her some more medicine and said, "I will be back tomorrow. Do what I tell you to do."

As soon as the doctor left, Kada and Olga made another batch of the paste and covered Peter's body. Olga knew the power that the gypsy remedies had and she was happy to help her. Kada told Agnes to watch for the doctor the next morning and as soon as she saw him walking across the bridge, she was to wave a white towel and Kada would take the cast off. She would wash and clean Peter before the doctor could enter the house. The only day of the week that the paste was not applied was Sunday, because the doctor drove his car and they did not know when he would arrive. Each day, Peter appeared to be a little better, but his teeth were turning brown from the medicine that the doctor was giving him. It took Peter a month to recover to the point that Kada felt that she did not have to apply the paste any longer. The doctor started coming only once every two days and finally only once a week. If there was a problem, she was to go to Stein's market, which had the only telephone in the neighborhood to call the doctor who would come as soon as he could. The doctor pronounced him fully recovered and told Kada to put some meat on his bones.

Peter had lost weight during his illness, almost a quarter of his entire body weight and Joe's chore each day, was to walk down the railroad tracks to a little farm, not far away. He would leave with a few pennies and an empty pail and he would come back about a half hour later with almost a full gallon of milk. The milk was not processed in any way; it was raw milk, but it was fresh, just a few hours before the cow had stored it herself. The neighbors brought over some canned goods, fresh baked bread and with the milk he drank, Peter began to gain weight and soon, was playing outside. He never had a lack of friends or people to talk to because everyone in the neighborhood knew who he was. Everyone reached into their pockets and came out with a piece of candy or a cookie to give to Peter. Agnes watched Peter play and marveled at the recovery of the boy and one day, she told Kada how she felt.

Kada said, "I am happy that the doctor had shown such an interest in the boy. The doctor had actually believed that he cured Peter, but I know better."

October of that year, Frank was born and by this time, Kada learned to control her weight and that of the baby during pregnancy. Frank was only eleven pounds and Dr. Drake delivered him with no problem. Olga took charge of Peter while Kada took care of Frank and since there was two and a half years difference in their ages, they would become friends for life. When they were young, they did not have to communicate with each other except for a look, a nod of the head or a wink and they were be in agreement as to what to do next. They would just go out and do it and neither Olga nor Kada could comprehend this mutual understanding. Where they found one of the brothers, they were sure to find the other.

CHAPTER THIRTEEN

When Steve arrived at work one day, he met Albert who was waiting for him. He had a message for Steve and he looked sad.

"Anna just left, she got a telephone call from Cohoes. John's daughter, Catherine was involved in a car accident in Troy, New York. She had been riding with her boy friend, Rudy when the car went out of control, down an embankment and struck a tree. The police investigation revealed that Rudy had been traveling at a high rate of speed in an open car and they were both pronounced dead at the scene of the accident. The funeral is Saturday."

Steve looked at him in disbelief and it was a minute before he spoke, "Can I have Friday off so I can go to the funeral? I need a day to get there, a day there and a day to get back."

Albert said, "It is all arranged. I can take you to the train station in Hartford, but you will need someone to pick you up or you will have to take the trolley to Farmington and walk the four miles home. I will have Anna call your brother and tell him, so some one can pick you up in Albany. Go with God, my friend"

When Steve arrived in Albany, Paul was there with John's car to pick him up and they rode to Cohoes in silence after Paul told him what had happened. "Hana is taking it very hard so you will be staying with me. I am working as a laborer for the railroad company and the hard work is beginning to wear me down. I am not bringing home much money and my father-in-law is complaining so things are rather strained."

"Why do you stay in Cohoes? You should go someplace where there is work."

"When things quiet down, I want to talk to you about some

plans that I am thinking about. I want to get your opinion before I do anything. We have four daughters now and I do not want to make any mistakes. If I had one son, maybe my father-in-law would be more kindly to me."

Steve washed and had a meager supper with Paul and his family. He went to see John to find out if he could be of any help. He found most of the rest of the family at John's home. Young John had taken a job in St. Petersburg, Florida, but he flew up so he could be there on time. Paul and Maria came in a little later. The entire family except for Olga, Kada and Steve's children was gathered under one roof. Hana was taking it very hard and the women, try as they might, could not penetrate the veil of tears.

All she did was cry, sway back and forth and mutter." "She was only twenty-six years old and had not lived before she was killed. I will never see her again."

Rudy's parents telephoned while they were there, but she did not talk to them. John spoke for a few minutes and then hung up. The funeral would be the following day at Sacred Heart Church, but it would be a closed casket and there would be no calling hours; her body was cut up very badly. She had been thrown into the trees and bounced from one to another. There would be a high funeral Mass and they would all go to the cemetery to bury her.

The Mass was a solemn affair, but it took only one hour and Hana had to be helped from the cemetery because she fainted when the casket was lowered into the ground. She was brought home and put to bed so Steve did not see her again before he left; she wanted to see no one, not even her husband. She had talked to young John before he left Sunday morning, but that was very brief. John called the doctor to look at her, but he said that there was no medicine that he could give her. The best medicine was time and that might heal her broken heart. He was wrong because two years later, Hana died. She was a frail, thin shadow of herself, refusing to eat. She would not see anyone and, one day, she just took her last breath.

Steve's train left at noon on Sunday and he called Albert, before he left. Albert felt so bad about his niece that he made some changes and promised to pick him up at five in the afternoon.

Paul spent the morning talking to Steve and asked, "Are there any jobs in Unionville? How was the housing market? I am planning to leave Cohoes with my family. I want to move to Unionville within a year. We plan to help my father-in-law sell the house and then put him in an old age home. He is having problems with his kidneys and I suspect that it is caused by all the drinking he has done at the club. He will be needing more care and with his pension and the money from the house, he could live very well in a home. It might even prolong his life because he would not have the opportunity to drink as much. I have to think of my wife and daughters."

Steve said, "You know that I will help as much as I can. With the threat of another war in Europe, there are more jobs, but you will have to hurry because house prices are going up."

Paul said, "Karl is not too happy in Cohoes and he has a friend that has moved to Barnesboro, Pennsylvania to work in the coal mines. Karl has worked in the mines in Slovakia and he is planning to move also. The mines are working at a hundred percent capacity and they need men."

Steve asked, "What about Mary and Joe? What are their plans?"
"I do not talk to Mary and Joe very much because I have my own problems to contend with."

Steve thought of the family while he rode back on the train. The family was moving out in all directions, Paul was leaving as soon as he could sell his father-in-law's home and Karl was moving to the coal mines of Pennsylvania. Joe and Mary were still in Cohoes, but there was no telling how long they would stay there. John lost his only daughter. His son was in a place called St. Petersburg, Florida and he had no idea where that was. It would be harder and harder for them to get together because America was such a large country and who knew where everyone will be a few years from now. There was no stable motive like land or a farm to hold them all in one place. He did not know what the future would bring, all he knew was that he had to provide for his family as well as he could.

CHAPTER FOURTEEN

When Peter was five years old and Frank was three, Olga became very ill. She was bed ridden and the family visited her every day. She had developed an upper respiratory infection that would not go away. Olga was seventy-five years old and she did not have the strength to fight the illness. Kada tried all the remedies taught to her by the gypsies, but nothing seemed to work. She made her the tea with the herb, thyme, added honey, but it did nothing. The doctor's medicine made her sleep all the time and she did not care for this because she wanted to spend as much time with her family as she could. She loved Peter and Frank and often said that they were her kind of little boys because they were always in trouble with their mother and father. Every time any one mentioned them, she smiled.

She said, "Little boys are supposed to get into mischief. That is why God has put them on this earth."

Steve always answered, "You did not let me get away with all the mischief."

She smiled and said, "You are being paid back for all the times you were high spirited. The grandmother's job is to just sit back and enjoy her grandchildren. You are the disciplinarian now and your job is to make men out of them as I have done with you."

Olga was closest to Steve's family because she had lived with them for most of her time in America. One day Olga and Steve were talking as they usually did after lunch, Steve sitting on the edge of the bed holding her hand. Suddenly, her eyes filled with tears and she began to sob.

She said, between the coughs, "I had a dream that Johan came to me and said that he waited long enough for me to join him in Heaven. He does not want to see me suffer any longer. He told me that he will come to get me soon, in a long boat and he will paddle through the darkest of waters so I can join him on the other side. We will be together and free of pain through all eternity."

Steve had talked to the doctor when he left that morning. It was the doctor's opinion that his mother looked better and at least, had not gotten worse. At that point, Paul came in to see his mother and Steve left to get ready for work. He found Kada in the kitchen as usual and said, "My mother told me of a dream that she had about my father. He told her that he will come and get her in a boat through dark water."

When he mentioned the dark water, Kada dropped the pan of water she was filling into the sink, turned white and hugged her husband.

He looked at her and asked, "What is the matter with you? It was only a dream."

"Steve, you mother is going to die. Please do not go to work today. The gypsies feel that when one dreams of deep, dark water, the closest person to you will die. She will not last the night."

He looked at her and answered, "I talked to the doctor today and he said she looked better."

Kada was on the verge of tears and she said, "What does the doctor know? Look what he did for Peter. It was not the doctor that made him better, it was my gypsies."

He said, "I am going to work, but if it makes you feel any better, you can stay with her all day, but do not to mention the dream."

Steve went to work and about seven o'clock, Joe was sent to bring his father home. He asked the rest of the crew to cover for him as they had done before when something important came up. He rushed into the room to find all of his children huddled around his mother. Kada looked at him with tears streaming down her cheeks. Peter and Frank were holding her hands because their grandmother had asked them to do that. She looked around at her family and died.

Kada could not control herself any longer, she beat her chest and said, "It's my fault that she died. Why did you have to tell me about the dream?"

"Why it is your fault? Do you think that the doctor would come because she had a dream?"

He grabbed her by the shoulders, shook her and shouted, "It is not your fault!"

The children did not know what was happening and they all started to cry. Joe took the blanket and put it over his grandmother's head, but it was too late. The boys could not let go of her hands and Steve had to pry them loose. He made everyone leave the room while he went to Agnes' house and called the doctor. He came about a half hour later, but the two young boys could not understand what happened to grandma.

Mr. Murphy, the undertaker came and took Olga away to prepare her for burial and he brought her back to the house the next day for the viewing. John, Joe, Karl, Paul and Mary arrived at various times. Steve made the boys sleep on the floor and John slept in Joe's room while Karl and Joe slept in a large bed used by Peter and Frank. Mary slept in Olga's bed. Food from the neighbors found its way into the kitchen, Medka, Magda and Josie set the food out for the people who visited and Steve bought two bottles of whiskey.

He said, "My mother wanted to see her family happy,"

Before the funeral was over, the contents of the bottles were gone. A high mass was held at St. Mary's with Father Sullivan as the principle priest. John had brought a priest with him from Cohoes who stayed at the rectory; she was buried in St. Mary's cemetery.

Mary announced, "Michael and I are moving from Cohoes to a little city in the north of Connecticut called Torrington. Michael has a friend there who had more work than he could handle and Michael is to become a partner in the business. They would be doing remodeling work, but hoped to go into house building where the real money was. I will not be working because I have decided to stay home and care for the children."

Karl said, "I am doing well in the coal mines and my sons are following in my foot steps. There is a large Slovak club in Barnesboro and I have become a member. We have ten children to date and more coming and I like my life in Barnesboro because we bought a house with a large piece of land. The property has a barn, chicken coop, and a pig sty. I raise my own vegetables, smoke my own pork and have two cows that are giving milk."

He joked, "The house is big enough for at least five more children, but Honcha had a little something to say about that."

He had to leave on Sunday because he went to work the next day.

When everyone left on Sunday, the house seemed empty. Kada washed clothes and bedclothes and the girls cleaned all of the dishes, pots and pans and put them away. Joe went out and chopped some wood while Peter and Frank prowled around the house to see what mischief they could conjure up. Steve was in Olga's room going over her private things and clothes that he packed in boxes to be given away. Olga was a small thin woman and her clothes would not fit everyone, but they were too good to throw away. He found fifty-four dollars that Olga had put away for one thing or another and he divided it by six. He sent each share to his brothers and sister. She belonged to the Slovak Rosary Society which paid two hundred dollars to her estate. She had given her rosary to Kada along with all of her prayer books. Steve found some pictures and the one taken at John's wedding, it was so faded that he could hardly make out the faces. It had been handled many times and the edges were curling because Olga must have looked at it so many times. There were pictures of children and even one of him in his dress uniform when he was in the army. He made piles of all the pictures and made a note to send them to his brothers and sister. Steve sat in a chair and thought about his mother because all that he had in front of him, was the culmination of a lifetime.

Olga did not leave many material things, but what she left to her family was priceless. She left an examples of good family values and a work ethic. She showed by love because she loved her children equally and treated them the same. It made no difference whether she was with John, Paul, or any of her children, she treated them and her grandchildren alike.

Olga had told him once, with a tear in her eye. "There is only one thing in my life that I regretted and that is the loss of my husband before he had a chance to see, touch, smell and love his grandchildren. God had taken him too early and that saddens me. I will have quite a bit to tell him when I see him in Heaven. He had given up so much for me and our children and when he went, he left a void in my life that I was never able to fill. He would have loved Peter and Frank, not as a father who was bound to discipline them, but as a grandfather who could watch their antics with humor. He might even had encouraged them, but he never knew them."

Sitting there in the chair in her room, Steve made an oath that he would pass on the traditions not only to his children, but to his children's children. They needed to know their heritage, where they came from and how they arrived at this point. He could not speak for his brothers and sister, but he would pass all the stories, customs and the family traditions on.

Out loud, he said to his mother, "I will carry on, mother, what you and father have started. You have given us a better life than you had and we can only hope from that. We have to give our children a better life then we had so they will prosper. You kept the family together even over the huge distances and we are better for it. I will not let you and father down!"

Steve sat in the chair a very long time and did not notice that it had gotten dark. A soft rap came at the door and he heard Kada call out in a whisper to see if he was all right. She wanted him to know that supper was ready. He said that he would be right out and tried to compose himself. He did not want to let the children see him with his eyes red. They would have understood, but now was the time to appear strong. He finally came out and the children were waiting for him. Olga's place was not there any longer and her chair had been placed in the corner.

They were having left-overs, and as Kada said, "A little of this and a little of that."

It was a silent meal, the dishes and the kitchen were cleaned up quickly. Even Peter and Frank were quiet and went into the living room to play. The Janek household would never be the same without Olga. It was an end of an era.

CHAPTER FIFTEEN

In September of the year Olga died, Peter started school which was in the center of town across the covered bridge. There were three buildings and Peter went to the one that contained the classes from kindergarten through fourth grade. The second building had grades five through eight and the third building had grades nine through twelve. Joe was in tenth grade, but this would be his last year in high school. Steve told him to continue, but he said that he wanted to work in the mill to help with the family expenses. Kada took Peter by the hand and walked him to school. She took him to the kindergarten class and left him with the teacher and eight other pupils. Peter could not understand what was happening because at home they spoke Slovak, he knew some English words, but not enough to get by. The teacher, Miss Miniter told him what to do by sign language and relayed her commands in English. At recess of the first day, the teacher told them to lie down and rest, Peter happened to be in a base cabinet trying to get a toy, but he did not understand what the teacher was trying to say.

She finally reached in, pulled him out by the leg and said, "Come."

So now, whenever he heard the word "come" he would look up at the teacher to see what she wanted.

At noon Kada came to fetch her son to take home and asked him, "How do you like school? Did you have fun?"

He answered, "I do not like it because I can not understand what was being said. Everyone talks funny and I want to stay home with my brother, Frank.

Kada told him, "You are going to school and you will just have to get used to it. You are going to learn because someday your father and I will need you to take care of us."

When they crossed the bridge, Peter looked across the street and Frank was waiting for him at the door. As soon as he saw Peter he dashed out of the house, looked both ways as he was taught and ran across the street to see his brother. Peter changed his clothes and they went out to the barn to play. Since the kindergarten class was only half a day, Peter went every morning with Joe and was picked up by Kada at noon. Kada told him that when he went into first grade it would be for the entire day and he was going to have to go with Medka because Joe would no longer be going to school.

Once the school year was finished, Joe went to work in the spinning mill across the street from the paper mill. With the extra money Steve and Kada decided to wire the house for electricity. They put a spot light outside so there would be light going to the outhouse. The path to the outhouse was made up of two boards laid together end to end. It got muddy in the backyard especially in the spring and winter and Steve was afraid that one of the children would fall and hurt themselves. He had an electrical contractor come and do the wiring. It took three days, Steve paid him seventy-five dollars; part of the money came from Olga's estate

Kada said, "Even though Olga is dead, she is still helping us."

The next thing that Kada wanted was an electric ice box and an indoor toilet, but they would have to wait until they saved enough money. It was their habit not to buy anything for which they could not pay. They saw their neighbors taking loans to pay for the improvements to their homes, but none of the Janek families would do that. That would mean paying the loan back with interest and they could not progress too far if they did that.

In the summer of 1940, Kada finally got her electric ice box. Mrs. Duka, at the end of the street decided to move in with her daughter in Collinsville and she wanted to sell her furniture. A price was agreed upon and the men of the neighborhood carried the "frigidaire" from one house to the other. They put it in the kitchen next to the sink, because they wanted to keep it as far away from the wood stove as possible. They plugged it in, the motor started and Steve told everyone not to open the door for a least a day. The old ice box was taken outdoors with the food still in it and the next day, the food was transferred. Steve showed Kada how to operate it and how to defrost it once a month because the frost would build up especially in the freezer portion. Kada was thrilled and she told everyone who would listen about her new electric ice box. This meant storing more food and fewer trips to Abel's market; the next step was the inside toilet. Now that food was plentiful, Kada gained weight as did her whole family. There was more food on the table than there had ever been in her whole life, but Steve who worked so hard at the paper mill, never seemed to gain weight. Kada made a practice of eating the food that was left over after her children ate as much as they wanted and since there was more food, she prepared more and she ate the leftovers. The boys, Peter and Frank grew bigger and bigger. The people who came from countries where food was scarce, associated the large child with being a healthy child, therefore the boys were very healthy indeed. It was a status symbol to see overweight children since this demonstrated that the family was wealthy enough to keep their families well fed. When company came to visit, the boys were paraded in front of them to show how well the family was doing.

 The sudden increase in weight caused Kada some problems. She could not maneuver as well and found herself sleeping later. She cut herself once, when she was slicing bread and the wound took an extremely long time to heal. She found the bleeding did not stop right away and she needed to keep a cloth on the cut to control the bleeding. Her monthly periods had stopped sometime ago, and being forty-one years old, she felt that her time for bearing children was over. In later September of 1940, she woke up to vaginal bleeding. She woke Steve and told him that she was hemorrhaging and sent him across the street to telephone the doctor.

He arrived as soon as he could and found that the bleeding had stopped, but he sent Steve out of the room and examined Kada. As Steve paced back and forth, he made sure that all of his children were around him except Joe who had gone to work. A few hours had passed when the door to the bedroom opened and the doctor came out holding a nine pound baby boy.

"Where did that come from?" Exclaimed Steve. "How can you be pregnant at your age?"

"God works in mysterious ways. I never knew that I was with a child, I thought that I was just too fat. The doctor says that the little boy is healthy and I have to stay in bed for three days. I can use the rest. Medka will stay home and take care of us."

Doctor Drake found another problem with Kada. He found that she was a diabetic and would require insulin every day. He gave Medka a box of syringes and a case of little bottles of insulin, which had to be refrigerated. He showed her how to measure the exact dosage and how to insert the needle into her mother's arm.

The doctor took Medka aside and told her. "You are to give your mother a shot after breakfast each morning. Here is a diet to follow with absolutely no sugar. It is very important that your mother eat the same foods and the same quantities each day. Keep an orange handy in the event that the food she consumed did not have enough sugar because the insulin would send her into shock. If that happens, you are to cut a piece from the orange or other fruit and force the juice into your mother's mouth to bring the sugar level back up."

Kada felt that this was the end of her life as she knew it. There had been illnesses in the Janek household that Kada could cope with, she brought Peter back after his bout with pneumonia and she treated her children for all the minor colds and stomach aches. This was new to her, this was life threatening and she was thankful that it happened in America where the doctors were better educated. She had loved Father Josef back in Ruzbachy, but she wondered if he would be able to handle this problem as well has her doctor had done.

Medka was young and intelligent and she would help her mother for the rest of her life. The three girls dropped out of school as soon as the law allowed and went to work. Medka did not return to school after Jerry was born. She stayed home to take care of him and her mother. Once Kada was on her feet, she went to work in the spinning mill to help the family. Magda could not wait for her sixteenth birthday and she too left school, to go to work. Josie had a few years to go until she was able to leave school, but she left as soon as she could.

CHAPTER SIXTEEN

As was the custom in the Stefan Janek household on Sunday evenings, the entire family was gathered around the radio listening to Jack Benny and Fred Allen. It was early December of 1941, Joe, Medka and Magda had not gone through High School because they found work and were helping to support the family. Steve was against this, but the youngsters were determined to carry their own weight as soon as they were able. Paul had moved to Unionville with all of his children and was living on Forest Street; on top of the first hill. The town of Unionville was located in a valley. On the southern end of town, there was a hill, a level plain with streets and houses and another hill. To identify the area where the residents lived, they indicated on which hill their home was located. He now had ten children, most of them working and Paul worked at a ball bearing factory in the neighboring town of Bristol. Maria had died a few years after they left Cohoes and Paul had married a woman named Sue who took over the household.

Steve and Paul got together a few times a week for the rosary at the church and also attended meetings of their Slovak Society. This society met once a month at different homes and dues were collected so if one of the members died, money could be provided for the burial expense. The family life for both of them ran smoothly because they had a roof over their heads and there was enough to eat. With the war in Europe looming over the horizon, jobs were paying more and the quality of life was improving.

As Steve's family was listening to Jack Benny, on that Sunday evening, an announcer broke into the program and said that President Roosevelt had an important announcement to make. The

President's voice came on and he said that the Japanese had just attacked Pearl Harbor in Hawaii with extensive loss of life and ships. The battleship Arizona had been sunk along with other ships of the United States Navy. The attack was unprovoked and without warning. The President felt that the country was at war and the cabinet was going to meet at once. All eyes looked at Joe because he was twenty years old, he had to register for the draft and he could go at any time. Peter was still too young, but if the war dragged on, he could be drawn into it. A tear rolled down Kada's cheek and she thought that now that the living became easier and they were beginning to enjoy themselves, this had to happen. No one listened to the radio except to hear if there would be any further news bulletins. Joe got up, went outside and brought in an arm load of wood to put into the wood box. It was still too warm to burn coal in the stove and they usually started burning coal around Christmas. The next day, the President came on the radio and said that the United States had declared war on Japan and would mobilize to fight the enemy.

Joe said, "I am ready to go into the Army, but I do not want to volunteer. I am going to try to get into a non-combat unit and possibly stay in the country."

Everyone was enlisting into the service of their country so that they could choose the branch in which they wanted to serve. Joe got his notice to report to Fort Devins, Massachusetts on May 30, 1942 and it was on his parents wedding anniversary. He took a train from Hartford to Boston where a bus was waiting to take him and others to camp. There was eight weeks of basic training at Fort Dix, New Jersey and he came home for a week before he was assigned to the Air Force and sent to San Antonio, Texas. Joe was going to school to complete further training in electronics. The school was six months long so he knew it would be 1943 before he obtained his permanent assignment.

Paul had two sons, Jimmy and Bob and there was two and a half years difference in their ages, with Bob being the oldest. Jimmy enlisted in the Marine Corp because he wanted to be in on the action. He was eighteen years old when he enlisted. He enlisted in that branch of the military because he wanted to go with four of his classmates with the understanding that they would train together and go through the war together. Bob wanted to go with them to take care of his little brother, but it was against marine regulations to send two or more members of the same family together. There was an incident where five Sullivan brothers were assigned to the same ship, the ship went down and all five were lost. It was such a tragic loss to the family, that the military decided that it would not happen again. Bob was disappointed, but he enlisted anyway and found his way into an ordinance company that took care of repairing the vehicles.

Joe's son, Andy, enlisted in the Navy and went through boot camp at the Great Lakes Naval Training Center. He was assigned to a warship that patrolled the east coast of the United States. He was not involved in any naval battles, but he did retire from the navy after thirty years.

It was while Andy was out to sea that he learned of his father's illness. They had found a tumor at the end of his spine that had been there for sometime and when Andy arrived in port, he was given leave to visit his father. When he arrived home, he found his mother and three sisters around his fathers's bed; they had been crying for sometime. His mother took him into the kitchen and while he ate, she explained what had happened and what was going to happen. The doctor said that he had a few days to live for the tumor had cut off all circulation to his hips and legs. Joe's upper body was large, but the lower part was skin and bones. He was under the influence of morphine because of the pain, but Catherine wanted her son, Joe to visit with his father while the rest of them left the room. She wanted her husband to know that his son was home with no distractions.

Joe passed away two days later with his entire family around him. His wife held one hand while his oldest daughter, Maggie held the other when he took his last breath. He looked up at his precious family, smiled, closed his eyes and died. The next day his brothers and sister arrived for the funeral and he was laid to rest with his niece, Catherine, John's daughter and his sister-in-law Hana. There would be many more of this family buried in this area of the cemetery before this generation passed on. Joe was the first of the five brothers to pass away in America and he left a wife, three daughters and a son. His oldest daughter, Kay joined the army and became a WAC. She achieved the rank of master Sargent and once the war was over, she took care of her mother until she passed away. She married a man that she met in the army and later moved to St. Petersburg, Florida.

* * *

The war years produced many hardships for the Stefan Janek family in Unionville, Connecticut. Meat, sugar and other foods were rationed and if it was not for their good friend Abel, food would have been limited. There was enough money, but there was nothing to buy. Once in a while, Abel would put aside some meat for Kada and when she was in the market, he would include it with her other purchases. He told her to keep it to herself because if the neighborhood knew that he had meat, there would a line in front of the store in a few minutes. Kada told Abel's wife, Leah about her various remedies and Abel, in return treated her like a privileged customer. This went on during the duration of the war and while everyone else in the neighborhood was looking for food, the Janek boys did not lose weight, but instead got bigger and bigger.

The boys were ten and twelve years old and wandered around the neighborhood at will. The summer was spent at the pines, a bend in the Farmington river they used as a swimming hole. The hurricane of 1938 had uprooted a huge oak tree and left it hanging over the water at the swimming hole. Someone had tied a rope at the top of the tree so the boys could swing out and drop into the water. The pines was up river from the bridge and people walking on the bridge could see the boys swinging over the water. On really hot days, the boys took off their suits and swam naked. Soon complaints came from the people on the bridge, so the boys rubbed sand around them selves, to make it appear that they were wearing suits; the complaints stopped. Girls were not allowed at the pines, but a few have been known to hide in the bushes and watch the boys. Across the railroad tracks, Mr. Mills had his field of watermelons, and cantaloupe and the boys never did go home because lunch was just across the tracks.

* * *

Steve had left the paper mill and had gotten a second shift job at the ball bearing factory, where his brother Paul worked. The money was better, but it was such a long distance away and neither Paul nor Steve drove. The factory had a service that matched up rides with people who agreed to car pool. They had to pay for the rides, but even with that expense, they still made more money. Another problem arose when Steve went to work at two in the afternoon and he was gone until eleven-thirty that evening. That left Peter and Frank to do what they wanted to do and once in a while, they would fish from the bridge. In order to get to the bridge, they took a short cut through Agnes' hedges. She had been trying to grow hedges across the property for many years and had succeeded except for the path that Peter and Frank used as their short cut. She had asked them to stop, but as soon as she was out of sight they forgot and reverted to their old habits. Agnes watched for them, but by the time she ran after them, they were gone. It became a battle of wills as Agnes would sit in a chair near the hedge to catch the boys. They would wait for her to go into the house to use the bathroom before they would dash through the opening and were gone.

One Saturday evening, the whole family was sitting on the front porch when Peter noticed Agnes getting ready to come over. He tilted his head towards her and he and Frank promptly left the porch.

Agnes told Steve, "I can not tolerate it any longer and something has to be done. I am spending all of her days watching for your boys and it is interfering with my duties in my home."

Agnes was the neatest housekeeper in the neighborhood. She had two daughters to help and her home was spotless. She would spend an hour tracking a fly until she smashed it with her swatter. There was not a pleat in her curtains out of place. The dishes were washed and put away right after use and there was not a speck of dust on any of the furniture. She was reluctant to bring it up because she and Kada were best friends, but the boys were winning and she could not permit that.

When Agnes left, Kada and Steve went into the backyard to find the boys and they found them sitting in the barn waiting for Agnes to go back home. They knew that they would be punished, but they did not know what the punishment would be. As was the custom, they sat around the kitchen table to discuss the problem. The boys promised never to do it again, but Steve had heard that before and it was too late for promises.

He told the boys, "Go out to the barn and bring back two pieces of split firewood."

On the way out, Peter pondered, "How is he going to use the wood and why is it only two pieces?"

Frank said, "Maybe he was going to hit us with them."

"But Pa has a strap that hangs by the door for that and he would not hit us with a piece of wood. He would not need two pieces of wood to do that. Lets get the wood and find out."

The strap, that they were referring to had found itself in the outside toilet where it could not be used again, but a new one always appeared.

They each picked out a piece and went back into the kitchen where Steve took the wood and placed each one in front of the table. Kada brought out three sets of rosary beads and gave each of the boys a set.

Steve told the boys, "You are to kneel on the wood and say the rosary. You have to say it slowly so that it could be heard by your mother who was going to say it along with you."

Every time the boys tried to speed it up, Kada would slow them down. It was a painful time, but they endured it and finally they finished. They had difficulty standing up, but they did not want their mother to know how difficult it was. They stood up straight, even though it was painful.

Kada put the wood into the stove and said, "You have to promise not to go through Agnes' hedges any longer, or you will have to go through this again."

The boys would have promised anything at that point in order to leave and rub their knees. They were dismissed and walked as calmly as they could out to the barn. The hay loft was their clubhouse and they used this to plot their revenge.

When the boys left, the girls came out of the dining room where they watched the punishment. Jerry could not understand what was happening, but the girls were livid.

Medka said, "It is cruel punishment, for so petty an infraction, and the boys are injured because Agnes had told on them. That is the type of punishment a barbarian would use."

She backed away when she saw the look in her father's eyes because this was not the time to push him any further. They had all expressed their opinion and what bothered them most was that their mother had allowed it to happen. Kada had been placed between her husband and her family, but she agreed that they had to slow the boys down by doing something drastic.

Steve said, "That was how I was punished and I had to do it only one time. With that punishment hanging over my head, I took the straight and narrow path from then on. This was a part of discipline, in the upbringing of the boys."

Their parents never had this problem with Joe, or the girls, but the younger ones were so close and their minds worked the same way. They pushed their parents to the limit and with this punishment, they had reached the limit.

What Kada and Steve did not know was that Peter and Frank had already plotted their revenge in the hayloft of the barn. There was a good likelihood that they would be caught so they went into the barn where the firewood was stored. They each picked out a piece of wood and with their jack knives, they rounded the jagged edges of the wood. The pieces of wood were placed in a certain place under a pile of wood where they would be sure they would not be found unless needed. They settled back and waited for a week. They were so good during the week, that Steve was lulled into the impression that his punishment worked. He was pleased with himself and went out of his way to be nice to the boys, but if he had known what they were plotting, he would have locked them up.

Each of the families in the neighborhood had a chicken coop in the back yard with a few chickens. When the population in each coop got over eight, someone had a fine Sunday dinner. Each had a rooster and enough hens so they could have fresh eggs and enough eggs for the next generation. Agnes had a neighbor named Mrs. Butka who did not get along with her. There was an incident many years before that both had forgotten, but all they knew was that they did not care for each other. There was a four foot fence between their properties that did not contain a gate and this told everyone in the neighborhood that they were enemies. If there was a gate, the neighbors would visit each other, but there was no chance of their getting along, ever, so there was no gate. They watched each other constantly so one would not get the upper hand. There were no trees near the fence so there would be no arguments about whose leaves were on each side. This, of course, did not go unnoticed by Peter and Frank and they chose to exploit the feud. Agnes had white leghorn chickens and Mrs. Butka had Rhode Island red chickens and they each had about seven or eight.

The boys waited for a dark night, each carried two burlap sacks. Frank went into Mrs. Butka's coop and placed the chickens into the sacks. Peter went into Agnes' coop and placed her chickens in his sacks. They met at the fence, exchanged chickens and turned them loose in the neighbors coop. Nothing was mentioned to anyone, but the following morning the entire neighborhood was in an uproar. Each neighbor accused the other of stealing her chickens, they shouted at each other and it took them all morning to switch the chickens back into the proper coop. Towards the middle of the afternoon, Agnes realized how it happened and guessed that Peter and Frank had done the deed. Steve was at work already, but Kada was home and Agnes relayed her suspicions to her. This made sense to Kada and they decided to wait for the boys to get home from school. They saw the boys turn the corner and head for home and they did not use the short cut which meant going through Agnes hedges. They felt that they were already in enough trouble when they saw Agnes on the porch. They walked up the path next to the house trying to avoid the front of the house, but Kada stopped them and made them come on the porch. From the look on their faces, both Agnes and Kada knew that they were guilty and nothing further was said.

Kada told them, "Go into the house and wait for me. Tomorrow is Saturday, your father will deal with you."

The next morning when the boys came down the stairs, the whole family was in the kitchen. The boys ate a good breakfast and Steve told them to go to the barn and each get a piece of wood. They left immediately and returned with their doctored pieces of wood.

They were just about to set the pieces down when Kada spoke, "There is something wrong here."

Steve asked, "What's wrong?"

Kada replied, "They did not give you an argument about getting the wood and they did not deny that they did it. They were ready for the punishment."

Steve took the two pieces of wood, put them into the stove and made the boys go out into the barn for two more pieces. The rosary was said without complaint and the boys went into the hayloft again. Their mistake was that they did not trim more than one piece of wood but they would not make that mistake again.

The boys would say the rosary once more and then they struck an uneasy truce with Agnes. On a hot summer day, the porch was covered with flies so each of the boys got a glass milk bottle. As the flies rested on the side of the house, the boys would put the opening of the bottle on them and trapped them in the bottle. When each had about fifty flies, they waited for Agnes to go down to the river and entered her house through the unlocked front door. They shook most of the flies out in her kitchen and left the way they came in. They were sure to take the bottles with them or everyone would be able to determine who did the deed. As luck would have it, Kada saw them leaving and went into the house to see what they had done. When she entered the kitchen, she saw insects everywhere. Agnes came in and went pale and Kada thought that she would faint. It took Agnes and Kada all day to kill the flies and Agnes had flies in her home for weeks later. She threatened to go to the police, even if Kada was her best friend, unless she called the boys off. It was time to stop it and she had to convince them.

Kada did not wait for Steve to come home, she had the boys say the rosary and then sat them down at the kitchen table to speak to them.

Kada was angry, "The pranks had escalated to such an extent that the police are going to be called in and I will do the calling. If it means that the both of you will spend time in the jail at the town hall, then so be it."

The boys had never seen Kada so angry and they looked at each other. As in one voice, they said, "We are finished and we will leave Agnes alone."

Kada said, "You go over to her home and tell her how sorry you are."

Neither boy was sorry, but they would play the game and go through the motions. Kada and Agnes would laugh about this period of time, but it was not humorous at the time it happened. Secretly, Steve could not get angry with his sons. Outwardly, he appeared disturbed, but inwardly he laughed at the pranks and thought that his mother would have found them to be just young boys and this was what they were supposed to do. He thought that they would both amount to something, someday, because they used their minds.

CHAPTER SEVENTEEN

Medka and Joe wrote to each other every week, but the letters were in English and Medka had to read them to her mother and father. There was a time when three weeks went by and she received nothing from Joe. Medka sent him a letter every week anyway, hoping that if he was shipped out, the letters would catch up with him.

A letter from Joe finally arrived and it was postmarked from an Army hospital in San Antonio, Texas.

The letter read, "Dear Medka, I was in an accident at the base while I was working on a bomber. I was doing some electrical work on top of the wing when, a crane carrying a beam swung around and struck me. The beam hit my right leg half way between the knee and hip and fractured the big bone of the leg. I am going to be in the hospital for another month and then I will go to another hospital where they had to teach me to walk all over again. If the bone does not heal, they will have to operate and put a metal support to help me walk. I will always have a limp, but at least I"m alive and maybe I can come home on leave."

The following Sunday, Kada and the women of the Slovak Rosary Society dedicated that week's rosary to Joe. While in the air force, Joe became interested in electronics and he was told by his counselors that he should pursue a career in electrical engineering, but he did not have a graduation certificate from high school.

His counselor told him, "Apply to a college and if you passed the test, he can go back to your high school and they should give you a diploma."

It sounded so simple so he spent his time in the hospital reading material on college courses and when he got to the rehabilitation hospital, he found that it had a library designed for people just like him. He read and studied every chance he could find and he could never satisfy his appetite for knowledge. When he was granted leave for the weekend, he could be found in the library; Joe had been bitten by the learning bug.

* * *

Just before they heard about Joe's accident, Steve bought a television set, it was a small set and the picture came in with some "snow", but they were able to watch it. Steve wanted his family to stay close to home and since he was away from home in the early evening, he wanted to give them something to do. They watched the "Texaco Hour" with Milton Berle and soon it became a habit to sit in front of the set after supper to watch fifteen minutes of news and wait for the regular programming. Between the news and the evening programs, there was an hour of wrestling and everyone in the family watched because Kada had become addicted to it. If she watched nothing else, she watched wrestling. One evening there was a rather close match and everyone was watching except Steve who was at work. The match was tied at two falls each and the next fall would win, but it was taking a long time. Kada was sitting on a chair brought in from the dining room because the rest of the chairs were being used. The man who was supposed to win was being beaten badly when he suddenly turned on his opponent, hit him twice and locked his legs around the man's neck.

The room was silent and everyone was looking to see what was going to happen when Kada jumped up from her chair, raised her fist to the heavens and shouted "Kill the son-of-bitch."

She looked around her and saw all eyes staring at her.

Medka jumped up and cried in disbelief, "Ma!!"

Kada realized what she had said, turned bright red and meekly sat down. The children could no longer keep a straight face and burst into laughter. That was the first time they had ever heard their mother swear and it surprised them more than it had her.

Kada continued to watch wrestling on television, but she learned to control her emotions. Once the children began to bring homework from school, they were not allowed to watch the television until their work was completed. Josie would sit at the dining room table with the two boys until it was finished. Peter was going to take the college courses, while Frank, who had an aptitude for mechanical work took the technical courses. He had hoped to go to one of the technical training schools, but it was difficult to arrange for transportation to Hartford every day. A bus came from Hartford, but it did not go close to the school, so Frank finished his education in Unionville. He was constantly helping his father, who taught him how to make repairs in the house. Steve did not go to work until two o'clock in the afternoon so he had time to work on his projects. Peter and Frank were charged with spading the garden, splitting the wood for the winter, bringing it into the barn and stacking it. It did not give them much time for other activities. Peter got a job at Abel's market during the winter and picked tobacco on one of the farms during the summer. Steve felt that the easiest way to keep his two sons out of trouble was to keep them working.

While Peter worked at Abel's market, he learned a few things about the facts of life. He was supposed to be restocking shelves with can goods, sweep the market and handle other menial chores. He rarely went into the meat cooler, but he saw a good deal of activity there. One day, Abel gave him a box to bury in the back yard behind the market. He dug a hole and poured the contents of the box into the hole. For a minute he just stood there looking at the head and entire hide of a calf. He felt a presence behind him and saw Abel in a bloody apron looking over his shoulder.

Peter heard his voice say, "cover it up quickly so no one will see."

He did not tell Peter what he was doing, but he asked him to bury the hides a few times a month. Peter told his mother about it, but he did not realize that she already knew. Abel had discussed it with her and when she came for her groceries, there was always a slab of meat in her bag at no charge. Meat was rationed during the war, but the Janek family ate well because Kada was adept at stretching out the food money. Steve, of course, had no idea that this was happening and would have stopped it if he had.

Abel's market was not open on Saturday because it was the Jewish Sabbath, Peter did not work at the market on those days, but he did work around the house. There was a garden to keep, chickens to take care of, wood to split and there was always "Tippy" to play with. Tippy was the Janek's dog, and one could not even venture a guess as to his breed. He did have some beagle or basset hound in his blood line because his legs were short, he had large droopy ears and his tail was always wagging. He was brown with white spots or he was white with brown spots; Peter could not determine which. He was an energetic dog and when someone was working in the yard, Tippy stood guard. Peter was in the barn stacking some wood that had fallen from the pile when he heard another dog in the yard. He went out to investigate and saw Tippy being swung around by a large red Irish setter. The big dog had Tippy by the hind leg and was swinging him around in a circle. Suddenly, Kada appeared from the kitchen with a pot of boiling water. She splashed the hot water over the other dog until he dropped poor Tippy. The other dog yelped around the yard while Peter got Tippy into the barn. The red dog stopped running and looked at Kada who looked him squarely in the eyes for what seemed like an eternity.

She raised up her arm giving the sign of the gypsy curse and said, "Lightning will strike you dead."

The dog suddenly broke from her stare and ran out of the yard. Kada tried to set Tippy's leg, but it did not heal and he had to be destroyed. Peter found out that a family, named Green who lived on Water Street owned the Irish setter and he stopped in to tell the owner about her dog; she offered no sympathy.

She did say, "I will chain the dog during the day to a large tree and at night, he will be chained to his dog house. The dog is my protection because I live without a man. My three daughters and I really need the dog."

Peter went home and told his mother who did not seem concerned. She said "The dog will not bother us any longer."

A few weeks after that encounter, the town was struck with a hail storm. The ground was covered with hail and except for the warm weather, it looked like winter. Suddenly there was a flash in the sky followed by thunder; a sign that the lightning was close. There were a few more flashes and the storm moved on.

Once the storm went by, Peter looked at his mother and she was smiling. Peter thought nothing of the incident until he happened to meet with a friend who lived close to the Greens.

His friend asked Peter, "Have you heard about the Green's Irish setter?"

Peter shook his head.

"The dog was chained to a tree and when lightning struck, the electricity came down the tree. It traveled into the chain, down to the dog and killed him."

Peter ran across the bridge and into the house where he found his mother at the sink, as usual.

He caught his breath and said, "The Green's dog got struck by lightning. It came down the tree and killed the dog."

She looked at him and she smiled as if she knew all about it, "We will not be bothered by that dog again."

The week before Halloween, Agnes spoke to Kada about the boys and said, "Your boys have been acting up again. I saw them going through my hedges and I am sue that they are up to something."

Agnes figured that Peter and Frank had something planned for Halloween and she would nip it in the bud.

She insisted that she saw the boys going through her hedges again, but this was untrue because the boys promised that they would not and they did not.

Steve asked them when they were in the barn alone, "You boys planning to do something to Agnes for Halloween? Are you up to your old tricks again? Are you going through her hedges again? If you are, tell me now and if you are not, tell me that also."

Frank said, "No, but do you want us to do something to her?"

Steve smiled, "No, and I believe you. Now, don't make me out a liar."

Peter said, "Pop, we haven't gone through her hedges since that time. we leave her hedges alone."

Steve believed them, but told Agnes that they would be punished. If he told Agnes that he believed the boys, it would appear that she was the one who was not to be believed and he would have made a enemy. Steve look the lesser of two evils and gave the boys a minor punishment. The boys realized that their father was in a situation that he could not win, and they took the punishment without an argument. As they sat in the hayloft, they talked of things that they would do for Halloween.

Franks said, "Agnes has challenged us and we have to get even. If we don't, she will keep on doing this."

On Halloween night the boys left the house quietly and made a full circle so that they could follow the river and go into Agnes' property from the rear. She was watching for them in the front, as they knew she would. She would not believe that they would go all that distance to come in from the other side. It was a dark night and they knew that they would not be seen.

They came to Anges' outhouse and pushed it back towards the river. There was a small embankment and they wanted to get it over so it would be more difficult to put back. Someone would have to go into the river on a cold October night to lift it back up. They were successful and went down the row of house and knocking them all over because they did not want to single her out. They went down the other side of the street and did the same, but they were reluctant when they came to their own privy; they did it as well so as to take suspicion away from them. The next morning, the whole neighborhood smelled and those that had to go to the toilet, could not find one standing. Peter and Frank got up early so that they could go to church with their mother and father because it was All-Souls Day and a holy day of obligation.

Steve asked them, "Did you boys do this?"

They said, "no."

They helped him set their outhouse back up and went to church. They always suspected that Steve knew that they had done it, but the matter was dropped.

It seemed like the boy's father knew what was happening all of the time. He save little jobs that the boys could do just to let them know that they were not getting away with things. He was letting them know in a subtle way that he knew. One of the jobs that he saved for them was getting rid of the trash in the house. The trash was stored in the barn, in fifty-five gallon drums that Steve brought home from work. There were about six or seven at any given time and there were covers on them. There was no place to dump them so when they were full, he did what they did in the old country, he buried it. The digging of the hole was a job for the boys. The only problem was that there was no system to determine where the empty spots were and Steve went strictly my memory. When the boys needed to be punished, he would have them digging in spots that had been used before and they would end up digging three or four holes. When they did not have to be punished, they only had to dig one hole. He never told the boys what he was doing and they never caught on. It was a dirty job because over the winter, the trash became fairly ripe, but the boys did their duty and the spring of the year would find them all in the yard trying to figure where the open spots were.

Another job that Steve reserved for the boys was spading the garden and turning the top layer of dirt over. This was done by hand, row after row. It was tedious work and to make matters worse, Steve wanted human waste from the outhouse spread over the yard before they did it. Once it was spread and the dirt turned over, their mother planted the garden. The boys never looked forward to spring and the first scent of human waste from a neighbors yard told them that they would be next. They always put on an old pair of shoes and changed them in the barn because Kada checked their feet before they stepped into her kitchen.

Steve and Kada discussed telling the boys that was really punishment, but Kada said. "You can tell them, but they would be extra good before spring and you will end up doing it yourself and you know that I am not going to do it."

After the outhouse incident, Steve decided to remodel the house and put in an inside bathroom. Since Joe was going to be coming home soon and would probably need a car, he would have to move the whole house over to make room for a driveway. There was no room between the house and the fence dividing the property for a car to go into the back yard. Steve set out to look for a contractor to lift the house three feet and move it over four feet. He would also remodel the kitchen and install the bathroom. The shed would be used for the bathroom with room left over for a walk-in pantry. He did find a man to lift and move the house for the price he wanted and work would start the next April.

In April, a crew arrived with a huge truck and large wooden planks that were twelve inches square and ten feet long. There were other planks that were only four feet long. The workers set up twelve stations under the house with the smaller planks until they had little platforms. They brought in twelve screw jacks and set them up on the platforms. The large planks were put between the jacks and the house. A backhoe came in and dug a four foot trench on the side of the house that would receive the house while a footing was poured with concrete and allowed to cure. The footings were on both sides of the house and the house would eventually rest on the foundation that was to be built on them. The workmen left and said that they would be back in two weeks to lift the house and move it the four feet.

Steve took his two weeks vacation from the ball bearing factory and went to work laying cinder blocks on the footings to the new height of the cellar. Peter and Frank mixed mortar before they went to school and hurried home to mix more so that Steve could spend his time laying the cinder blocks. When they came home from school, Peter would hand the blocks to his father while Frank mixed the mortar and he always made sure that there was mortar for his father to use. The lines of blocks were laid quickly, they worked until dark and were able to complete that portion of the foundation within a week. The dirt taken from the excavation was stored in the yard and was to be used to fill the hole once the house was moved. Peter could not understand how his father learned to lay the blocks.

He asked his mother, "Who taught Pop how to do all these things?"

She replied, "Your grandfather, in Slovakia, taught all of his sons how to do many things, just as your father is teaching you. Your grandfather learned it from the workers who came to the abbey and the church. This is a father's job and your father is passing on these skills to you. You will be expected to pass it on to your sons. When you were little, your father has always told you that there is no substitute for hard work and if you wanted something you should not wait for someone to hand it to you; you have to work for it."

The first Sunday that they could rest, the family sat down to a good family dinner. Kada had killed a chicken, cut it up and made in into a stew. She had mashed potatoes, fresh cabbage, fried with animal fat, and fresh baked bread. Kada had not gotten beef from Abel for some time, and she wanted her family to have a good meal. She even boiled some coffee on the stove for the older children and as they were finishing the meal, a knock came on the back door. Kada got up to answer it and found her brother-in-law Paul standing there with tears in his eyes. She pulled him through the door and called for her husband.

Steve rushed into the kitchen, led his brother to a chair, asked, "Paul, what's wrong?"

"I have some very bad news."

His eyes showed signs that he had been crying for some time, when be said, "Two officers from the Marines came and told me that Jimmy was killed in action in the Pacific. He went in with his buddies to capture a small island held by the Japanese on the first wave. The enemy was waiting for them, Jimmy was killed by machine gun fire and died instantly so he did not suffer. I did not know where else to go to share my grief and I immediately thought of my brother and his family. I cannot talk to Sue because she buried her head in a pillow and is sobbing so uncontrollably that I had to call the doctor. The doctor came and gave her a shot and she was now sleeping."

Steve embraced his brother and Kada placed a cup of coffee in front of him.

After he controlled himself, he said,"We got a letter form Jimmy a week ago and he said that something big was in the works and we will not be hearing from him for a while. That was the last time that we heard from him."

Paul did not know what to do next and he appeared that he was in a daze.

Steve said, "Wait until the marine corps tell you what to do and in the meantime, we will go see Father Sullivan and arrange for a funeral Mass in a few days."

The two brothers sat in the living room for the rest of the afternoon and Steve let his brother talk without interruption. Paul brought back all the memories that he could think of while Steve made them a highball. When Paul felt better, he walked him up the first hill to Paul's house. He kissed all of his nephews and nieces and left Paul in their care.

The funeral Mass was held in the middle of the following week and the funeral director, Mr. George handled it with no cost to Paul. He told Steve that it will be paid by the military. Jimmy was buried in a military cemetery in Hawaii. He was killed on Iwo Jima, a tiny island which was a stepping stone for the invasion of Japan. The whole town turned out for the funeral and Mass and there was no room in the church for another single person. Jimmy was twenty-one years old when he died fighting for his family's adopted country and the Janek family paid a very dear price to live in the United States of America.

* * *

The following week, the contractors came and started work on the house. They had two sets of planks, one going in one direction and one in the other. The ones going the length of the house went under the porch in front and under the shed in the back. On Tuesday morning, the main water pipe into the house and the electricity were disconnected. One man stationed himself at each jack and as the foreman called "pull" each man turned the handle of his screw jack one complete turn. The house creaked and moaned, but it started to go up slowly. Within an hour, the house was lifted up four feet and the men put braces all over the cellar from the ground to the floor of the house. They dropped the jacks down one foot and put steel rollers on the large planks. The contractor fixed jacks at one end of the house against the foundation of the house and the jacks were turned to move the whole house over the foundation. When the house was aligned with the foundation, the house was lifted, the rollers taken out and the house rested on the twelve jacks. The crew left and said that they would come back in a week to drop the house on the foundation.

Steve and the boys finished the job the following week and the house rested on its permanent foundation. It had been lifted thirty-eight inches in the air and moved to one side a distance of four feet. The temporary water and electrical hook-ups were made permanent and Steve built temporary stairs to the porch and back door because there was now a four foot drop. The property had a driveway and was not resting on the old field stone foundation, almost at ground level any longer. It took Peter and Frank a few days to fill in the hole on the drive way side of the property and it began to look better.

Steve next tackled the remodeling of the kitchen and by this time, the boys had finished the school year.

Steve told his sons, "Don't take jobs for the summer. You are going to help me remodel the kitchen and put in a new bathroom."

It would be the first inside bathroom in the neighborhood and everyone would be watching to see how much it cost to finish. When he left for work at two o'clock, Steve usually left orders for the boys to complete some project or another so he could start early the next morning. After two days of taking apart the walls of the shed, Steve was ready to start framing the pantry and the bathroom. He had saved all of the nails that he took out and put them into a pail.

When he left for work, he gave each of the boys a hammer and an anvil and said, "You have to straighten the nails so I can reuse them in the morning."

The boys did this boring job for about an hour when a group of their friends came by and talked them into going to the pines. The temptation was just too great for two young boys and they abandoned their work to go with their friends. It was a hot day and this was the only way to cool off. When they returned in time for supper, they were in trouble with Kada. She gave them something to eat, but they had to straighten nails until dark. Their hearts were not in the task and not much work was accomplished.

The next morning, Kada talked to Steve and he had to take the time to straighten nails before he could start framing. When he left for work, he told the boys, "Since you are not going to do any work, you will go nowhere."

He took them into the cellar and tied their hands and feet so that they could not move. He went to work and left them there to be untied by Kada when she returned from work at five o'clock. Peter was not tied as tightly as Frank and he was able to crawl on his knees and elbows along the floor. He went up the cellar stairs and into the dining room where the eating utensils were stored. Peter took a butcher knife in his teeth, as he had seen in the movies, and crawled down the cellars stairs to where Frank was lying on the floor trying to blow a fly off his nose. He had Frank roll over and cut his ropes with the knife in his teeth using a back and forth motion. He got Frank loose without cutting him and then Frank returned the favor. Since they were going to be punished anyway for cutting the rope, they thought that they would make the rope unusable by cutting it into small pieces and they spent that afternoon at the pines swimming.

The next morning, when Steve saw what had happened, he accepted defeat graciously and changed his tactics. He appealed to their sense of family, but that did not make an impression so he offered to pay them a small amount for each hour that they worked. This would enable them to go to a movie once in a while at the Luxor theater and he managed to get some work out of them. He felt that he was not having too much luck ordering them to do the work so he appealed to their sense of greed; even if it did cost him some money. The boys kept their own hours which they gave to him on Saturday morning. They did not dare lie about that because the punishment for lying was the rosary at the kitchen table on a piece of wood.

The work was completed by the time the boys went to school. Peter went to seventh grade and Frank went into fourth. Since Frank was born in October, the school officials felt that he was not mature enough to handle first grade, so he repeated it. In fourth grade, he had a teacher by the name of Mrs Ray. Frank, being a large boy, usually did what he wanted and this teacher was a strict disciplinarian. Frank was put into her class, for this reason and she was supposed to handle him. He had always been taught not to start anything, but if someone else did, he was allowed to finish it. No one could talk down or harm a Janek without a reprisal. About a month into the school year, Mrs. Ray, with her back to the class, heard a whispered remark and she assumed that it was Frank. Since his reputation had preceded him, she chose to make an example of him in front of the class. She had him come up to the front of the class and Frank was just as tall as his teacher. He was probably about twenty pounds heavier. She did not give him a chance to explain, but told him to put his hand out, palm up. With his hand up she slapped a ruler down on it very hard.

Frank could not understand why he was being punished because he did not even hear the remark that he supposedly made. With lightning speed, he took the ruler away from her and with one motion, he took her hand and brought the ruler down on it. She was stunned when he did it and stepped back as he was handing the ruler back to her. There was a platform, on which her desk rested and in taking a step backward she went down and landed on a desk in the front row. She got up and told him to follow her into the principal's office.

Mr. Kent, the principal, knew the Janek family and he also knew Mrs. Ray. He sent his secretary to find Peter as a witness to what was going to happen. He wanted to avoid a confrontation with Kada because he had faced her in the past and he always came out second best. Peter came into the room looking at a calm Frank and a pale Mrs Ray. Mr. Kent explained the teacher's version and now he wanted to talk to Frank in front of Peter.

Peter asked Frank, "Why did you hit Mrs. Ray with the ruler?"

Frank answered, "She hit me first for no reason. She hit me in front of the whole class."

Peter asked, "Did you make the remark?"

Frank asked, "What remark?"

Peter was looking directly into Frank's eyes, "Did she ask you if you did it?"

Frank answered "No, I don't know why she hit me, when I did not do anything."

Mr. Kent asked Mrs. Ray, "Do you know that Frank had actually made the remark?"

She said, "I assumed that it was Frank since he is a trouble maker."

Mr. Kent dismissed the teacher, "I will handle the matter from now on and you are to go back to your class."

Mr. Kent addressed Peter and said, "Frank should not be striking teachers"

"We have been taught that we are not to push first, but if we are pushed, then we should push back and that is exactly what Frank did. I will have to stand behind my brother and I probably would have done the same thing if someone hit me for no reason."

Mr. Kent dismissed both of them and asked Peter to stop by at his office before he went home. They both went back to class and Frank held no malice for Mrs. Ray. She never tried to hit him and he never hit her back.

When Peter stopped into Mr. Kent's office, he was handed a note addressed to Kada Janek. On the way home, they stopped on the bridge and opened the letter. It said that Frank had struck a teacher and he should be punished. Peter threw the note into the water and they both watched it as it floated down stream.

As they watched the paper float down the river, Peter said, "If you ever hit another teacher, I'll tell Ma and then you will punished. I'll save your ass this time, little brother, but you had better do what they tell you to do. If Ma finds out, we are both in trouble."

When Peter returned to school, Mr. Kent waited until the first period ended and caught the boy in the hall. He asked Peter what his mother had said about hitting the teacher and Peter had a well rehearsed reply.

He told the principal, "My mother is not going to punish him since he did nothing to her or her family. If you want to punish him for something he did at school, then you should do it. She suggested that he be kept after school for an hour to do extra work. He could clean blackboards, or put the chairs onto the desks so that the floor could be cleaned."

Peter knew that Mrs. Ray would not let the boy go unpunished. While the punishment was minimal, Frank would not get off scot free. He did strike a teacher and he could not be allowed to so this sort of thing. Mr. Kent called Frank and said that his punishment would be to stay an hour after classes closed and clean the blackboards for the rest of the month. Kada knew nothing of the incident, nor did the rest of the family. No other member of the family went to this school so the danger of her finding out was minimal. Frank never struck another teacher although on a few occasions, he came extremely close.

CHAPTER EIGHTEEN

Joe stayed in the hospital in San Antonio and was sent to the rehabilitation hospital in South Carolina where he stayed until the war ended. The doctors were reluctant to let him leave the hospital unless he was discharged into someone's care. The person had to be responsible because he still walked with a limp and needed help once in a while. Joe wrote to Medka who went down to the hospital to pick him up. Her friend, Maisie had a car and offered to go down if Medka paid for the gas and the hotel for the night so without telling anyone, they started on the long trip to bring Joe home. Medka did not want to tell her parents about the trip because she did not want to worry them and there was the possibility that they would not release him into Medka's care. Magda knew and she was supposed to cover for her in the event that her father got suspicious. On the following Sunday evening, Medka walked into the house first.

Kada saw her come in and said, "Do you know that you have a little soldier boy following you? Did you run off and get married?"

She recognized Joe and rushed to give him an embrace. She started to cry as Steve came into the room. It reminded Steve of the time that he came home during a blinding snow storm from the last war. Joe hugged his brothers and sisters who put his luggage aside so no one would trip over it. The laughter and shouting could be heard from the Janek household until early in the morning; the family was united again

Joe took two weeks off to visit his friends and relatives before he took steps to start a career. He went to see his Uncle Paul and expressed his sorrow for the death of his son. Paul had still not gotten over it, but he appreciated the visit by Joe. Timmy's buddies who were with him when he died, stopped in to visit his family and told Paul how it happened. Jimmy died instantly and he did not suffer. The remaining four stayed together and adopted Paul as their father. All he had to do was mention something to be done and it was done. The four ex-marines stayed friends for the rest of their lives.

Joe got on the bus and went to a junior college in Hartford. He would be getting paid by the government under the G.I. Bill, if he could get into the school.

He went to the admissions office and told the woman at the desk, "I want to go to this school. I have only one year of high school and had to quit school to help support my family. I studied in Texas and South Carolina for eighteen months and I want to take the entrance exam anyway. The G.I. Bill would pay for the tuition, so money is no problem and I could take the bus so I will not miss any classes."

Joe was determined and the woman was impressed with his determination and although it was unusual, she would talk to the dean of the school and she told him to wait. She left the room and she returned in ten minutes with a man dressed in a tan suit and highly polished brown shoes. What little hair he had was slicked back and he had thick glasses that rested on his nose. There was a thick brown mustache under his nose that hid his upper lip and made a shadow over his lower lip. Joe thought that he looked like a man in one of the disguises that men wore where the glasses, large nose and big bushy mustache were used for comic purposes. Joe could not help but smile and the man smiled back showing large teeth and now he looked like Teddy Roosevelt, thought Joe.

Mr. Thomas Astor, the dean of Hillyer College invited Joe into his office where he had papers stacked over the floor, desk, chairs and a bookshelf. They talked for about an hour and with each question Joe looked him squarely in the eye and answered him.

He settled back in his chair and asked, "What have you set as a goal?"

Joe answered, "I want to become an electrical engineer."

"You know, Joe "he said, "Hillyer is only a two year school."

"I know that, but Hillyer is only a start and I plan to go on." Joe said, with a look of determination in his eyes.

At the end of the hour, Mr. Astor asked, "Where do you live?"

Joe said, "Unionville, which was part of Farmington."

"Mr. Ellis is superintendent of schools in Farmington is also the principal of Farmington High School." Said Mr. Astor, "I know him very well. Many of his students come to our school. Let me call him right now. Does he know who you are?"

Joe answered, "He knows my family,"

Mr. Astor called his friend while Joe waited in his office. From the conversation they were having, Joe's hopes soared and when the conversation ended, Joe waited for Mr. Astor to speak.

A bright smile came across the face of the dean and he made a decision on the spot. "I will allow you to take the entrance examination in one month because classes begin in only six weeks. If you do well on the test, I will forward the results to Mr. Ellis who will make a decision as to whether you should receive a high school diploma. If I receive the paper, you may start school."

He pointed out to Joe, "Although you are well read in the technical aspects of your chosen profession, the examination is geared to general knowledge which is taught in high schools. You should use the month wisely and study. Here is a list of subjects to study and also a note to allow you free access to the school library."

He knew that Joe did not have the books to read and study and he wanted him to sample the environment of a college. The dean felt that if Joe was going to be discouraged, this would be the time to do it. In his heart, Mr. Astor felt sure that he would not be discouraged and he saw something in Joe that made him want to help this young man; it looked like Joe was on his way.

The next month Joe took the bus into Hartford every day except Saturday and Sunday and then he brought books home to read. He received a letter in the mail from Mr. Astor naming the date, time and place for the examination and he would be taking the test alone. Joe did not know this, but Mr. Astor made a trip once or twice a day past the library to check on him, studying.

On the day of the examination, Joe felt that he was ready and as he left the house to walk to the bus, Kada kissed him and said, "Your, grandfather, Johan would have been proud of you. You do the best that you can and do not worry about what will happen if you fail. You will not fail because I have seen good signs in the sky and I know that you will do well."

He arrived at the college an hour ahead of time and he was so excited that he did not eat the lunch that Kada prepared for him. He sat down at one o'clock and started the examination. The next time he looked at the clock on the wall, it was four o'clock. He had only one more hour to go before the woman collected his papers. Joe had read somewhere in his studies that it was not advisable to go back over the test and change an answer so he went with his first impulse. At four-thirty, he was finished.

He stacked his papers and walked up to the desk to turn them in and the woman asked, "Do you want to take advantage of the final half hour?"

Joe said, "I am finished."

The woman told him, "Many students that take this examination do not finish."

Joe smiled the smile of a confident person. "When will I know the results.?

She said, "It will be a few days, but since the time is so short, the correspondence will be by phone and not by letter."

Joe came into the house and Kada was waiting for him. She wanted to talk and as was their custom they sat at the kitchen table. She would bring out a quart of Schmidt's Tiger Head Ale, a loaf of black bread and some pickled herring. Kada loved this snack and did not let an opportunity go by when she could bring it out. They sat, drank, ate and talked by the kitchen stove. Joe did not appear too excited because he felt that he had done fairly well.

Kada said, "Your father and I talked it over and we do not want any board money while you are going to school and any money that you collect from the government will go toward your education."

"I will work the summers, but I am going to need money when I go to another school which will probably be farther away and I will have to live there."

Kada said, "I had some good signs about your future. Encourage your younger brothers to follow in your foot steps."

She wanted Peter, Frank and Jerry to finish high school and to go to college. They could not help them financially, but they could live home without paying board while they went to school.

Two days after he took the test, he received a call from Mr. Ellis and it was good news "I have received the results of the entrance examination and you scored very high. I am mailing you and Mr. Astor a high school diploma. I have just gotten off the phone with Mr. Astor and you have been accepted as a student by Hillyer College. You will start school in two weeks. I want you to come to my office and I will help you apply for G.I. benefits."

Things were moving very fast for Joe and finally he became so excited, that he stuttered when he talked to his mother.

Kada said, "I knew all along that you would go to college. You will be the first one in the family to go beyond high school."

She kissed him, "The whole family is proud of you. You did not finish high school and you are going to college."

Joe went through the two years at Hillyer very easily. He saved what money he could and Steve gave him fifty dollars to buy a car so he would not have to ride the bus. With the gift from Steve and the fifty dollars he saved, he bought a 1938 Buick coupe with a rumble seat. It was a straight eight cylinder and burned quite a bit of gas. The engine was very powerful and the only thing on the road that it would not pass was a gas station. He only used it to go back and forth to school because he could not afford the gas to go anywhere else. He named the car, "The Buyok" which meant "The Bull," in Slovak. He had planned to sell it once he left for school somewhere else and applied, with the help of Mr. Astor, to various schools for scholarships. Joe received many replies, but picked the

University of Denver because of its reputation as an excellent engineering school.

He was accepted as a scholarship student at the University of Denver after he was graduated from Hillyer College with an Associate Bachelors Degree. He sold the buyok and went to Denver. While at the University, he applied for a fellowship at Carnegie Tech in Pittsburgh, Pennsylvania. He was graduated from the University of Denver with a Bachelor of Science degree in Electrical Engineering and went to Carnegie Tech. There, he taught part time while they allowed him to earn a Masters Degree in Electrical Engineering. He was offered a job with the Sperry Corp. in Long Island, New York. The main reason that he accepted the position, in the east was so he could be next to his family and help them out financially. Joe met a young lady by the name of Mary Murphy, who had recently came from Ireland. They married, had six children and finally settled in Seattle, Washington with a stop in Phoenix, Arizona. Joe spent many years working for Boeing Corp. when he retired to stay in Seattle. He accomplished all of this without graduating from High School.

CHAPTER NINETEEN

In Peter's junior year at Farmington High School, he took a job with the spinning mill and worked the second shift as a bobbin boy. The shift began at three in the afternoon and was over at 10 o'clock in the evening because he would have to start school at nine in the morning. He had to leave school at two thirty to go to his job at the mill. Peter did his homework when he got home at ten o'clock or when he had some free time between classes. He used his time to make the best use of it and weekends were used to make up the homework that he could not complete during the week. Besides the money made at the mill, the main lesson that Peter learned was that he knew he would not make working in the mill his life's work for. He wanted an education and he wanted to follow the path that his big brother took. He put his money away for his future education expenses and he worked for the mill until his senior year of high school.

One day in the summer of that year, Steve mentioned to Peter that he had to go to the bank and pay his interest. Peter had heard him say this every year, but paid no attention to it.

This time, he asked his father, "What is the interest that you are always talking about?"

Steve said, "The president of the bank told me that I should not pay the loan on the house off completely because I will lose my good credit rating."

"You have been paying the interest on five hundred dollars for the last ten years without paying the loan off? How much money do you have in the bank?"

Steve took out his book and showed Peter that he had twelve hundred dollars in his savings account.

Peter said, "Pop, I can't understand why you left five hundred dollars on his loan and paid the interest for all these years when you could have paid the loan off ten years ago and not paid all that interest. I want to go to the bank with you and find out why."

When they arrived at the bank, Peter asked to speak to an officer of the bank. Mr. Donnelly came out of his office with a smile and his hand out. Peter did not care for him when he first laid eyes on him and disliked him even more as they talked. The banker was dressed in a gray suit with a vest and a gold chain between the two pockets of the vest. Peter wondered what kind of watch he had on his chain and if his father had paid for any of it. He wore a stiff collar over a white shirt and a gray bow tie. His hair, what was left of it, was cut close and Peter assumed that he had the money to spend for a professional hair cut: not like his father. He reminded Peter of a "fat cat" while his father was a poor mouse that he played with.

He looked the banker right in the eye and asked, "Why did the bank tell my father that he was not to pay the loan off because he would lose his credit?"

The banker became defensive and answered, "No one at the bank told him that."

Steve said, "Mr. Taylor told me and he probably told other people."

Mr. Donnelly smiled and said, "Since Mr. Taylor had died, we cannot not very well ask him."

Peter turned to his father and asked, "Do you want to pay the loan off so you will not have to pay anymore interest?"

His father nodded so Peter handed Mr. Donnelly the bank book. "Transfer five hundred dollars to his loan and pay it in full. He also wants a receipt and a release of mortgage from the town because the bank will no longer have a lien on it. I'm sure that my father's lawyer, Mr. Ryan knows nothing about that so I will make it a point to tell him. He is still a director of this bank, isn't he?"

The banked nodded and took the bank book.

Once the transaction had been completed, they walked out of

the bank. As they were walking across the bridge, Steve said, "I would like to know how many other people are just paying the interest thinking that they would lose their credit rating if they paid their loan off in full."

Peter answered, "I hope that another bank will come into town so this bank will have some competition and they will not be doing things like that to our people. The next time there is a meeting of your society, tell all the members what we have done today. The bank will have many people come into the bank to pay off their mortgages."

* * *

Medka made an announcement at dinner the following Sunday. She brought a quest by the name of Andrew Koskoff and she had been seeing him for about a year. The family had met Andy before because he worked with Steve in the ball bearing factory and he had been over to the house many times. This was the first time that Medka had invited him for dinner. They had an announcement to make and since the entire family was there, they decided that it would be a good time.

Andy stood up and announced, "We have decided to get married at the end of September. We have cleared it with Father Laughton, since I was brought up in the Greek Orthodox faith, the priest said that we could be married in St. Mary's Church."

Medka got up and said, "We have the wedding party picked out and the wedding list so the wedding could be at the end of September.

Kada started to cry because her oldest daughter was getting married. It was a happy meal and everyone wanted to know what they could do to help. Medka's sisters knew of her plans, but they had been sworn to secrecy and they were happy that it was finally out in the open.

The next morning, Steve went to the town hall and spoke to the first selectman. He asked to rent the hall in the basement of the town hall for the reception; the selectman said there would be no charge. He reserved it for the last Saturday in September and the wedding plans were complete. The girls had a wedding shower for Medka the week before and right after that, the friends and relatives started cooking. Everyone that was going to the wedding stopped in at Steve's house on Friday night to toast the couple, to bring the wedding gifts and to tease the couple.

Medka was a beautiful bride and they borrowed some the customs of their parent's native country. The young couple were at her home on the night before the wedding so she could say goodbye and as was the custom, Andy asked Steve for permission to marry his daughter. Steve, after much discussion and soul searching, reluctantly agreed to allow his daughter to leave his protection and marry this man. He gave Andy Permission and everyone there cheered. There was, however, no march of the matriarchs which disappointed Kada, somewhat. The wedding ceremony went well at St. Mary's church and everyone met in the hall afterward. The guests provided much of the food while Steve and Kada provided the liquid refreshments; there was an abundance of both. Steve had hired a polka band from Bristol who started playing at two o'clock in the afternoon and went on and on.

Steve and Kada had counted on the reception winding down about eight o'clock, but everyone was having such a good time, the band did not stop playing. People went home to bring more liquor and food and the celebration went on. The bride and groom left at eight o'clock and the party was still going strong. They finally began to go home at three in the morning; the wedding and reception lasted eighteen hours. Steve had to pay the band more money, but he felt that it was worth it. The women took the food and liquor home only to bring it back for the "cleaning crew." The party started after church on Sunday and somebody brought a record player with polka music while more people filtered in. The bus driver who parked his bus in front of the town hall came in when he heard the music. He had lunch and had a few dances before he drove his bus to Hartford. By five in the afternoon, the food was gone, all the people were gone and the hall was spotless.

There were two jail cells that were tucked away in a corner of the cellar, shut off from the rest of the building. On Saturday night two men, who had too much to drink were put there by the police. They had supper supplied by Kada on Saturday night and when they were released on Sunday, they helped clean up.

The day after the wedding, Josie announced, "I am getting married at the end of October. I have quit school and have a job at the convalescent home in Bristol."

The woman that owned it, had a son named Robert who started seeing Josie. Once in a while, when she worked late, Mary Price, the owner of the home let her sleep over. Steve did not want to lose control of his daughter at that age and he told her to come home every night or find another job. The more he tried to impose his will upon her, the more he pushed her to stay over. Robert asked her to marry him and she accepted.

Josie went to her mother when Steve was at work and asked, "Ma, I need your help with Pa."

Kada promised to do all that she could.

She only had one question and she took Josie by the shoulders, looked her squarely in the eye and asked, " You are not pregnant, are you?"

Josie gave her an equally determined look and answered, "Ma I am not pregnant. You taught me better that." They were married in St. Mary's church after Robert agreed to turn Catholic. The reception was very small and was held at Steve's home because he did not have much money after Medka's wedding.

The final blow came after Josie's wedding when Magda said, "Pappa and Mama, I am getting married at the end of November."

Steve and Kada were not prepared for this, but Magda was in a family way and time was important. She had been dating Albert Rivers, a young man who worked with Robert Price and he introduced him to Magda. They both worked for the Stanley Works in

New Britain. Al and Magda were married in St. Mary's Church on the last day of November with the reception held at Al's home. Only relatives and a few friends were invited. They wanted to keep the wedding very small for obvious reasons and because Magda was beginning to show. They rented a small house in New Britain and five months later a little girl was born.

Agnes, who had attended all of the weddings said to Kada, "Magda's dress seemed to ride a little high in the front."

Kada had an answer for her when she said, "The first baby does not take anytime at all, it is the second child that takes nine months."

* * *

Before school started that year, Peter sat down at the kitchen table to discuss things with his mother. She went into the old electric icebox and took out a quart of Schmidt's Tiger Head ale, bread, onions and pickled herring; the discussion started.

Peter said, "Ma, I am going to quit my job before I become too dependent upon it and I will be stuck in it for the rest of my life. I want to play football for the high school and this will be my last chance to do it. There will be other jobs and I could work a year after graduation. I could add that money to my savings to go to college."

She let him talk because he had already convinced himself and just wanted reassurance. Kada did not like football because people were injured playing that sport, but Peter said that he would take the chance. She did not forbid him to do it, but she would be afraid for him the entire football season.

Some new events happened in Peter's senior year of high school that were to change his life for the better. A young lady named Barbara Levesque transferred to Farmington High School. She was a pretty girl with bright blue eyes and light brown hair. Peter had signed up for French class because he needed a language course to graduate and Barbara took the same class. Peter sat next to her that first day and could not stop thinking about her. The teacher, Miss Murphy noticed this and put them together on projects whenever she could. Peter would wait in the upstairs window where he could watch her getting off the bus the first thing in the morning. He watched her all day and seated himself so he could see her during classes. All the other girls got off the bus with their hair tied up in pin curls and they would go to the girl's room to comb it out, but Barbara was perfectly groomed and prepared herself before she got on the bus. He did not realize that she knew that he watched her all the time, but she did.

Peter tried out for the senior play and got a very small part. Although he was in the play, he asked Barbara to go with him and she accepted. He was so happy that he ran down the stairs, tripped and ripped his pants. He arrived home and his mother noticed the tear in the pants when he told her what happened, she forgave him.

She told him, "Next time, control yourself. New pants don't grow on trees."

Peter weighed two hundred and thirteen pounds when he went out for football and the coach, Mr. Walters decided to harden him up and put some muscle on his body. When everyone else did two laps around the field at the end of practice, Peter did five. Peter had the Janek stubbornness and did everything that he was told. He would not give the coach the satisfaction of knowing that it was bothering him. The more that Peter did without complaint, the more the coach made him do. While at practice, Peter would look over to the side of the field where the cheer leaders were practicing and he would catch Barbara watching him. Barbara opened up a whole new life for Peter. The football team was very successful even thought by the end of the season, Peter was lean and trim at one hundred and seventy pounds. He had started at left tackle on offense, went to defensive tackle and to line backer when he lost the weight and became more mobile. The team won the state championship for that size school, and went undefeated for the entire season.

Peter and Barbara started seeing one another and dated the entire school year. The custom in the school was that if a couple went steady, no one else would consider going out with them.

After graduation, Peter took a job with a wholesale auto parts store delivering parts. He bought a 1937 La Salle that never did run correctly because it had a short circuit in the wiring and the battery would not start the car. It was common to see the couple stuck along side of the road when one of their friends went by. This caused problems with Barbara's mother because she thought that they were using the car as an excuse when in fact, they were telling the truth. Peter saved his money for that year because Barbara had one more year in high school. She had to be home each night and they saw each other only on weekends. He always parked the La Salle on the hill so he could start it by rolling it down the hill, in second gear with the ignition turned on.

The following year, he started college at New Britain Teachers College. This was a state run school with a low tuition while Barbara took a job in Hartford where she and her mother moved. Peter stayed at the automobile parts warehouse, working part time to help with his expenses. The manager told Peter that he could set his own hours when he did not go to school and he even set up a shower so Peter did not have to waste time going home to change for school. One day blended into another and the days went by quickly.

Peter got home late one night from seeing Barbara and turned on the television. The only thing on was the news and he listened as the announcer told of the North Koreans pouring over the thirty-seventh parallel; they had invaded South Korea. President Truman called America to arms and it looked like they were going to draft young men into the army. Peter and Frank had registered for the draft, but they were going to take the older ones first so Peter prepared to go before Frank. Frank was still in high school, but if the war lasted for a while, he could go. Peter was more worried about Frank than himself or to put it another way, he was more worried about the people that Frank would come up against. That summer, Peter became concerned that he would be drafted, so he talked to Barbara.

He said, "Since we plan to get married, we should do it before I went into the army. I will get $91.30 every month if I am single and that money would be sent to you if we are married. I will get $43. a month in addition while I was in the army. With you working, we could put away enough to buy a house when I get out after two years."

There was just enough money for the wedding and the rings, but Peter talked to one of his friends at the Hartford Store and told him that he was planning to get married.

His friend said, " My brother-in-law is in the jewelry business and I could bring in a selection of wedding rings to the store next week. You would have to pick out an engagement ring and two bands and bring them back the same day."

The following Saturday. Peter was handed a pouch with seven diamond rings and three wedding bands and he was told to take them to his girlfriend so she could pick out the ones that she wanted. He waited for Peter to return and Peter did not give "trust" a second thought, but the friend must have trusted him.

It took no time at all to get to Barbara's home. He pressed the door bell and it was opened by Barbara's mother, Toni. She was annoyed because Peter had come over so early and unannounced, but he was too excited to care.

He said, "I would like to see Barbara." and Toni stood aside to let him enter. He found her sitting on the floor in front of the television cross-legged, in her bathrobe that made a pouch in her lap. Peter threw the rings in her lap and said, "Pick one!"

Her face lit up and she looked up at Peter who repeated, "Pick one and tie a string around your finger for size and its yours."

Even Toni was impressed that Peter could be trusted with all the jewelry. Barbara picked a one-half carat solitaire ring and two bands. She gave him her size and he left.

Once he returned home that afternoon, Peter and his mother had one of their sessions at the kitchen table. They drank the ale, ate the herring, while they discussed Peter's problems.

Finally, he said, "Ma, I'm getting married."

He looked for a reaction from his mother, but could not see any. Slowly a smile began to spread across her face and when Kada smiled, the whole room lit up. She looked at her son and said, "We like Barbara and she will make a good wife. We know that you will never be a priest so you will have my blessing and I'm sure that your father will give you his. Have you set a date yet?"

"We have not talked about a date yet and I have not even asked her mother."

She said, "You should talk to her mother as soon as possible. You will have to get along with her for a long, long time and it would not be right to start off on the wrong foot."

Peter kissed his mother, finished the herring and left the room.

On the next Sunday afternoon when Peter and Barbara were having a hamburger, Peter brought it up. He said, "I want to talk to your mother about our getting married."

Barbara said, "This is not the right time." My mother said that she did not want me to marry someone who will be going into the service and who will leave me with a baby to care for. She did not want to see me walking around with a small baby while my husband was out of the country for an extended period of time."

When the couple met the new priest, Father Cannon, he gave Barbara a form that had to be signed by her mother. Since Barbara was under twenty-one, she was considered a minor in the eyes of the church. Barbara gave the paper to her mother who refused to sign it, but the couple made their plans anyway. In the end Toni decided that she had better sign the paper because she did not want them to a elope.

They set a date for June 20, 1953 at St. Mary's church and the reception was to be held at the Farmington River Inn where Medka worked as a waitress. There were sixty people invited and the owner charged a minimal fee because the couple was paying for the wedding themselves. She included the wedding cake, and the wine for the toast in the cost. It was a beautiful wedding and reception and what it lacked in size, it made up in enthusiasm. The couple left for their honeymoon, part of which was spent in Joe's apartment in Queen's New York. Joe and his wife had been married the year before and decided to go away for a few days. Peter always suspected that his brother, Joe made the apartment available because he knew that the newlyweds had very little money to spend on their honeymoon; such is the family.

The couple settled in a small apartment in Unionville, close enough to the center so Barbara could take the bus to work in Hartford. The summer passed quickly and Peter began his third year of college, but in November, he received his draft notice and he was to report to Fort Dix, New Jersey. His report date was January 4, 1954 and the police action in Korea was still being fought up and down the peninsula. Peter did not want to go to Korea, or into the army for that matter, but he had no choice. He left Barbara after he moved Toni to live with her and for the next two years, he would be gone.

It was a tearful good-bye when Barbara took him to the railroad station in Hartford on that cold January morning. She stayed with him until the train went out of sight and returned to the empty apartment to begin the longest two years of her life. She did not feel that it was proper to take away her husband so soon after they were married. How were they expected to begin a life of their own if he was taken away at this critical time? She became depressed, but the chain of events would bring her out of it.

Before he left, Peter said to her, "I will be back to take care of you and we will be together again. We have our whole lives ahead of us so be patient, sweetheart and things will work out. God will take care of you. Write often and say a prayer for me once in a while. It is not like I'm never coming back and two years will go by quickly."

As Peter boarded the train, he wondered how he could go

through two years without her. He did not speak to anyone on the train because everyone was in the same boat and they just wanted to be left alone. He stayed at Fort Dix for basic training for eight weeks and was assigned to Camp Chaffe, Arkansas for another ten weeks of artillery training. Peter felt that he was going to Korea, but orders came down to ship him to postal school in Indianapolis, Indiana. He was only one of a very few that escaped the assignment to Korea from their training company. After completing his classes, he was assigned to Fort Eustis, Virginia where he would stay for the next nine months.

Enlisted personnel were allowed to live off post at this base. He went home on leave and brought Barbara down to live with him in Colonial, Williamsburg. Barbara began working at William and Mary College to help support the apartment and it was as if Peter had a regular job and went home every evening. Life in Williamsburg was pleasant because they settled into a routine. Peter would finish his mail route and was allowed to go home without reporting to anyone. He was usually home by three o'clock in the afternoon and made supper for Barbara who came in at about five o'clock. There was much to do and much to see in the quaint colonial village of Williamsburg. There was always someone walking around in a colonial costume and once the tourists went home, there were very few people around. The movie theater was not crowded and the prices seemed to go down in the restaurants so the couple could eat out more often.

Once in a while, Peter was assigned to the kitchen for K.P. duty and that meant that there was more food in the house. Fresh vegetables and various cuts of meat found their way into the Janek kitchen. The Janek family always managed to eat well. It must have been the training that Peter received from his mother when he worked at Abel's Market. Everyone wanted to be friends with the mailman because the mail was the cheapest way to communicate with the young soldiers. With the people that Barbara had gotten to know at the college and Peter's friends at the base, they were never short of company. It was a good life, but they both knew that it would not last as long as the conflict went on in Korea. Peter kept track of the negotiations that went on with the warring parties. He did not tell Barbara, but it was just a matter of time before she went home and he went somewhere into the world.

One night, as they were having supper, Peter said, "If we could continue this life, I might consider staying in the army."

All Barbara said under her breath, was, "Over my dead body."

Finally, one day, Peter received a phone call from a friend on the base. The friend, who came from West Hartford and worked in personnel said, "I have to pick two men to be sent to Germany in January and two men to go to Korea two weeks later. You have your choice as to where you want to go. If I were you, I would rather go to Germany even if it for a longer time. If you went to Japan, there is no telling where they will send you."

Peter answered, "Do I have to go anywhere?"

"Yes you do. There are only a few of you postal men available and I have to know right now."

"O K I guess I have to go to Germany. How long do I have?"

The answer came back," I'm cutting the orders now."

Peter had three weeks leave coming so he had a chance to bring Barbara home. He and Barbara took all their possessions, packed them into their 1942 Plymouth coupe and started north. He reported to Fort Dix on February 3rd and left on a troop ship for Bremerhaven, Germany. This was the same port that his uncles John and Paul used when they came to America. He spent ten days on that ship and was sea sick the entire time. The trip across was pure agony and he lost six pounds in ten days.

When he arrived in Germany, he was assigned to the post office in Darmstadt, about twenty miles south of Frankfort. It was a small office with only ten people including the Commanding Officer. Duty there was good because there was no K.P. and no guard duty. Peter even paid a man to make his bed and clean his area around the bed each morning. He had breakfast at eight in the morning and started work at eight-thirty. At eleven-thirty, he went to lunch and had the rest of the day off. Time was heavy on his hands and he could not understand why he was over there when there was so little to do. Surely, the army could combine some duties and allow half of them to go home.

He waited for letters from home and wrote almost every day, although he only mailed two letters a week home. A few weeks into his tour of duty, he received a letter from Barbara telling him that she was pregnant and due to deliver in October of 1955. He was disappointed that he could not be there for this most important time, but he was due to come home two months after the baby was born. He wrote right back and asked Barbara to have pictures taken of her at frequent times so he could see her stomach grow.

A few week later, he received a letter from Medka saying that his Uncle John had died in St. Petersburg and he left one son, but no one knew where he was. The funeral took place so quicky that no one was able to go down to Florida for the last rites. He was seventy-six years old, lived a good life and always said that he wanted to live out his life in a place that was warm. Uncle John had been the first to come to America and through his efforts, all of the rest of them came. If it had not been for Uncle John, Peter might have been born in Ruzbachy instead of Unionville.

In her next letter, Barbara said, "Your father was saddened because his brother died without his family around him; no one should die alone."

Peter looked for the letters from home while he put letters in the slots for the different sections on the base. When he came across a letter from Barbara he would stop, open it and read it even though there were mail clerks waiting for their mail. He stopped smoking because cigarettes were rationed and he could use his cigarette coupons at the PX to buy them. He used them to barter with the German civilians that worked on post. He used packs of cigarettes as payment for making his bed and doing his cleaning chores around his sleeping quarters.

One day, while he was talking to a German civilian who had been reading the German newspaper, the man asked Peter, "Where are you from in America?"

Peter said, "I come from a little state smaller than Germany called Connecticut."

The man showed him a picture of a bridge that had collapsed because of a flood. It was a picture of the bridge that spanned the Farmington river in Unionville and it was lying in the water. He also had pictures of Winsted, Connecticut showing half the town ravaged by flood waters. He had not received any mail from home for a week and thought that it was odd because he looked forward to seeing how large Barbara's stomach had grown. He now realized why he had not heard. Their apartment was in the flood plain and must have been hit by the water. The old homestead was directly in the path of the waters and Peter was worried about his parents. He bought a "Stars and Stripes," but that contained nothing about the flood. He thought that it was just like the army to withhold this information.

Peter went to see his commanding officer, Captain Dean to see if he had heard anything and he said, "I heard about the flood, but I did not pay much attention to it."

Peter became excited and said, "My wife, Barbara is in the flood plain, she is eight months pregnant and I'm worried."

The Captain said, "I'll make some calls and tell you what I find out."

Peter checked with him every day, but he had no news and suddenly, three letters came from home. He read them in the order of their postmarks. The first letter said, "It has been raining quite a bit, but so far, things are fine. The river is rising, but we do not expect it to reach us. We are on an alert to evacuate at a moments notice."

There was a picture of Barbara at a lake with her mother. Some friends had stopped to take her with them and her mother went along. The letter went on, "I am feeling fine and I never felt better."

A tear came to Peter's eye as he thought that his wife looked beautiful. She even had her hair cut short. It must be hot in the middle of summer in her condition, he thought.

The second letter began, "Medka's husband, Andy, came down the hill and he waded through knee deep water to get us out with all the food we could carry. Andy took care of my mother and me and we are at his home, high on the hill. We are out of danger. My father had gotten through by going in a round about route and brought enough food to last us for a week. I will end this letter because my dad will take it to Hartford to mail. No mail is being accepted an the Unionville post office."

The third letter said, "The water is down and we are back home. Since the apartment was on the second floor, we suffered no damage." She sent him pictures that she had taken and those from the newspapers.

"No one in the family was injured and Frank had gotten to the house on Railroad Avenue before the flood waters came. He opened all the windows so the water could flow through. They had quite a bit of damage, but the Red Cross was helping and the house was still standing."

Peter thought that Frank was one smart kid.

Now that he had confirmed that everyone at home was safe, he settled down to his daily routine. Peter volunteered to drive the mail to the airport just for something to do in an attempt to cope with the boredom. At the end of September, he was told by his captain to take the day off. Peter decided to stay in the dormitory to write some letters and he needed to take care of some chores such as shining his boots and wash out some clothes. He knew that it was unusual that he was given a day off on a workday for no apparent reason, but he decided not to look a gift horse in the mouth.

He fell asleep after lunch and was awakened by one of the men in his unit, "The old man wants you to report to him at the post officer at four P.M. He also wants you to go to the PX and buy a six pack of ginger ale when you reported."

Peter took a shower. It was nice to take a shower and shave when no was around because he could take his time and there was no one to share the mirror with; he had it all to himself. All fresh and shaved, he picked up the ginger ale and reported to the captain promptly at four.

The captain handed him a telegram from Barbara's friend saying, "You are the father of a five pound six ounce baby girl. Congratulations."

It was only the end of September so the baby was born early and the telegram came as a complete shock.

Captain Dean asked him to sit down and said, "I feel bad about not doing more for you when the waters were rising. You must have been worried."

He put a bottle of southern comfort on the desk with two glasses. Peter knew what the ginger ale was for and they drank the entire bottle of whiskey. They talked and laughed and by eight o'clock it was gone so the captain took Peter in his car and brought him back to the barracks. His buddies put him to bed and he stayed there for the entire next day. The men of the postal unit took up a collection and gave Peter sixty dollars to send to Barbara so she could buy something for the baby. Peter could not wait to write a letter and send the money to Barbara. The new baby was toasted many time in the gasthauses of Darmstadt.

Peter and Barbara decided on the name for the baby by mail. If it was a girl it would be Anne and if it was a boy, it would be Peter. Pictures began coming in showing Anne in her bassinet, in the bath, sleeping, smiling and any other pose Barbara could make her do. Peter had expected to go home at the end of December and he wished that he could be home for Anne's first Christmas. In the first week of December, orders came down saying that he would be rotated to the United States on December 15th. The trip home would be by air, but there had been two airplane crashes in the past two months, killing returning servicemen.

Peter wrote to Barbara, "I will be coming home by ship, it will take me ten days so don't worry about me. You will not hear from me while the ship was at sea. I love you and my little daughter that I have never seen. Boy, it will be great to be together again and be a family. I can't wait to get out of here. See you soon."

He flew out of Frankfort on December 15th, 1955 in a four engine, noisy propeller airplane. They made one stop in the Azores and landed at Andrews Air Force Base in New Jersey on December 16th. As soon as he landed, he looked for a phone to tell Barbara that he was in the United States and he wanted her to pick him up. When he finally reached her, she recognized his voice, but there was dead silence on the other end. She did not expect to hear his voice and she was in shock. The next thing he heard was sobbing, and he knew that they were tears of joy.

"I'm in New Jersey," he said, "Can you come and pick me up? I want to come home."

Between the sobs, she said, "I will come get you where ever you are."

"I'll call you with the date so be ready. I love you and I want to see my daughter."

"She is waiting for her daddy."

Five days later Peter was home in his apartment in Unionville. Toni decided to move back to Hartford so the young couple could be alone. She found an apartment within walking distance to her work at the typewriter factory so she was happy. Peter, Barbara and Anne started their life together as a family.

CHAPTER TWENTY

After looking for work, Peter found a job at United Aircraft as an engineering aide in the experimental division that tested new jet engines for aircraft. Joe told him to try that and go back to school to get his degree. After a few days of tedious paperwork, Peter started night school at Hillyer College, where his brother started. Hillyer College had changed its name to the University of Hartford while Peter was there and became a four year college that presented bachelor degrees. He worked a forty hour week and went to school from six-thirty until ten o'clock two days a week. Peter was taking one half of the credits that a full time student would take during the day. He did this for two years and found that he had to take a day off from work once in a while just to get caught up on his sleep. He had to report to work every morning at eight o'clock in the morning and it was an hour's drive from the apartment to the factory so he had to be up by six o'clock to be there on time. He did not have time to drive home for supper on the nights that he went to school. Peter did not arrive home until eleven o'clock at night on school nights. On the nights he did not go to school, he completed his homework and sometimes when a special project came up at work, he was asked to work until late at night and even on weekends. The money was good, but it was taking its toll on Peter's body.

Barbara was an excellent money manager because she had been handling her own finances since she was in high school and she took care of the money in the family. With the money that she had put away while Peter was in the army, plus what she had saved, they had enough for a down payment on a house. They found one that they liked and could afford and as soon as they moved in, Barbara announced, "I am pregnant again."

Peter smiled and said, "We must find out what is causing this. It must be the water."

"We both know that it is not the water. With your work and school, I don't know where you find the strength. You Slovaks must be inbred with the strength."

In her sixth month, she woke Peter in the middle of the night and said, "I am having labor pains. They are ten minutes apart"

Peter looked at the alarm clock and saw that it was five in the morning. He called the doctor and after many rings, he answered.

He did not use an abundance of words, "This is Peter Janek. Barbara id having labor pains and they are pretty bad. I don't want to move her."

"I'll be there as soon as I can."

Peter saw the baby coming out and baptized it at that moment. He laid the baby aside, comforted his wife while he waited for the doctor to arrive. The doctor arrived at six o'clock.

The doctor said, "Even if I had been here, I could not have done anything. He weighs under two pounds and did not progress to the point where he could have lived."

Peter still did not have a little boy, but they agreed to keep trying. Somehow, Peter went through the days, weeks and then months of working, going to school and trying to keep their new home looking new. Barbara became pregnant again and the baby was due in the middle of April.

One cold day in February, Barbara and Annie were outside taking a walk, when it started to snow so Barbara decided that it was enough for one day and started for the house with Annie in tow. The phone rang just as they entered the house and she left Annie alone for a minute to pick up the phone. The cellar door was open a crack, Annie stuck her little fingers in and opened the door. She was an inquisitive child and peeked down the stair when she lost her balance and fell down the cellar stairs with a screech. Barbara dropped the phone and ran down the stairs. She scooped

Anne up and began checking her to see if any part of her was injured. Anne was not injured because her snowsuit was well padded, but the fall had frightened her. Just then Barbara had a sharp pain in her abdomen, she knew it was too soon for the baby so she decided to rest until Peter got home. As he walked in the door, Barbara saw that he was covered with snow.

Before he took off his coat, she calmly spoke. "I am having pains and I'm pretty sure that I am in labor."

"How far apart are they?",he asked as he dialed the doctor.

"Oh, about ten or fifteen minutes apart. I have been waiting for you to come home."

The doctor's office answered after about the sixth ring. After Peter explained, the nurse said. "Bring her into the hospital, at once. The doctor would meet you there. You are lucky because the doctor's last patient had just left and we were going home because of the storm."

He called a neighbor to take care of Anne. The neighbor asked Peter to take his car because it had good snow tires and at about six o'clock, Peter and Barbara started to drive to the hospital through a blinding snow storm. Most of the roads on the twenty mile trip were state roads and were plowed or in the process of being plowed. Every few miles, Peter would ask. "How far apart are the pains now?"

Barbara would reply the latest time between contractions. Each time she answered, Peter tried to go a little faster, but he could feel the rear of the car begin to slide. He wished that a policeman would stop him and he could either transfer her to the policemen's car or get an escort to the hospital. He muddered to himself. "Where is a cop when you need one. If I was speeding, there would be one on my tail in a minute."

He prayed to himself and talked to Barbara who was beginning to perspire. It could have been from the pain or from the high heat that Peter had in the car. He finally pulled into the emergency entrance at the hospital, the contractions were two minutes apart and it was seven-thirty. Peter parked right at the entrance, jumped out and ran in for help.

He said. "I have a pregnant women delivering a premature baby in the car."

As soon as he yelled, he saw two men running toward him pushing a gurney. The fact that it was snowing meant a slow night for the emergency room personnel and he had no trouble getting help.

They took Barbara out of the car and told Peter to move the car that was blocking the entrance. The last thing he saw was one of the orderlies lifting her, putting her backside down on the gurney and they disappeared into a room. When Peter came back, one of the orderlies told him that there was no time to take her into the delivery room so the doctor was on his way to meet with Barbara. Peter had to give the clerk all of his information along with his insurance numbers. He was told to go into a little room fondly called the "sweat shop" where all the fathers waited for the news. He no sooner walked through the door when the phone rang and he was handed the receiver.

The doctor at the other end identified himself as Dr Goldstein and said. "You have a son, but I need to talk to you. Meet me in the room where your son was born."

All types of problems ran through Peters mind. Was Barbara alright? Was there a problem with the baby?

When Peter reached the room, he found a tall man in a green cover-all. He had a green cap with no visor on his head and a surgical mask hanging on his chest. The mask an the top of his clothes was wet, but the doctor was smiling so that made Peter feel a little better.

He sat Peter in a chair and stood before him. "You people must live right. Your son weighs only three and a half pounds, and he is not quite fully developed which means that he will have to stay in the hospital two months or until he reaches the weight of at least five pounds. If he had gone full term, there would not be a problem. It was fortunate that you arrived at the hospital when they did because if the baby had been born in the car he would not have survived. You will need a pediatrician to take care of the little boy and there happens to be an excellent pediatrician in the hospital who is examining your little boy, he will talk to you. His name is Dr. Thomas Murphy, he is one of the best in the business and he will explain the baby's chances. Have you agreed upon a name for the boy?"

Peter said without hesitation, "Peter, and we will call him Pete."

Peter went in to see Barbara who was medicated, but not enough that she could not talk.

He asked, "How do you feel? Is it all right to call the boy Pete?"

She was smiling when he told her of the developments up to date and he would come back after he talked to Dr. Murphy.

She looked up at him and then with tears in her eyes, she said, "I'm sorry."

Peter kissed her and replied. "Sorry? You did a great job of holding off until we got here. You did everything right and now we have a little boy. I don't care what it takes, but we have a son and we will take him home soon. You have nothing to be sorry about. We will get through this, you just wait and see. Peter is a Janek. He will fight! And he will survive!"

A nurse came in and told him that it was time to leave. Dr. Murphy was waiting for him so he kissed his wife and saw that her eyes were already closing when he left the room.

He met Dr. Murphy in the room where the premature babies were kept. His first impression of the doctor was that he was one of those doctors who loved to practice medicine, not one that was doing it for the money.

Peter asked, "What are Pete's chances?"

The doctor replied. "If his lungs were perfect, then I would give him a 50-50 chance. This baby is extremely strong. He squeezed my finger when I put it into his hand. He weighs only three and one half pounds, but babies such as your son are survivors, they will be survivors all the rest of their lives. The next twenty-four hours will be the critical time. If his lungs fill up, then his chances will improve. Crying will make this happen."

He sent Peter home to care for Anne and told him to come back the next day and he would talk to him further. The snow had stopped, but the secondary roads were still covered and Peter did not get home until midnight. He went next door, got Anne, put her in her crib and the rest of the night was spent with Peter watching Anne sleep, breathing in and out. The next morning, he called the office and explained the situation to his supervisor who told him to take as much time as he needed. Peter had never missed a day at work, he went in whether he was ill or not.

He told his supervisor, "I want to take a week of my vacation time."

His supervisor said, "You take a week of sick time and leave your vacation for later. You stay home with your daughter and we will talk some more when you return to work."

He stayed home with his daughter and his neighbor watched her while he went in to see Barbara every day.

When Peter talked to Dr. Murphy the day after Peter was born, the doctor told him, "Little Pete did exactly what he was supposed to do. During the night he cried and his lungs filled with air. They are still pumping oxygen into him, but they expect him to breathe on his own within a few days."

He went in to report to Barbara who was looking better and she even joked, "My stomach disappeared and now I can get out of a chair without a block and tackle. A nurse told me that I could get up this afternoon,"

Peter pushed the wheel chair to the room when Pete was sleeping so she could see their son. Barbara had not seen him yet. The first thing she said when she saw him was, "He looks like a sausage, a long, skinny sausage.

Peter said, "That is the most beautiful sausage that I have ever seen.

Peter took Barbara home five days later and she was looking forward to seeing Anne. When she arrived home, Anne would not let her out of her sight. She did not know if Barbara would leave her again and she wanted to be sure that she did not. From that time on, until Anne went to kindergarten, she would get up from her bed when her parents left the room and listen at the bedroom door to be sure that she heard her mother's voice. Peter and Barbara had to open the door gently because Anne was usually asleep on the floor next to the door. Each night, they would place her back in her crib for the night.

The days went by slowly for Barbara, she wanted her son to come home, but the doctor said that the hospital had a rule not to release newborns until they weighed five and one-half pounds. The first few days in the hospital, he lost three ounces, but he gained them back by the time his mother left the hospital. They called the hospital every day to learn how he was improving, his weight gain, eating and general condition. Peter usually called from work because it was not a toll call and even with the limited insurance on Pete, money was tight. He would write everything down and give Barbara a full report at the evening meal.

When Peter returned to work, everyone wanted to know how Pete was doing and he must have answered a hundred questions. Word had gotten around the department that Pete weighed only three and a half pounds. People that never saw him, were saying prayers for him. He was on prayer lists of many churches because everyone was concerned about the little boy. Peter called the hospital at noon each day and one of the engineers had made up a chart to hang on the wall so the date and weight could be recorded. The title on top of the chart was "Pete's Progress." Each day that Peter called, he would make a dot on the date and weight and draw a line from the previous day and that way, everyone could see his progress at a glance.

Everyone checked the chart before they left for the day so they could tell their wives and husbands about his progress. The line went up an ounce every two or three days, then it went to an ounce a day and towards the end, it went up by two ounces a day. When Pete had a bad day and lost weight, Peter had to answer many questions. After forty-five days, Pete was approaching five and a half pounds and he could come home the following weekend. Peter was told to stay home for a couple of days to enjoy his son. The people in the department took up a collection and on that Friday, they handed Peter a card and one hundred dollars in cash for Pete. Peter promised that he would bring Pete into the office as soon as he was able.

When the entire family was together, Pete caused some problems. In the hospital when Pete whimpered, he was picked up, no matter what time of day or night it was. He was hugged, talked to and loved and he expected this treatment when he came home. He could not understand why he got the attention in the hospital, but was not getting it at home. It took Peter and Barbara a whole month before they could get Pete to sleep the whole night through, but it finally happened. This was the first test of wills between Pete and his parents and it was the first sign of discipline even at this early age. If they had relented towards Pete, they would have to relent during the time that Pete was growing up and he would have expected it. The Janek family values were being utilized at this time and no one really realized it.

Barbara and Peter decided to wait for a least two years before they had any more children. Between Peter's school at night, a full time job during the day and the problems with Pete, they were both tired. Peter liked his work and was good at it, but without an engineering degree, he was at a dead end job. He looked around him and saw people that had been there for ten, fifteen and twenty years in the same job, with no chance of promotion. He would be getting merit raises once a year, but he would never see the time when they could buy whatever they wanted. He started to look for other work, checking the newspapers and even going to the State of Connecticut employment office.

The first question asked, "Do you have a degree?"

Peter would answer, "No, but I am in school and will have one in a few years."

He would be told, "Your options a limited. Come back after you have your degree."

They needed a new car, but they could not afford one, even

with low payments. The family lived in a neighborhood where all the residents were about the same, age with one or two small children. One of his neighbors, Jim Jones worked for an insurance company, where he was a claims adjuster. He said that there was an opening, but they wanted someone with a degree and they preferred one in pre-law. Some how, Jim arranged an interview with the claims manager and this could turn their lives around.

The claims manager was a tall, thin, easy going southerner with a pleasant manner. They talked for an hour in the corner office of the building that had glass on two sides so everyone on the floor could see what was happening and the manager could see what was going on out side of his office. Peter felt that he was in a gold fish bowl and everyone was watching him.

The claims manager said, "I have respect for the Yankee mind and you have a good mixture. Your parents came from eastern Europe where people are trained to be logical and you grew up with the Yankee mentality. A claims man has to have a logical mind and I will tell you a story to illustrate this.

I was vacationing, with my wife in the state of Maine. It was a misty day when we came to a high mountain with a road winding its way to the top. The top of the hill was covered with mist so we did not know whether to venture a trip to the top or not. We wanted to see the view. I saw a farmer plowing the field at the base of the mountain and walked out to him. I told him that we wanted to see the view from the top, but did not know if we could see it because of the mist. Do you know what he told me?"

Peter moved his head back and forth.

He went on, "He said that we should go to the bottom of that mountain and look up, If we can see the top, chances are when we get to the top, we can see the bottom."

Peter smiled and thought that he would have to remember this story for his father.

"This is what I mean by logic. You take nothing for granted. You have to see before you make a decision. Every action has to have a cause for that action to take place and I feel that you will do very well in this line of work."

At the end of the interview, the claim manager said, "I am going to ask permission from my home office to waive the education requirement. I will let your know in one week, either way, of our decision."

Peter thought that the interview went very well and he was excited when he got home. Barbara had some news of her own to tell, "I am pregnant again!"

Peter threw his arms into the air, "I can't not understand it. We have been so careful and we have to be careful with this baby, remembering the trouble that we had with Pete. There is nothing that we can do about it now so we would just have to live with it." Barbara asked Peter, "Don't mention it to my mother because I want to tell her in my own way, at the right time and it will be a trying time."

A week after the interview, Barbara received a call from the claim manager who asked Peter to call him. She relayed the message to Peter at work and he waited for noon when everyone had gone to lunch.

The claim manager said, "We will waive the education requirement since you are going to school at night and I had to assure them that you would finish."

Peter knew that he would have to finish now, since the manager had given his word.

"There are some conditions with your employment with the company. The starting salary is thirty-six hundred dollars a year, but without a degree in hand, we can offer you three thousand. After a probation period of six months, we will give you a raise of six hundred dollars if you proved to be able to perform. There is also a company car and an expense account that goes with the position. If you accept, you will have to go to the home office and be interviewed by two officers of the company. They have the authority to turn you down or to have you fill out an application on the spot. If you passed the interviews, you will start in two weeks."

Another problem popped into Peter's mind while he was driving home that night. Barbara was pregnant and the new company would not pay for the delivery or the baby's stay at the hospital. They would only pay for the pregnancy if the baby was conceived while he worked there. He thought that if he waited until the baby was born, then this job might not be there. He had the people in the insurance company convinced that he could do the work and they might cool to the idea over a period of time. He had to talk it over with Barbara so there would be no problems later. It would also mean that he would have to work some nights as all the people that he would deal with, could not be seen during the day and that might interfere with school. When he arrived home, he got out a piece of paper and wrote the pros and cons in each column; he put all of his cards on the table. The biggest problem was the salary because he was now making forty-one hundred dollars a year, but the company car would eliminate much travel back and forth to work, insurance and other car expenses.

After he and Barbara discussed it, she asked "Do you want to do it?"

The answer came back. "Yes, I think so."

"Well," Barbara said, "then do it."

And the first of the next month, he was working for the Allied Insurance Group.

When the weekends came, Peter had so much to do and he tried to finish all of work so he could spend more time with his children. He hated to hear the phone ring, but Barbara handed him the phone and told him that it was his father.

Steve had some bad news and it apparently had gotten to him because his voice sounded very low. He said, "My brother, Karl died in Barnesboro, Pennsylvania. I am going to Barnesboro and I will need someone to drive me."

Peter had not known his uncle very well and he had only met him once in his life. Joe was in Seattle while Frank was with the Army in Germany. Jerry was no help and Medka had said that her husband, Andy would drive him, if no one else could.

Peter said, "I cannot go because I just started a new job and I have to help Barbara with the children since she is pregnant again. I am sorry, but I just cannot go. I will send a Mass card with you."

Mainly to change the subject and also because he did not know what else to say, he asked, "How many children did uncle Karl have?".

His father answered, "He went through two wives and had fourteen children. He was seventy-three years old, but he drank quite a bit,"

That last bit of information was supposed to justify his death at the young age of seventy-three.

Peter's first few weeks at the new company were challenging and exhausting, but the company assigned him to a supervisor who had the best training reputation with the company. He sent Peter out with various members of his unit to learn the investigative reporting and negotiation techniques necessary to adjust claims. Peter had been brought up to trust everyone and to take what they said as fact. He had to completely retrain himself because claims adjustors were fair game to the public. People felt that insurance companies made a lot of money so it was up to everyone to take as much of it away as possible.

Peter's temperament was such that it was ideal to achieve success in the business. He investigated throughly, reported promptly and negotiated to save money. His reports were right to the point, contained all the required information and his estimates for the ultimate settlement of the claims were excellent. Soon he was working on his own and was given the territory of Torrington where his Aunt Mary lived and that allowed him to come home for supper before he went to school. He and Barbara had saved up enough to handle the birth of the child coming in April and he did get his six hundred dollar raise. The company car saved them more money than they anticipated and they had started to save for a bigger home.

In the middle of February, Barbara said, "Guess what! I am having labor pains."

Peter looked out of the window and saw that it was cold, but it was not snowing. It was five in the morning and one could see all the stars. Peter telephoned the neighbor and dropped Anne and Pete next door. There was not the urgency that there was with Pete and there was little traffic on the roads, Peter got to the hospital in forth-five minutes and Barbara spent fifty minutes in labor. He thought that he had plenty of time when he settled down for the wait, but the telephone rang and Peter found out that he had another little boy who weighed four and a half pounds. Dr. Murphy was on his way to the hospital and everything appeared to be under control. The little boy was born five weeks early, was in good shape, but he would have to wait until he weighed five and a half pounds before he went home.

Dr. Murphy said, "Unlike Pete, this baby had a full set of lungs and he used them whenever he could."

Barbara went home four days later and the couple waited for their son to gain some weight so they could take him home. They named him Andrew after Kada's brother in Slovakia.

After a thirty day wait for Andy to get big enough to come home, they went to pick up their baby. The nurse brought the baby out, fully dressed with the clothes that Barbara had brought and they waited for the two day supply of formula that was given to him. The baby never stopped screaming and his face was all flushed from the exertion. He had black hair and brown eyes and the couple looked at him very carefully to see why he was crying. Peter thought that he might be hungry and they were going to ask the nurse to feed him prior to the long drive home, but she came into the room with another baby. The nurse had given them the wrong baby and Peter now checked the identification bracelet. He saw that the name of the baby that was dressed was Brennan. He checked the other one and it said Janek. The nurse was embarrassed and she quickly undressed the Brennan baby and put the clothes on Andy. They picked up the formula and left the hospital before something else happened. Andy was a pink color, he did not cry and was content to enjoy the ride home.

On the way home, Barbara said, "Some mother I am when I do not recognize my own son."

Peter smiled when he said, "You have not seen him in a month and children grow rapidly at that age."

Barbara frowned, "That is no excuse, I should know my own child."

With Andy now at home, they had three little children in one room; they had to have a bigger house. They found one in a pretty section of Unionville and with a small down payment, they were able to assume the mortgage from the previous owners. Peter had checked out their mortgage and saw that the sellers had paid on it for eight years. That money was mostly for the interest and the payments would start paying a little more of the principle. His training with the insurance company was paying off because he was investigating his own transactions more thoroughly.

The new home had three bedrooms instead of two. The boys were in one bedroom, Anne had one of her own and the other was the master bedroom. Peter spent his weekends filling in the yard with dirt, building walls, painting and general repair. They were closer to his parents and when they went out, they could get Steve, Kada or Toni to baby sit. Peter's salary was growing and Barbara was thinking of going back to work, but he thought that she should wait for a few years.

CHAPTER TWENTYONE

The age difference between the boys was a few days short of eleven months and they were inseparable. They seem to look at each other and they knew exactly what they were going to do. They would disappear and Barbara would find a closet emptied on the floor or they would turn the water faucet on outside and let it run. Barbara was constantly listening to water running until Peter took the handles off the water spouts.

The previous owner had built a fireplace behind the house. It had an area to broil food and a chimney in back of this area that allowed the smoke to escape. The family used the fireplace to cook their summer meals and roast hotdogs on a stick. The boys found this a convenient place to play and would come into the house covered with soot and ashes.

Peter was visiting his mother one day and said, "My boys do not have to talk to each other to communicate, they just look at each other and they know what they are going to do."

Kada smiled and said, "When you and Frank were young, you did exactly the same thing. I prayed to God that someday, you would have two sons and they would do the same thing to you. It is God's way of paying you back for all of the problems that you caused me. Now I can see that he is punishing you as you have punished me."

Peter thought back to those days and smiled. He would have to tell Frank, the next time he saw him.

Peter was moving dirt around the yard one Saturday morning. He would dump a load and the two boys would jump into the wheel barrow for the ride back to the pile. Barbara called out that

Medka was on the phone and he dumped the boys out of the wheelbarrow and answered the phone.

He said, "Hello" and then could not get out another word. Medka said, "Your Uncle Paul died. He was eighty years old and he died in his sleep. Barbara might want to make a dish because we are all going over there tonight. The funeral will be Tuesday and there will be a wake Sunday and Monday nights. I'll talk to you later, I have to call Cohoes as soon as I hang up."

There was only one daughter living with Uncle Paul, Eva had left her husband and had decided to live with her parents. She refused to get a divorce because it was against the church law. She had called Medka and told between sobs, "My father passed away last night. I tried to wake him up this morning and he was cold. Of the five boys who came over from Slovakia, your father is the only one left. Call everyone in your family and in Cohoes. I will call aunt Mary in Torrington. She was sixty-five years old and not well, but her sons will come to the wake and funeral."

Uncle Paul had two wives and ten children including the boy, Jimmy, who was killed in the war. The funeral was large because the Janek family had grown and so had the friends of all the family members. Eva was left to care for her stepmother who was seventy-eight and she was bed-ridden with a broken hip. This determined old woman would live to be ninety-two. She never missed a Sunday at Mass unless she was physically unable to go. At the age of ninety, she still went to church in a wheelchair. Two men had to carry her up the steps so she could take part in the mass. The priest had to make a special trip to the back of the church to give her communion while the rest of the people waited. She went to church until the winter before she died. Eva retired early to take care of her stepmother and she and her husband never did get a divorce or had gotten together again.

A month after Uncle Paul's funeral, Frank came home from Germany. He brought a bride and two sons. One son was born before they were married and one son was born after they were married. Frank's bride was named Hilda and she knew hard work and survival. Frank went to work in Torrington while Hilda went to work for a factory that made explosives in Simsbury, Connecticut. They made very good money, but Frank took a part time job, repairing small engines. He was not afraid to take anything apart and fix it because he had a knack of knowing how things ran without the training. Peter and Frank became close again and Frank kept all of Peter's equipment in running order.

Frank and Hilda finally bought a home in Simsbury, to raise their two children. Frank had adopted Hilda's first son and he was being raised as a Janek.

* * *

The Christmas of 1962 was a happy time. The three children still believed in Santa Claus, although Anne was having her doubts. They were able to spend more money than they ever did on toys for the children. Barbara made nut bread and other foods that were taught to her by Kada. The whole family and their children met at Steve and Kada's home on Christmas Eve and the house was very noisy. There were fourteen children running around the huge tree in the corner of the living room. Steve had put in a furnace with central heat so the old wood stove had been taken out and this gave the children more room to run around. Steve and Kada were beaming from ear to ear because all of the grandchildren were under one room; The children could do no wrong.

Medka had three girls, Magda had two girls and a boy, Josie had two boys and a girl. Peter had two boys and a girl, Frank had two boys and Jerry was not married although he planned to be, by the next spring. Barbara held her own with her sisters-in-law who had more time with Kada to learn to cook the traditional foods.

Kada liked Barbara and told her, "Pete and Andy remind me of Peter and Frank when they were young and I wish you good luck when the boys get a little older."

Kada had a smile on her face. She knew what to expect while Barbara did not. Kada and Steve took care of the children, most of them had fallen asleep, while the rest of the family went to midnight Mass together. Peter thought as they walked to church that he was seeing a close family, rich in family values. He hoped that he could pass these values on to his children so that they could pass them on to their offspring.

When they returned from Mass, they collected all of their own and left for home. It was one-thirty in the morning, Peter still had to assemble some toys while Barbara had to take some out of hiding and wrap them. When they finally went to bed exhausted, they knew that it would only be a matter of a few hours before they would be up again. It seemed that Peter had just laid his head on the pillow when he felt someone shaking him.

He awoke to see a wide-eyed Pete shouting, "He came! He came! Come look under the tree."

He shooed them all out of the room so he could get up and when he got to the living room, he saw the three children going over the name tags. Barbara went to the kitchen to make breakfast because, on Christmas morning, they always had kielbasa, scrambled eggs and toasted nut bread. She allowed them to open one present and the rest would have to wait until after breakfast.

Breakfast went down quickly and the children waited patiently until Barbara and Peter finished theirs before they rushed into the living room. There were ribbons, bows and wrapping paper flying all over the place, Barbara thought that it had taken her hours to wrap all the presents and they tore them apart in minutes. Pete had opened his and grew quiet.

Peter noticed how quiet his son was and said, "What's the matter Pete?"

Pete answered while looking at the fireplace, the half eaten cookies and the half glass of milk. He answered "How does Santa Claus get up and down the chimney with the boxes?"

Pete went to the fireplace and looked up. The flue was closed and he asked, "How did he close that little door?"

Peter said, "You will have to ask him if you can catch him." Pete answered, "I would like to know how he does that. Next year I am going to stay up and watch."

Peter smiled as he probably had said the same thing to his father. Andy could care less as long as he had his toy truck and Anne had her play stove that had taken an hour to assemble.

Christmas and New Year's Eve passed and the family settled down to its normal routine. Peter went to work and after breakfast, Barbara got Anne ready for the school bus which picked her and fifteen other children in front of the Janek home. Anne was in first grade and Pete would go to kindergarten the following year. Once the bus left, Barbara got Pete and Andy dressed to go outside while she enjoyed a quiet cup of coffee. She usually made a full pot and by the time Peter came home at night it was gone. It was a cool day and the wind from the east made it seem colder. She told them to play in the pile of sand that Peter had bought to mix with cement for the wall he was building. She would look out of Anne's window every once in a while to check on them. She had just finished her coffee when Andy came to the back door.

He was all excited, trying to tell her something and finally he said, "Pete stuck."

She threw on a sweater and ran out of the house behind Andy. She looked at the fireplace, in the back yard and saw her son half way down the chimney with only his arms sticking out. She found herself standing on top of the chimney with her full skirt blowing up and down, but she did not realize it and she did not feel the cold wind that was blowing. Pete's jacket had gotten caught in the chimney when he lowered himself down and bunched up on the bottom when she tried to pull him out. He was screaming for Barbara to get him out and Andy was jumping up and down, all excited. Barbara had visions of calling the fire department or having the fireplace dismantled to get her son out. When she pulled on Pete, she noticed that he came up only a few inches before the coat caught. She jiggled him up and down hoping that the coat would straighten out and she could free him. Slowly, he started to move out as she pulled. The bottom of the coat finally cleared the chimney, but she still had to twist and pull before he came completely out.

She cradled Pete in her arms and ran into the house with Andy at her heels. Once inside, she took off his clothes and checked his body, his arms hurt from the pulling and he would have some bruises, but he was all right. She finally realized how cold she was and turned up the heat. She took Andy's snowsuit off and sent them to their room while she sat down to catch her breath.

The phone rang and it was her next door neighbor asking, "Is Pete all right?"

When Barbara assured that he was just fine the neighbor asked, "Would you do it again, my husband did not see it."

Barbara said, "It is too bad that he missed it, but it will never happen again,"

She hung the phone up and went to talk to Pete.

She sat down next to him on the bed and asked "Why did you try to go down the chimney?"

Pete looked up at her and replied, "Santa Claus does it all the time and if he can do it so can I."

He was so serious, that she could not laugh and she could not punish him. She and his father had told him ever since he was really small, that Santa came down the chimney without any further explanation so Pete felt that he could do it. She was thankful that he had not, somehow, gotten on the roof of the house and try to go down the real chimney. She could not wait for Peter to come home so she could answer him when he asked how her day had been.

CHAPTER TWENTY-TWO

Steve finally retired. When he and Peter talked about his retirement, Peter took him to the social security office in Hartford so his father could file for his benefits.

Steve said, "You mean that the government is going to pay me to stay home and I do not have to go to work anymore? This is a great country to pay me retirement benefits and I do not have to work any more. My father worked on the farm until he died and no one paid him anything."

Medka had talked him into becoming a citizen of the United States in 1935. He was reluctant to give up his roots even though he would never go back, but with the urging of the girls, he finally gave in. They gave him a social security number and he became an American. He knew that they were taking some money out of his pay all those years, but he did not know why and he did not want to show his ignorance; he just kept quiet. Now he had money coming in every month. His mortgage was paid up and he did not own a car so all he had to pay was electricity, phone, taxes, heat and food. Both he and Kada had clothes in their bedroom that had never been worn. They were birthday and Christmas presents that they had gotten from their children over the years. The clothes that they wore every day were fine and they never wore out. Each of them had dressy clothes that they wore on Sunday and they took them off right after church. They had worn the same clothes for many years and had no need for new ones. Kada had even managed to put part of his monthly check into a saving account.

When Steve heard about Pete's escapades with the chimney, he laughed and said, "I like that boy. Pete is a true Janek because, if he does not know the answer to a question, he will ask. If the answer does not satisfy him then he would go out and find it."

He looked forward to a visit from the boys. Medka had three girls. Magda had two girls and a boy, but they lived in New Britain and he did not see the boy often. Josie had a daughter and two sons, but Josie's older son did not visit as often. Andy and Peter were just the right age to play with. Maybe Jerry would have sons, he was due to get married in six months.

In April of the following year, Peter stopped in to see his father and told him the story about Freddie, the rabbit. A neighbor up the street was moving and he did not want to take his large white rabbit with him. He kept the rabbit in a large cage on stilts. Peter and the three children walked down to see the rabbit and the children were thrilled.

Anne said, "We will take care of it."

Pete said, "I'll help."

Andy as usual, was noncommital. The boys carried the cage up the street while Anne carried the rabbit. The cage was set up behind the now famous fireplace in the backyard and the rabbit had a new home. At supper that evening, the family discussed names, and each had a suggestion. Andy wanted the name, Bunny. Anne wanted Peter, but her father disagreed. Pete wanted the name Bugs, but the others agreed that the name Bugs just did not suit him. Peter had a supervisor named Fred who had six children and since rabbits were known to multiply rather quickly, they all thought that name was appropriate; Freddie became a member of the household.

Anne went to school the next day and researched rabbits to see what to feed Freddie rabbit. When it turned really cold, she found out that they should bring the cage inside. The rabbit turned out to be very tame and they brought him in the kitchen to play with them. He would eat lettuce right out of their hands and allow himself to be cuddled. The winter passed with the children becoming more and more attached to the big white rabbit.

The neighbor living on the other side of them had a large

German Shepard named Whiskey that was allowed to roam freely around the neighborhood. One day when Peter got home from work, he found Freddie outside of the cage with his neck broken. He went upstairs and found the three children sobbing in the kitchen.

Barbara said, "Whiskey somehow had gotten the cage door open and killed Freddie. I chased the dog away and called Sally to tell her what happened and I told her that they should tie their dog. Sally told me that the dog was only doing what his instincts told him to do and that was to hunt for food. I told her that you would decide what to do about the dog when you got home from work. She is so stubborn that I did not want to argue with her."

Peter called her husband, Jim and said, "The next time I see your dog loose, I will call the dog warden and have the dog locked up. It will cost you money to get him back."

He hung up the phone and took the children into the backyard. They dug a hole, put Freddie in a box and dropped him in the hole.

Before he covered the box, Peter gathered the children around him told them, "Freddie has gone to a better place and he did not need his body anymore. He went to heaven to be with the relatives that went before him."

They covered the box and the children said goodbye to Freddie.

The next day when Peter came home from work, he went out back and noticed that Freddie was back in his cage. He found Pete sitting there watching the rabbit.

Pete looked up at his father and said, "Freddie does not belong in the ground, he belongs in his cage."

Peter took his son upstairs to talk to him. He went through all the reasons why Freddie should be in the ground and not in his cage. He took the boy back outside, buried Freddie again and told Pete, "You have to leave Freddy in the ground."

Peter knelt to his level and asked, "Do you understand?"

The young man nodded and they went to supper. Freddie was not mentioned at supper.

Peter had an easy time the following day so he came home early. He went right into the backyard where he found Pete looking at Freddie who was back in his cage. He took Pete up stairs and told Barbara to keep him occupied and away from the windows while he went down to bury Freddie in a different place. He covered the grave with pine needles to try and disguise it.

The following day being Friday, Peter had to stay in the office the entire day. He was required to spend one full day in the office, each week, to catch up on his reports. When he returned home that evening he was confident that Freddie had stayed buried and went directly into the house.

Barbara asked, "Have you gone in the backyard yet? You should."

He found Pete looking at a well matted Freddie in his cage. He had no idea how he had found the grave, there were no holes dug in the yard so how had he known where Freddie was buried? Peter said nothing, but took his son upstairs, washed his hands and took him to his room. The boy could not get the concept that Freddie was dead or he just refused to believe it. With Andy and Anne, it was no problem, but Pete got it into his head that Freddie was not dead and refused to see him in the ground.

The next morning, Peter took the cage apart and put it into the trunk of his car, put the smelly Freddie into a plastic container and made a trip to the town land fill. He set the cage on the ground and threw the plastic container as far as he could. It would be a long time before the children got another animal for a pet.

CHAPTER TWENTY-THREE

Peter asked for some time from work so that he could study for his final examinations because graduation day was approaching. He was given a week's vacation by the claims manager. He told the manager that he expected to be graduated on May 25th of that year, and the manager asked to see his Bachelor of Science degree in Business when he received it. Peter's mother and father along with Barbara and the children went to see Peter in his cap and gown go up to the platform to receive his degree. Barbara stood on her feet and clapped and the children seeing this, stood up and clapped their hands too. Peter looked up when he descended the stairs and saw his family; he smiled when he saw his family standing there, clapping. They had sacrificed much of their time so he could have the time to complete his education and he put the certificate under his arm and clapped for them. Many people saw this and turned around to see Peter's family giving him a standing ovation. That moment when Peter descended the stairs, made the six and a half years of coming home late, requesting quiet so he could study and the meals that he missed because he was late, all worth it. They all went to Peter's home, Barbara took pictures of Peter with his mother and father to send to Joe. She took pictures of Peter with the children to preserve the day. They had a great dinner and toasted Peter's success. If it had not been for the support of his family, he would not have finished because there were many times when Peter felt like giving it up, but he did not want his family to see him quit. Weather permitting, the children were outdoors most of the time, but now it was finished; after six and a half years. Steve and Kada were proud, and even prouder that they were invited to the graduation ceremonies because now they could tell anyone who would listen, about their educated son.

When Peter went to work the following Monday, he went into the large corner office and showed the claim manager his certificate. He shook Peter's hand and spoke with him for a few minutes and when Peter stood up to leave, he shook his hand again. As Peter was going out the door, the claim manager asked him to close it and he looked back to see him punching the numbers on his phone. He was calling his superiors at the home office to tell them that Peter graduated as he said he would do.

Six months later there was an opening in a claim unit and Peter was promoted to claims supervisor. They gave him a six hundred dollar raise, but took away his car and expense account. The raises would be larger from now on and the company offered him an investment program. They would allow him to buy stock in the company without a broker fee and would take the money out of his paycheck each month. Peter elected to take fifty dollars a month out of his pay for the program, but he did not tell Barbara or anyone until he got his next raise six months later. He spent seven years in the program, having invested forty-two hundred dollars and when he sold it later in life, he received a sizeable amount for his retirement.

Peter spent the next two years working as a supervisor when tragedy struck the family. It was on a hot August night when the phone rang at Peter's home. Barbara answered it and did not say a word as she handed the phone to Peter, but tears were streaming down her cheeks.

Peter took the phone and heard his sister Josie's voice, "If you wanted to see your mother alive, you have to rush to her home because she had suffered a massive heart attack and she was failing fast."

He jumped into his car, raced down to her home and found the whole family, along with the doctor around her bed. Medka was holding one hand and Magda was holding the other, while he went in and kissed his mother. She blinked her eyes a few times to tell him that she knew that he was there and at that moment, the doctor put his stethoscope on her chest and announced that she was gone. Kada was sixty-five years old when she died and she left this world with her family around her. She did not look frightened, but she smiled at her children and the important thing was that she did not die alone. She was closest to her daughters and they had a bond that few families have. The girls took their father out of the room, made him coffee and said that they would take care of him. Peter took charge of the funeral since he was the oldest male in the family who was living in town.

There was much grief in the family until the funeral was over. The time went by so slowly because they were either waiting to go to the funeral parlor, or the Mass at St. Mary's church. People came from Cohoes, Barnesboro, and Joe came from Seattle, Washington. Steve took it very hard as he remembered the years in Ruzbachy when they crossed the Atlantic, in Cohoes and finally in Unionville. They spent a lifetime together and loved each other throughout their marriage. They raised seven children and Peter was happy that she had a chance to see him graduate from college.

Frank said it best, "This is an end of an era and our father will need the support of all of his children. The dead will be remembered, but the living have to be taken care of."

Peter, in all his years living with Frank, never did see the profound side of his brother. He was never so proud of anyone as he was of Frank at that moment.

Steve lived in their home for a year and his children persuaded him to sell it. He was lost in the house and his children often came to see him and found him talking to his dead wife. It was as if he refused to believe that she was gone and he could still speak with her. Since Medka's husband died, she was taking care of her home and children by herself. She had a small apartment next to her garage that she rented to single people and her last tenant had just moved out. It was perfect for Steve because he could help Medka with some of the repairs or at least give her advice as to what should be done. Peter and Frank helped her with repairs as best they could, but their time was limited with work and their own families. Medka did not charge her father rent and he ate most of his meals with her.

When he wished to be alone with his thoughts, he made something for himself or Medka would bring a dish over so he could eat alone. She wanted him to maintain his independence, but she did not allow him to want for anything. It turned out to be a relationship that they would both enjoy.

CHAPTER TWENTY-FOUR

The regional supervisor in Waterbury, Connecticut became ill and had to be replaced and the company sent Peter to take his place. It meant running an office with eighteen people in it and Peter accepted the challenge. With the extra money, he and Barbara were able to sell their home in Unionville and buy a much larger one in a nicer neighborhood in Farmington. It meant a longer commute to Waterbury, but the rooms were much bigger and there were two bathrooms, much to the delight of Anne and Barbara. The boys took the larger room and Anne took the smaller one on the second floor. They put on an addition for a family room and a large two car garage. Anne was going to be sixteen soon and she wanted to work after school to save for her education after high school. The family would need another car, which would be used by the children. Barbara wanted a swimming pool in the back yard and she offered to get a job to buy it because it could not come out of the budget. Peter had learned very early in life that you did not buy anything unless you were able to pay for it. The children were excited, so after many conversations, Peter finally relented and the swimming pool was installed. Peter and the boys put a fence around the property and landscaped it. Barbara really wanted the pool to keep the children at home rather than keep them under constant peer pressure away from home.

The pool turned out to be an excellent reason for them to stay at home because they invited their friends and gave it Peter and Barbara opportunity to see who their friends were. Peter had talked with the boys about the drinking of alcohol and the drugs that were creeping into the community.

Andy told Peter, one day, "Dad, we know where the drugs are and where we can get them, but we chose not to do so."

Those of their peers who did so were outcasts in their circle of friends and not someone to look up to. Years before, Barbara had the usual conversation with Anne on the facts of life and discussed problems with boys as they came up.

Anne got a job at a drug store after school, and applied for entrance into a highly recommended school of nursing. She always wanted to be a registered nurse and her parents encouraged her.

The claim's manager retired and a new one was brought in to clean house of all the dead wood, as he called it. Peter's office in Waterbury was staffed with people who were well liked and respected by their customers. They were also fiercely loyal to the company. The new claim manager decided to install a new program where he instructed Peter to give his employees one hundred and ten percent of the work that they were doing. If they failed to do it, they would be rated below average and would not be given a raise. If they did the work at that level then they would be rated average and given a minimal raise. If they did more than what was asked, then they would be rated above average and given a bigger raise. The next year the process would be repeated and if someone was rated below average for two years, they would be let go and replaced with entry level people. The people that were in his office were there for many years and Peter suspected that the claim manager wanted to replace the loyal people with entry level people at a much lower salary. He told Peter that he would not tolerate a decline in productivity.

Peter resisted the new method of supervision which was called "Management by Objective." Finally the claim manager came to the office and demanded that the program be carried out or he would replace Peter with someone who would. Since this interfered with Peter's principals and the way he was taught, the Slovak tenacity kicked in; he would not treat his people in this manner. He was demoted to a claim representative and sent to the Manchester office. Peter was told by the claim manager that he would never be allowed another raise or to expect any promotion. The day after his talk with the claim manager, Peter began looking for another career. He knew that he would not work for a large corporation ever again, but he spent a year working in the new office because it gave him the freedom to explore other possibilities. He did hear that the company closed the Waterbury office a year and a half later and the claim manager was transferred to the home office. The claim manager was told that he did not fit into the company's plans and a few years later, he was separated from the company.

While he was living in Farmington, Peter had joined a service club because he felt that it would be a good way to make contacts and learn what jobs were available in the area. He met a man by the name of Harold Patski, who was an accountant and had a part time insurance agency business. Harold was told by his companies that he either become a full time agent or he would have to sell his business. They would not allow him to place business into their company on a part-time basis.

One day as they were working on a fund raiser, He approached Peter about his dilemma and said, "I have to sell my business, you interested?"

Peter answered, "I have no money to buy it."

Harold smiled, "You don't need the money now. You can pay me over a period of time at no interest. I"m going to lose it anyway." He took Peter to the American National Insurance Company marketing department and introduced him to the officer in charge of new agents. The vice-president agreed to transfer the license to Peter and he was now an insurance agent.

The only matter left was how to resign from his present job without causing a problem with the claims manager. The claims manager did not consider the event to be of any importance, but did report it to the general manager who asked to speak to Peter.

The general manager, Phil Jacobs had known Peter for fifteen years and knew that he would work hard at whatever he did. He wanted Peter to write for his company. They sat down to talk.

"Peter, I'm going to offer you contract to write for our company. I have an agency school for new agents coming up and I want you to go to it. The school will run for five weeks and I can get the company to pay your salary for the five weeks and we will call it vacation time. If you leave now, your pension will not be vested, but if you wait until February third, we can get it vested. It won't be a hell of a lot of money, but every little bit helps. Peter, we need good loyal agents and I think that you will do very well."

"Any problem with the claims manager?"

"Let me handle him. What do you say?"

Peter stood up. "Thanks, Phil. You won't be sorry."

On February 3,1972, Peter left the employment of the large insurance company, and went into business for himself. He had no salary coming in and the little money that he had saved to live on, would be depleted in six months; he had to build up his business rapidly. He was working from his home so he had no rent to pay and he was paying his phone bill anyway so that was not a business expense. He had cards printed and felt that he had to have a post office box because his address was in a residential area. He went to the post office every day to get his mail just to meet the people that were down there so he could give them his card. He made a list of all the clients that he bought from Harold, the business that he had and the business that he hoped to write. He started with the A's and made phone calls, made appointments and went out to visit his people at all hours of the day or night. Word had gotten out that Peter would visit anyone, at any place and at any time, but he had to go to his clients homes. He had no office to meet with his clients; he had to look for an office.

Peter moved into his office two months later. He had to pay rent, phone and other expenses, but he now had a place of business. He hired his sister, Medka to be his secretary, to mainly answer the phone and type letters. The Town of Farmington opened its insurance program for bid and he went after it. He worked on it for a whole month and waited for the opening of the bid. Peter's bid was low, but the town council, that was politically motivated to other insurance agents, tried to give the contract to the second lowest bidder. The bid had to be voted on at a town meeting and Peter attended this meeting to try to convince the council to accept his bid. When the matter of the insurance came up on the agenda, many people got up to speak on Peter's behalf. Some were insurance agents who lived in town, but did not bid on the business and some were his friends.

One agent stood up and said, "If the low bidder did not receive the contract, then the town should not ask for bids any longer because no one will bid. The town will be paying a higher price for insurance, in the long run. If the bidding procedure is not followed to the letter, I will never bid on the business."

The town council voted and awarded the contract to Peter and the commission on the town business gave Peter enough money to feed his family for six months. He started to write business in town and his agency was growing. He was beginning to receive letters and he needed to answer the correspondence so he wrote his letters in long hand and gave them to Medka to type. They came back in such poor quality that he gave them back to her to retype. They still came back with type overs and words misspelt so Peter decided to have a talk with her.

He called her into his office and said, "These letters are of such poor quality, do you have a problem with the typewriter?" She said. I have something to tell you."

She finally looked up and said "I cannot type."

Peter thought about how he was going to fire his own sister, but instead he had Barbara type the letters at night and used Medka to answer the phone.

Since business was growing, Peter was taking business from the other agents to such an extent that he received a call from one of the partners of an agency in town called the Quality Insurance Agency. He wanted to know if Peter would consider merging into one large company. The other agency already had an office and a secretary, and it had more companies with which he could place business, so Peter merged with that agency. He paid Harold off from the town business since he would be sharing in the profit of the larger agency. Within two years, he bought one of the partner' share and one half of the office building. He was now one half owner of the Quality Insurance Company and would spend the next fourteen years building up the business so he could retire.

CHAPTER TWENTY-FIVE

As Peter was working on building his business, Anne was graduated from high school and entered the school of nursing. She went to classes part of the time and worked on the floor as a student nurse the rest of the time. She had to live in the school dormitory while attending school.

Two months into the program, Anne called her father, "Come and get me, I want to come home. I want to leave school."

He drove into Hartford, picked Anne up, and said, "Leave your stuff here and let's talk about this. This is serious and you have been training for this all your life. Let's go home and you, your mother and I will talk it out."

Once home, Anne said, "Something happened at school that upset me and everyone at school."

She started to cry and they did not press her because she would tell them when she was ready; her parents were patient. They did not want her to make any statements that she would regret later.

Finally, she stopped sobbing long enough to tell them what had happened. "A very good friend of mine had committed suicide. She did not want to become a nurse, but her parents made her go to the school. The hospital sent her to a mental hospital for that segment of her education and she had become despondent. She had wanted to scare her parents into allowing her to leave school and she took some sleeping pills. She took too many pills and they could not revive her. She died last Thursday night."

Anne and her father spoke all weekend, they went out on Sunday with Barbara, rode around and finally ended up bowling and having supper; anything to take her mind off her friend.

At supper, Peter asked, "Please try if for one more day. I will stay by my telephone all day and if you call, I will come to take you home. If I do not hear from you, I will be at the dormitory at six o'clock and take you to supper."

She agreed and the following day, when he did not hear from her, he came to the at the dormitory at six o'clock. Peter liked going to the dormitory with all the teenagers running around. When the elevator door opened, he usually heard a shout, "Man on the floor." They was a flurry of activity and young ladies were running from one place to another. Peter would hold the open button on the door until the activity died down, before he would step out.

Toni, Barbara's mother had an apartment close by the school. Arrangements were made with Toni for Anne and Carol, a friend of Anne's to go to Toni's apartment for dinner, every Tuesday evening. After that incident, Peter decided that he would go into Hartford on Wednesday evenings and take Anne and Carol out for supper. This continued while Anne went to the school.

In 1975 when Anne was in her second year, her grandfather, Steve became ill. Medka called Peter and told him that his father had developed a cough, but Steve had smoked all of his life and it was not unusual for him to have a cough. Kada, when she was alive, told him that if he did not stop, she would start smoking. She thought that if he saw her smoking, he would stop, but she could never go through with it and he kept on smoking. He said he would quit, but he would sneak a cigarette in the bathroom and flush the evidence down the toilet. He always coughed when he first got up, but Medka said that it was going on for a few days and it was getting worse. Peter drove over and they took Steve to see a doctor. He examined him and had him admitted into the hospital because he had pneumonia. They gathered up a few clothes and drove him to the emergency room of Hartford Hospital and he was admitted at once. Peter went directly to the student nurses dormitory and left a message for Anne. He told her where her grandfather was and asked her to help him all that she could. As soon as she was free, she went to his room and from that time one, every young lady who had on a student nurse's uniform was known as Anne. The administrators would not let Anne work on the floor where her grandfather was, but Anne took care of that.

She made it a point to find out who was going to be on that floor and talked to them. She warned them that her grandfather would call anyone with a student nurse's uniform, Anne and they should answer to it. She had the entire student body organized to take care of him and on her breaks, she went in to see him. The other patients in his room were amazed at how much attention he was getting. Anne would call her father when he could not come in, to tell him how his father was doing. Peter was worried and on the eighth day of his confinement, he talked to the doctor.

The doctor said, "You father is not getting any better. All those years of smoking have made his lungs leather-like and he is not getting enough oxygen. We are going to place him into the intensive care unit where we can monitor him closely. His heart is strong and his other organs are functioning properly, but the blood supply is not bringing enough oxygen to his brain. For an eighty-two year old man, he is extremely strong."

After two days in the intensive care unit, with all the tubes and wires sticking out of him, Steve died. He died alone and he must have been frightened because his children were not there at his last breath. The nurse on duty said that he was asleep, when she checked him he woke up and looked around and took his last breath.

The entire Slovak community came to the funeral. Joe came from Seattle and all of Steve's friends and relatives came from all over the country. His children lined up in the receiving line at the funeral parlor. There had to be two viewing days to accommodate all of the visitors. Anne came from school and she brought some of the student nurses who had taken care of him.

They had only known him for a few days, but as one of them said, "He was a beautiful little old man who did not want to cause problems for anyone."

Peter and Medka were co-executors of his estate and he left a sum total of sixteen thousand dollars. One half went to Medka who took care of him all those years. The rest was divided among the remaining six children. It just seemed to Peter that it was a very small amount to be a sum total of a man's entire life. He thought about this and realized that this was only a small portion of what he left his children and grandchildren. He left them the strength of character that they possessed and the ability to see right from wrong. He taught them to treat people as he wanted to be treated. He taught them a sense of fairness and the ability to accomplish anything with hard work. He took nothing unless he gave something in return and he worked for everything that he processed. The sixteen thousand dollars he left his children, was earned with the sweat of his brow and that was what made it valuable. The lessons he taught would be passed on to the generations that followed him. He did not leave only sixteen thousand dollars, he left a way of life for others to follow in his footsteps.

CHAPTER TWENTY-SIX

Anne graduated from nursing school a year later. The ceremony was held at St. Joseph's Cathedral in the Arch Diocese of Hartford and it was the last, three year class to be graduated from that school of nursing. Peter, Barbara and Toni attended. Peter watched the sixty-four young ladies walk down the center aisle in their white caps and starched uniforms, each carrying a single red rose. A lump formed in his throat, a tear ran down his cheek and he realized that all those trips into Hartford were well worth it, because Anne was beautiful. Her radiance set off a glow that made him sure that Steve was shining down upon her. There was a reception at the hospital that afternoon. All the dignitaries from the school attended and Peter knew that his daughter was part of the cause of the celebration. He was proud of Anne, his family and all those that came before and could not be there to celebrate. Anne had her whole life ahead of her and she would do well.

Peter's business was growing and he had little time for himself on weekends. Barbara suggested that they buy a summer place by a lake somewhere which could be used as a retreat. They looked for six months and finally found a five bedroom summer house in Wales, Massachusetts where they could hide from Friday afternoons until they came back Sunday evenings. Pete was attending college at the school Peter attended before he went into the army. Andy was still in high school, but he was working part time at the local McDonald's fast food restaurant.

The progress of the family seemed to be moving along smoothly until Anne announced that she was getting married. She was maid of honor for her friend, Carol and had met the groom's cousin at the wedding. They had been dating for the last year and decided to marry. His name was John Delaney and he worked in New York in the commodities market. They planned to live in Stamford, Connecticut and John could commute to New York while Anne would try to find a job in Stamford.

Barbara thrust herself into the planning of the wedding with all the energy that she could muster. Peter had taken Anne aside one day and made her a proposition. "I will either pay for your wedding for two hundred people, or I will give you the money and you can get married on your own."

Anne replied, "Dad, you only have one daughter and that's me! I want a big wedding!" Spoken like a true Janek.

Peter asked Barbara to proceed with the wedding. She arranged for a hall for the reception, a caterer, flowers, cake, wedding dress, invitations and the liquid refreshments. The wedding took place in October and it was timed so that the leaves would be in full color. It took place at eleven in the morning and was followed directly by the reception. At six o'clock the liquor ran out, but no one wanted to leave. The people took up a collection and paid the band to play longer. Since they did not have another engagement that evening, they stayed for another two hours; they were having a good time. Pete and Andy went back to the house to get the reserve liquor and the party continued until 9 o'clock that evening. It was a great wedding.

The newly married couple settled in Stamford and Anne began work at St. Joseph's hospital. They rented an apartment close to the hospital and a short walk to the train station. Barbara saw it as a long distance to go to visit, but Peter looked at it as a good place to stay for a weekend visit. Anne showed her skill and furnished the apartment tastefully with the least amount of expense. She worked a shift that required her to work weekends periodically so the visits were not frequent. Peter was happy that Anne found someone that she loved and together, they would make a life of their own. The night before the wedding, Peter and John sat at a bar and discussed the wedding. They gave each other their views and they were compatible so Peter was not worried abut his daughter.

CHAPTER TWENTY-SEVEN

With the business growing, Peter became worried about his taxes. He looked around for different investments and he found it advantageous to invest in rental property. He and Barbara decided that it might be nice to retire to Florida so they took a trip to see how the market was. They drove down to a town on the East Coast to spend the night and they liked the city so they looked around for property. The State of Florida, to stimulate the housing market, raised a sum of money through a bond issue that it loaned out to residents of Florida at a very reasonable rate. Peter and Barbara found such a home that had a bond mortgage that was assumable. After some negotiation of the price of the home, Peter asked the real estate agent. "How much would you require to bind the contract?"

The real estate agent called the lending company who said that anyone with a job could assume the mortgage.

The agent said, "A hundred dollars should do it."

Peter and Barbara bought their first piece of property with a travelers check. The closing was all handled by mail and the real estate agent found a family to rent it. The couple was on its way to retirement in Florida.

The following year, they bought another home with the money they saved on taxes and bought a third one the year after that. Barbara handled the properties from their home in Farmington while Peter sold his insurance policies. The following year, Peter's partner was looking for three other investors to buy a condominium in Hawaii, on the island of Maui. The condo cost one hundred and eighty thousand dollars, but the seller was willing to take a mortgage for one hundred thousand so each investor had to bring twenty thousand to the table. A property management company would handle the rentals that would pay for the mortgage payments and the Janek family were part owners of a condo in Maui.

Peter was working late in the office, one night and he received a phone call from Frank, "When are you going to Florida because I need a vacation and Hilda and I want to go along. Maybe we will buy a condo or something."

They met and arranged for a trip for two weeks in March of that year. Peter had just bought a new car and they would drive it down. This was the first new car that Barbara and Peter ever owned because they had always bought cars that were in an accident. The mangled autos could be purchased cheaply and Peter would pay a body shop to put it together again. They now had the money to buy a new car and Barbara felt that it was about time that the Janek family owned a brand new car. It took them the usual two days to drive down and they stayed in a condo for two weeks. Peter wanted to inspect their properties and possibly look for another one, but they did not find anything reasonable, so they used the time for sightseeing and fishing.

One day they decided to drive over to Tampa and take in one of the attractions. Frank and Hilda had never been there and although it was a few hours away, they all set out to see it. The day went along normally until they arrived at the hospitality building and since the park was owned by a beer company, every one was allowed two free glasses of beer. They also served food with tables set up outside, overlooking a pood with sea gull swimming around. Hilda loved to feed the birds and she always had packets of crackers in her handbag, in the event that she came across some birds. While they were waiting in line to get their beer, Hilda took out a package of crackers. Frank pointed to a sign that asked people not to feed the birds, but Hilda chose to ignore it. The gulls swarmed down while people were trying to protect their food and drinks. She finished her feeding frenzy and the four of them each picked up a beer. The plan was for Frank and Peter to have two beers while the women went across the little bridge to the oyster pool.

The brothers watched the women cross the bridge and they settled back to enjoy their cold beer. They each had on shorts because it was a rather warm day. Suddenly, a seagull flew over Frank and chose that time to deposit his waste. It hit Frank on his left knee and also splattered onto his right knee. He looked at his knees and his face became bright red, the veins stuck out of his neck and Peter thought that they were going to burst.

Frank got up, raised his head, clenched his fists towards the heavens and shouted at the top of his voice, "There are five hundred thousand people in Busch Gardens and you picked on me to shit on!"

Peter could not keep a straight face as the situation looked comical to him.

Frank looked at Peter and shouted, "What are you laughing at?"

Peter replied, "You, I'm laughing at you. Why don't you wipe it off and let's get out of here?"

In the meantime, the women hearing the commotion, started back across the bridge. Hilda had assumed that Frank was at the bottom of it so she was hurrying back to calm him down.

Frank saw Hilda on the bridge, he shouted, "It's all your fault. You fed the gulls all those crackers and now they shit all over me!"

When Barbara saw what was happening, she stayed back so she would not be connected with the incident. Peter had already backed into the corner and was waiting for the drama to be played out. Hilda wiped his knees off, they drank their remaining beers and left the park, but the drive back to the east coast was filled with tension.

From that day on, when Peter and Barbara went anywhere in the car and Peter smiled for no reason, Barbara would say, "It looks like the gulls shit on Frank again.",

Peter would just nod and smile.

Anne and John were trying to have a child. In November of 1981, Anne had a little girl named Elizabeth; Beth for short. She was a pretty baby and was very well behaved. Since she was the first child, her parents gave her much attention and she learned very quickly. Anne and John bought a home in Ridgefield with three bedrooms and they both became active in the community, especially when it involved the church and the schools. Marie was born in 1984, she was on the heavier side and she had Kada's disposition. Marie loved everyone and when Peter would sit down for a quiet moment, he would always find Marie sitting on his lap.

She would look at him with her big bright blue eyes and say "Grandpa, are you OK? Is there anything I can do for you?"

This cheered Peter up and he often said that if Marie was around all the time, he would never feel blue.

Little Mary was born in 1987 and when Anne took her daughter to her doctor for her six months check up. The doctor said that she appeared healthy, but she looked a little pale. He did some blood work and phoned Anne that evening.

He said, "Mary has a rare blood disease that does not allow her body to manufacture red blood cells. Without red cells, her blood cannot carry nutrients to the vital parts of her body. I have made arrangement to have her admitted to Yale-New Haven Hospital which is best equipped to handle this type of illness. It is imperative that she be admitted into the hospital immediately."

Anne took her right to the hospital which was some distance away. At the hospital, she was told that Mary was only the fourth youngster who was identified with this type of illness. Two of the children had died and the other one was still being treated. What they were going to do was give Mary a transfusion from her mother and perhaps that would kick-start her body into manufacturing its own red cells. They used one half pint of her mother's blood for the transfusion.

Anne called Peter and Barbara that evening with the news and

Peter said, "I have no doubts that Mary will recover. She is a Slovak and Slovaks are known to be survivors. Don't worry, I know, deep in my heart, that she will recover."

Two days passed and Peter and Barbara heard nothing, but Peter still was not worried. After Mary was given the transfusion she was brought home because there was nothing anyone could do for about four weeks. That was how long it would take for her to start producing red blood cells. She was scheduled for another blood test at that time and that would determine the outcome of further treatments. The test came back and Anne called Peter and Barbara as soon as she found out. Mary was manufacturing her own red cells and she would not have to go back to the hospital. She would be monitored regularly to make sure that she continued to do so.

When Anne told Peter the good news, he said, "I was not worried, we are survivors."

CHAPTER TWENTY-EIGHT

Frank called Peter one day in January with some bad news; he had just come from his doctors office. He had been bleeding from the rectum. He thought that it was hemorrhoids and the bleeding would stop, but it had not. The doctor did a biopsy and found that he had cancer of the colon. It was malignant, but the doctor felt that it had not spread. He had to see a specialist and he probably would have part of his colon removed. By the middle of February, he was scheduled to go into the hospital and have the operation. They took eleven inches of his colon and they felt that they had gotten all of the cancer, but they would have to wait; they put him on a course of chemotherapy with the hopes of giving him a complete cure. In July, the test showed that the cancer had spread to the rest of his colon and he had no choice, but to have it all taken out and replaced with a bag.

That fall, Peter would stop to see him as often as he could. He would tell Frank that he needed to take pictures of houses that he insured and took Frank with him. Frank loved to go to his favorite tavern in Torrington for a submarine sandwich and a beer and they usually stopped there for lunch. Peter really did not have to take pictures, but it was a way to spend the day with his brother and best friend. Frank thought that he was just going along for the ride, but Peter had two things in mind. He wanted to spend as much time as possible with his brother and he wanted to be there if Frank needed him. He wanted to take care of his little brother. They talked about the old times; before Frank got sick.

Frank had time on his hands because he was always active and he offered to fix Peter's snow blower. Peter had an old red ford truck that he used to take trash to the dump so he brought the snow blower to Frank. A few days later, he got a call from Frank to pick it up. The snow blower was in Frank's drive way, nice and clean and it started right up so they loaded it on the truck.

Peter asked, Why don't you let me pay your for the repair? Or, at least let me pay for the parts?"

Frank answered, "I don't want money, not even for parts. Just get this god-damn blower out of my sight."

Peter could see that Frank's well known temper was starting to rise, but there was something wrong. He persisted, "What's wrong, Frank?"

Frank was calming down and he opened the overhead door of his garage. When Peter looked in, he saw that the inside was covered with potato skins. They were over the ceiling, the work bench, the walls and the floor.

Peter asked, "What happened?"

At this point, Frank smiled. "You are not going to believe this, but I fixed the blower and I was testing it in the garage when it got away from me and ran over fifty pounds of potatoes."

Peter started to laugh, scraped some potatoes from the stool because he needed to sit down. Frank could not compose himself any longer and he started to laugh.

Peter asked, "Do you want me to help clean it up?"

"No," said Frank, "It will be a good job for my son, Freddy. Besides, I want Hilda to see it when she comes home from work."

Peter thought that he had better leave because he would just start laughing and provoke Frank, once again. The last thing that Peter remembers seeing in his rear view mirror, was Frank standing in the middle of the road, shaking his fist at the snow blower as it moved away.

Peter decided to take a trip to Florida before Christmas of that year because he bought a new truck and he wanted to bring some furniture down. They had sold the cottage in Massachusetts and bought a house on the Connecticut shore. Peter found many antiques in the cottage in Wales and he took them out before they sold it. He wanted to take them to Florida because they would eventually move there and since he felt fine; now was the time.

Once everything was in Place in Florida, he called his brother Frank. He asked him, "How are things going?" He did not hear an answer. He asked again and he heard a weak voice answer. "I'm just lying here in a pre-natal position waiting to die."

Peter's voice choked up and he said, "Hang in there, little brother, I'm on my way up."

They had planned to leave the following Monday, but Hilda called Saturday morning, "Peter, your brother, Frank passed away during the night. The last thing he said before he went to sleep, was to tell everyone that he loved them if he did not wake up again."

Peter said, "I'll fly up for the funeral on Monday and then fly back." Peter sat in the nearest chair, put his hands over his face and wept.

He caught a flight to Hartford Sunday afternoon and went home. Anne, Pete and Andy were there and Anne took charge. She made supper for all of them and with Toni taking care of the girls, they all went to the wake. All of Frank's nieces and nephews were there and all of his brothers and sisters except for Joe from Seattle. Joe felt that he could not do anything so he did not fly out for his brother's funeral. Frank was buried in a cemetery down the street from his home and his wife did not dispose of his clothes or personal things for two years. Hilda went to the cemetery three or four times a week and talked to his grave stone and Peter suspected that she could not accept the fact that he was gone. Peter missed him terribly and he never went to the cemetery after the funeral. He did not want to remember his brother as a tombstone, but he wanted to remember all the good times that they enjoyed together.

It was about six months later that Peter noted that he had pain in his back. It radiated down his right leg and he decided to mention it to his doctor on his annual check up. Peter had a history of back pain so his doctor referred him to a neurosurgeon who found nothing wrong with his back. Peter felt that the pain would go away, but it got worse. He went to an orthopaedic surgeon who he knew from his days as a claims representative, many years ago. This doctor took x-rays of his right hip and asked Peter when he wanted the hip replacement done. They agreed on the first of September and Peter went into the hospital. Anne came from Ridgefield before the operation and brought in some pictures drawn by her daughters. She put them on the wall where Peter could see them before he turned out the light and the first thing when he woke up.

He stayed in the hospital six days after the operation. Barbara helped with the therapy and within five weeks he was back to work. The doctor told him that x-rays showed that he would need the left hip replaced within two years. He started to walk back and forth to work, a distance of three and one half miles a day in hopes of prolonging the second replacement, but it only brought it about sooner.

Peter had his second hip replacement in March of 1989. He did not take as long to heal because he went back to work in three weeks, but work was not the same. He did not have his brother to call when he felt down and his younger brother, Jerry was not as close to Peter. He was nine years younger and Joe was eleven years older; their interests were not the same. Jerry had a daughter and two sons and they devoted their time to Jerry's wife's, side of the family. Their cousins from that side of the family were more their ages and they had more in common with them.

In June of 1990, Peter retired. He sold his half of the insurance agency to his partner, took the money and invested it. Peter and Barbara sold all, but one piece of property in Florida, invested that money and moved to Florida; it still was not the same without Frank. They sold their home in Farmington, paid for the home at the shore and go there every summer to see their children and grandchildren. Pete married a woman who had two children and they own a lovely home. He has his own family now, works as a computer programer for a large machine manufacturer and travels the world over. Andy married a young woman, a little younger that him and they have a little daughter who will play with grandpa at any given time. Andy works as a parking lot gate installer and service representative. The values of the Janek family have taken hold. It is time for Barbara and Peter Janek to rest.

EPILOG

The year was 2001 and Peter Janek is sitting on the screen porch of his home in Florida. It is the first of March and the temperature is in the 80's with low humidity. He watches a hawk flying over head, soaring from one thermal wave to another. His wings are not moving as he glides freely across the sky. Here is a symbol of freedom with nothing to stop him from doing what he wants to do. As of January 1, 1993, Slovakia became a free and autonomous state and the people of that country had voted to separate from the Czechs and govern themselves. If only Father Damian, Johan Janek and Steve Janek had been alive to see this. They and generations before them, had worked and prayed that they world would recognize them for what they are, hardworking, intelligent and industrious people; capable of governing themselves. Peter survived and is alive to see the transformation and he is sure that some where, the three of them are standing arm in arm and smiling on that development.

Peter looks back on the events that have brought him to this point in his life. He remembers his own life in America and wonders what it would have been if he had been born in Slovakia. He would be trying to eke out a living on the small farm at the base of the mountains. He thanks Father Damian and all that came after him for installing in him the character, and work ethic of the Slovak people.

It is a legacy that was given to him by the priest so many years ago. Peter was sure the he was up there somewhere smiling on his handy work. He looks at the values of family lives falling apart all around him. He looks at his children and his children's children and he could see the values being passed on. He sees Beth with her ballet and the resolve that she places on it. Marie who works hard at everything she does and Mary who survived a most serious threat and is now moving head long into life. He sees the way his uncle and aunt's children behave because they are interchangeable with those in all the Janek families. Aunt Mary's sons who built her a home free of charge before she died at the age of 92, still advising her children.

He thanks his parents because he never realized how hard they worked for the family, how many sacrifices they made and the guidance they gave.

As he sits there, deep in his own thoughts, his granddaughter, Beth comes to him with her blue eyes flashing and asks, "Grandpa, can I sit on your lap?"

He patted his knee and she sat down.

She looks at him, "Grandpa, do you think that I am too old to sit on your lap?"

He smiled and answered, "Beth, you will never be too old to sit on my lap."

He thought to himself, "This is what it comes down to, this is what is important, the children that we produce to keep the values." Now is the time for rest. The dream has been realized and Peter will never forget his heritage

BVG